# HER
# FIERCE
# WARRIOR

## PAIGE TYLER

sourcebooks
casablanca

Published by Sourcebooks Casablanca, an imprint of Sourcebooks, Inc.
P.O. Box 4410, Naperville, Illinois 60567-4410
(630) 961-3900
Fax: (630) 961-2168
www.sourcebooks.com

Printed and bound in Canada.
MBP 10 9 8 7 6 5 4 3 2 1

*With special thanks to my extremely patient and under-standing husband. Without your help and support, I couldn't have pursued my dream job of becoming a writer. You're my sounding board, my idea man, my critique partner, and the absolute best research assistant any girl could ask for.*

*Love you!*

# Prologue

*Fort Bragg, North Carolina, May 2000*

ANGELO RIOS SLOWED DOWN WHEN HE GOT TO THE gate, and held out his military dependent ID card for the MP standing guard. The guy barely glanced at it before giving him a "hooah" and waving him through. Angelo had been driving his old beater car through the Fort Bragg gates several times a day ever since he'd gotten his learner's permit two years ago, when he'd turned sixteen. He knew all the MP and civilian guards by name and they knew him. Fort Bragg might have thirty thousand military personnel and three or four times that many civilians, but in a lot of ways, the base was like one big extended family.

"Hey, Angelo! When do you report?" one of the younger MPs, Private First Class Spencer, shouted from the traffic lane beside him.

"About three weeks," he yelled out the window as he drove his old Monte Carlo through the serpentine pattern of concrete barriers placed there to make sure no one sped through the gate too fast.

Angelo grinned as he made a right at the next road and headed toward the housing area. On an army base, everybody knew everybody's business, including the fact that he'd be leaving for Basic Training at Fort Benning soon. He couldn't wait. He'd wanted to be a soldier like his father ever since he could remember, and now he was finally going to be able to put on a uniform.

But while his dad was thrilled with his career choice, his mom was a different story. She absolutely hated the army and everything about it, especially life at Fort Bragg. Angelo could understand why. His dad had been deployed almost constantly over the last half-dozen years or so. Not only did that mean his mom had to take care of the family on her own, but also that she had to do it while living in terror that something might happen to his dad.

After twenty years, she thought he was finally getting out, but now his dad was considering staying in. Angelo didn't blame him. The way his dad saw it, there weren't a lot of civilian jobs out there for a man who only knew how to shoot, kill, and blow things up.

It hadn't helped that Angelo picked the same weekend to tell her that Dad had signed the delayed-entry paperwork, so Angelo could join early, then ship out as soon as he turned eighteen and graduated high school. But seriously, what did she think he was going to do? He wasn't going to get a job at the local Walmart or one of the nearby textile mills, and he sure as hell had no shot at college. He was done with sitting in classrooms. He was born to be Army Special Forces, just like his dad.

Even so, he felt a twinge of guilt as he pulled into the driveway of their ranch-style housing unit. He wished he could make his mom see that she didn't have to worry about him, that he'd be safe, just like Dad had been all these years. But Angelo knew she'd worry anyway. And cry a lot. She did that every time Dad deployed, then again every time he called from whatever crap hole in

West Africa or the Caribbean he was in. Angelo hated to see her cry.

He climbed out of the car with a sigh. Maybe Dad would change his mind and retire. Then maybe Mom could finally be a married woman who actually saw her husband.

Angelo unlocked the front door and walked into the house as quietly as he could, not sure if his mom was asleep. She slept like crap these days, and at odd hours. When she wasn't waiting for a phone call from his dad, she was glued to CNN, praying nothing was going on in whatever part of the world Dad was in. Whenever she did get some rest, it was usually with the help of sleeping pills—but more often with the aid of alcohol.

He didn't need to look around to know his two younger sisters, Venus and Lydia, weren't home. The house was never this quiet when they were around. No doubt they were at a friend's house. And since the television wasn't on, that meant his mom was almost certainly sleeping. Just in case she wasn't, he should let her know he was home.

He walked past the living room with its Native American meets Mexican decor and down the hallway that led to the back of the house. The door to his parents' room was ajar, so he stuck his head in. It was just as he thought. His mom was asleep, her back to the door, blanket pulled all the way up over her shoulder.

He turned, about to head to the kitchen to grab something to eat, when something stopped him. He couldn't say quite what it was, but something was…off.

He walked back into the room and slowly circled around to the other side of the bed. That's when he saw the empty wineglass and the equally empty brown plastic bottle his mom's prescription sleeping pills came in.

Angelo's stomach clenched.

*Please, God, no.*

He might have called out her name, but he wasn't sure. He shut everything out and focused on his mom's face. Her hand was tucked under her cheek and her eyes were closed, like she was sleeping. For a fraction of a second, he thought she was. But the blanket wasn't rising and falling with her breathing like it should have been.

Angelo yanked off the blanket, so he could roll his mom onto her back. He'd worked a few summers as a lifeguard at the base pool, and he automatically started prepping her for CPR.

He froze the moment he touched her shoulder. She was as cold as ice and already stiff. He put his shaking fingers along her neck to feel for a pulse, knowing he wouldn't find one but needing to check anyway.

His mom was gone.

Angelo dropped to his knees beside the bed and closed his eyes.

He didn't know how long he knelt there. He wanted to cry, but the tears wouldn't come. So instead, he stared down at the floor and wondered whom he should call first. Dad's A-team was somewhere in West Africa, but he had the phone number for the first sergeant and sergeant major memorized, and the MP station was the first number on speed dial on every phone in the house.

He decided to go with the MPs.

He was reaching for the phone on the bedside table when he saw the piece of folded notebook paper sticking out from under the handheld's base. Fingers numb, he plucked the paper from under the phone and unfolded it. He wondered briefly if he should touch something that could be evidence. But this wasn't a crime scene. This was his house.

His dad's name was at the top of the page, and in handwriting that got harder to make out as it went down the page, his mom apologized for leaving them and said how much she loved all of them. But she couldn't live this way anymore, waiting for the call to come saying her husband was dead and knowing she would now have to wait for the same call about her son.

She asked his dad to keep the girls safe and promise never to let either of them marry a soldier. There was something after that about Angelo and how proud she was of him, even if she wished he hadn't chosen to join the army, but tears blurred his vision so much he couldn't read anymore. He wiped them from the letter where they'd fallen, hoping he hadn't smeared the writing too much. Then he folded it and slipped it back under the phone.

Angelo wiped his eyes on the sleeve of his T-shirt, then reached for the phone and punched the number one speed-dial button. As it rang, he mentally prepared himself for what he would have to do next, starting with finding his sisters, then getting a message to his dad. It might take a while for his dad to get home, so Angelo and his sisters would be on their own until then. But he would take care of them. It was what his mom would want.

It was the least he could do for her.

# Chapter 1

IT WAS EARLY MORNING, THE SUN BARELY PEEKING over the mountains. Darkness still clung to the deserted, dilapidated buildings around Minka Pajari as she slunk through the village. She was only one rugged mountain pass away from home. Four or five hours of walking, and she would be back with her family and this terrible nightmare would be over.

But when she heard the men who had been following her for the last ten minutes break into a run, part of her realized that the nightmare wasn't over yet. Another part insisted the nightmare would never be over. Not for her. Not after what she had become.

Minka wanted to run, but the beast inside her demanded that she turn and fight. She was so tired, and really didn't want to do either of those things. She'd been going for so long without food and barely any water. All she wanted was to be left alone.

Instinct told her they wouldn't leave her alone.

Minka had escaped her captors weeks ago, or at least it felt like it had been weeks. Getting home to her village had been much harder than she'd thought it would be, though. It had taken her many days to even figure out where she was, then many, many more days to slowly traverse the mountainous terrain between where she'd been held and the small farming village near Khorugh where she lived with her parents. This part of the country— the Gorno-Badakhshan Autonomous Region—was very rugged and rural. Strangers, especially women traveling without male companions or money, weren't treated with kindness, and she'd been forced to dig for food scraps in piles of garbage and sleep in caves or abandoned buildings. What she'd endured during her captivity taught her that she no longer had to fear these minor, momentary forms of discomfort, though.

No, the only thing she truly feared now was the beast the doctors had unleashed inside her. During her slow journey home, she had learned that the creature's appearance was hard to predict. At the slightest provocation, her claws and teeth would extend and her sight would change, making nighttime seem like daytime and daytime painfully bright.

If she was frightened, startled, or threatened, the changes went even further. Her muscles would throb with power, and her face would change. She'd seen her reflection once in a stream and been startled to see that she looked almost catlike.

Sometimes the changes came on for no other reason than because she was sad or lonely or afraid. Those times truly terrified her, for with a curse like this, she couldn't imagine a time when she wouldn't feel those things.

Worse than the physical changes was what she felt happening to her soul. Where once she'd been a calm, compassionate person, now all she ever felt was anger and rage.

She had taken to traveling only at night, seeking cover in wooded areas, and avoiding villages and people whenever she could. While she feared being attacked or mistreated by people, she feared what the beast inside her would do to those people more.

Now, Minka wasn't sure if she'd be able to keep from hurting someone. She'd wanted to go around the village, but it was squarely in the middle of the path that headed toward the mountain pass. Two of the men following her had swept around, to get ahead of her, and she had to turn into the village to avoid them. Minka said a silent prayer, hoping she could pass through without incident, but she feared her prayers weren't even being heard anymore.

She was so busy second-guessing herself that she didn't see the men who'd arrayed themselves in a line along her path until she was almost on top of them. Her heart beat faster at the ugly expressions on their faces.

She stopped and slowly backed away from them, but it didn't matter. Two more men closed in from behind.

Minka didn't scream as they converged on her, afraid it would only spur the men to do something even more violent than what they already had planned—and afraid it would bring out the monster inside her. So she just stood there.

Two of the men grabbed her and lifted her off the ground while a third grabbed her ankles. As they carried her toward an abandoned building, she begged them in Tajik and in Russian to leave her alone, but they only laughed and called her horrible names. The man on her left shouted at her for being out alone without a male chaperone.

Inside the building, she tried to shove them away and get her back to a wall, but they continued to taunt her. When one man tore at her tattered shirt until it completely ripped away, they grew silent, their eyes latching on to her nearly naked body. She moved back against the mud wall behind her, trying to cover her bra with her arms.

But Minka knew her hands wouldn't stop these men from getting what they were after. After all the pain and suffering she had already endured, she was going to die just a short distance from her home in total disgrace and humiliation. She was never going to see her family again. That might be for the best, though. She didn't want her parents to see what she had become, what she was turning into even now.

The men didn't notice the change. Not at first, anyway. They were too interested in other things. But they noticed when the first man tried to kiss her and she sent him reeling back, his chest ripped open to the bone.

Minka thought for sure the rest of the men would run then. But they only cursed and came at her all at once. They threw her to the ground, one of them kicking her while the other two pulled out knives.

She hadn't wanted to hurt them, and if they had killed her quickly, she would've almost been grateful. But it was clear they wouldn't get around to killing her for a while. They would toy with her the way the doctors' guards had toyed with her, making her scream in pain.

But the beast inside her would never let her be tortured again.

Minka was off the floor in a flash, slashing and biting, pushing the men back to give her space to move. For a moment, she saw the door, clear of attackers and open to her escape, but she ignored it. The beast wasn't interested in running now. It was interested only in tearing and ripping and killing.

The men's shouts of pain and terror got louder as they ran for the door and scrambled toward the windows. But their cries only made her anger flame hotter, driving her into a fury she'd never felt before.

Minka desperately tried to rein in the beast, but it was like she was on the outside of the abandoned house looking in. She knew she was the one tearing the men apart, but she was no longer in control. She wasn't sure she ever would be again.

—⁓—

Sergeant First Class Angelo Rios glanced at his watch. They needed to get moving, or it'd take all day to get back to camp. He and his Special Forces A-team had been doing a recon sweep back and forth through the rugged terrain of southern Tajikistan when they'd heard about a small town near the mountain pass that had been hit hard by a recent storm. Repairing buildings damaged by high winds and torrential rain wasn't the kind of work Special Forces usually did, but Angelo and the team's new lieutenant figured it'd be an easy way to gain a little goodwill with the locals, which definitely *was* an SF mission.

Angelo squeezed the last of the cheese onto a cracker from his MRE—meal ready to eat—and shoved it in his mouth. With breakfast done, he stuffed the empty wrapper into his rucksack and swung the pack over his shoulder. The rest of the team got the message and did the same.

"So, do you think Kendra will ask you to be the godfather?" Staff Sergeant Carlos Diaz, the team's communications expert, asked Derek, a smile tugging at the corners of his mouth.

Angelo let out a snort. Diaz had been ribbing the team's medic, Staff Sergeant Derek Mickens, for a month straight about his most recent crush, Kendra Carlsen. The Department of Covert Operation's admin assistant turned kickass field operative had married Declan MacBride, the DCO's freaking huge bear shifter, after spending a week alone with him in the jungles of Costa Rica a few months ago. And to top it all off, the couple was now expecting twins.

Derek gave Diaz a less-than-amused look. "Give it a rest already."

Diaz grinned, his teeth a flash of white against his tanned skin. "No way. After all the time you spent trying to convince us that you and Kendra had a *connection* after dancing with her at the captain's wedding, I'm going to be reminding you about this when we're all old and gray."

Derek muttered under his breath as he tightened the straps on his own rucksack. "Yeah, well tell me this: What does that big bear shifter have that I don't?"

Angelo chuckled along with everyone else. The only member of the team who didn't laugh was Second Lieutenant Ben Watson, and that was only because he was the new guy and didn't know why the whole thing was so damn funny. Angelo felt bad about Watson being out of the loop, but it wasn't like he could just come out and tell the lieutenant about the secret government organization called the Department of Covert Operations; or about humans known as shifters who possessed naturally occurring genetic mutations that gave them certain animal traits, like claws, fangs, enhanced speed and reflexes, and improved senses; or about man-made versions of shifters nicknamed hybrids; or any of the other crazy crap the team had been involved with in the past year or so. How did you explain to someone that there really were monsters in the world, complete with sharp teeth and even sharper claws? Worse, how did you explain that some of those monsters were actually the good guys?

Angelo was about to point out to Derek that the DCO's resident bear shifter had seventy-five pounds of muscle and six inches on him, not to mention a face that didn't scare small children, when screams of terror from the far end of the village silenced the words in his mouth.

Angelo had his M4 in his hands and was running toward the sound as the rest of the guys spread out behind him, checking for incoming threats. He rounded the corner of a dilapidated building and was heading down a dirt road lined with more crumbling buildings when a man covered in blood ran toward him. Two more men followed, fear clear in their eyes and blood staining their clothes.

At first, Angelo thought it was an IED—an improvised explosive device—but that didn't make sense. He hadn't heard an explosion. He slowed down anyway, worried he was leading the team into an ambush.

One of the men pointed behind him, shouting something in Tajik. Angelo's grasp of the language was pretty good, but the man was speaking way too fast for him to make out what he was saying. Then he figured it out.

*Monster.*

He opened his mouth to ask where the "monster" was, but the man was already halfway down the road. Angelo picked up the pace only to skid to a stop in front of a mud-covered shack a few moments later. He knew he was in the right place because there was a guy who looked like he'd been sliced up by Freddy Krueger on the ground in front of it.

Angelo got a sinking feeling in his gut. He'd seen damage like this before.

He jumped over the dead guy and was through the door before he even thought about what he was doing—thinking only slowed you down in situations like this.

Angelo raised his M4, ready to pop the first threatening thing he saw. If he was right about what had attacked those men, it would take multiple shots to kill the thing.

But what he found stopped him in his tracks. Derek and Lieutenant Watson skidded to a stop right behind him.

There wasn't a square foot of wall space in the one-room shack that wasn't splattered with blood, and in the middle of it stood a pretty, dark-haired woman, gazing down at two dead men at her feet. Her shirt was on the floor beside them, one of her bra straps was torn, and her skirt was ripped. Her feet were bare and covered in dirt, and her long hair hung down around her face, almost to her waist.

Angelo felt a rage build inside him like nothing he'd ever felt before, and he was torn between staying where he was and going after the rest of the men who'd tried to rape her and killing them, too.

He glanced at her hands, hoping to find a knife there and praying he was wrong about what she was. But she didn't have any weapons—unless you counted the wickedly sharp claws on each slender finger. And given the amount of blood in the room, those hands certainly qualified as weapons.

As if just realizing he was there, the woman lifted her head and looked at him with glowing red eyes. She growled, baring her teeth and exposing some seriously long canines.

How the hell had a hybrid turned up in Tajikistan? More importantly, what the hell was he going to do with her?

"What the fuck is that thing?" the lieutenant asked hoarsely even as he raised his carbine and sighted in on the woman's chest.

The woman growled again, louder this time, and crouched down on all fours, like she was getting ready to pounce on them.

*Shit.* Things were about to get ugly.

But instead of leaping at them, her eyes darted around, like she was looking for a way past them. Unfortunately, they were blocking her access to the door and windows, and she knew it. For some reason he couldn't explain, Angelo suddenly didn't see a hybrid monster like those he'd fought in Washington State and down in Costa Rica. He saw a woman who was scared as hell.

"Derek, get everyone outside and away from the building," Angelo ordered softly, never taking his eyes off the woman. "We're freaking her out."

"Freaking her out." Watson snorted. "Are you kidding me? She's the one freaking me out."

"Outside, LT," Angelo ordered again, more firmly this time. "Trust me on this one."

He knew the lieutenant wanted answers, but he didn't have time to give him any. Behind him, Derek was herding the officer toward the door.

"LT, remember when we told you that you'd be seeing some weird shit in the field that they never mentioned in training?" Derek asked. "Well, that weird shit just started. But trust Angelo. He knows what he's doing. He's dealt with these things before."

Their voices faded as they moved outside.

The woman's eyes followed Derek and Watson until they disappeared from sight; then they slid to Angelo. He slowly lowered his weapon, carefully set it on the floor, and raised his hands, speaking softly in Tajik.

"It's okay. You're safe now. No one is going to hurt you."

The red glow in her eyes flickered, then began to fade. Angelo released the breath he'd been holding. Maybe he'd be able to get out of this situation without killing her. He couldn't explain why that mattered to him all of a sudden. She was a hybrid and clearly dangerous. Some might consider killing her to be a mercy—and the only sure way to keep her from hurting anyone ever again.

From what he'd seen, the woman had had a pretty good reason to attack those men. But more importantly, Angelo knew for a fact that not every hybrid was beyond reach. Tanner Howland from the DCO was one of those. The former Army Ranger had learned how to control the rage that defined his kind, and if he could do it, maybe she could, too. At the moment, she certainly seemed to be trying.

Angelo kept up his calm chatter, reassuring the woman that she was safe, and soon enough, her eyes turned to a normal, beautiful brown. There was still anger there, but there was also confusion, maybe even hope.

Raised voices echoed outside, drowning out Angelo's soft words. The villagers had worked up their courage and come looking for blood. The woman's head snapped in that direction, and like a switch being flipped, the veil of calmness that had descended over the female hybrid disappeared.

She tensed, anger warring with what looked like frustration mixed with honest-to-goodness fear on her face. As those emotions ricocheted, her eyes changed from red to green to brown over and over, in a dizzying display like nothing he'd ever seen before.

But then, just as it seemed like she might have a chance, the internal struggle was over, and the hybrid leaped at him.

Every instinct in Angelo's body screamed at him to lunge for his weapon, or at the very least to pull out his knife. But he ignored his instincts and instead set his feet for impact, blocking her slashing claws with his forearm, then ducking down and tackling her. It wasn't the nicest way to treat a woman, but considering the fact that she was trying to kill him, he decided she'd just have to forgive him.

He twisted at the last second, letting his shoulder take the impact. He'd planned to immediately roll his weight onto her, hoping to keep her from getting away by pinning her to the floor like a wrestler, but the hybrid didn't give him a chance. She spun in his grasp, trying to break his hold on her. He wrapped his arms around her, doing his best to trap her clawed hands safely against her breasts as he pulled her back down. She twisted in his arms again, trying to sink her teeth into his shoulder. He hugged her tightly to his chest, whispering over and over that it would be okay, that she was safe, that no one would hurt her.

When she buried her face in his neck, he just about freaked, sure she was going to tear out his throat. He resisted the urge to shove her away and go for his gun, instead continuing to talk to her. Unbelievably, she didn't bite him. She kept struggling to free herself, though. But after a few moments, she went still, all her fight gone.

Angelo glanced down at her. Her cheek was resting against his chest, her eyes closed, and her fingers curled into the front of his uniform. He wasn't sure if she was asleep or had simply passed out from exhaustion. Either way, her breathing was rhythmic and even. The sight of her made his heart ache. This close, he was finally able to see past all the dirt and blood. While he'd thought she was pretty when he'd first seen her, now he realized she was absolutely beautiful—and that she looked vulnerable as hell.

"Damn, Tex-Mex," Derek said from the doorway. "You're good with the ladies when you want to be."

Angelo didn't laugh. "Get on the satellite phone and call Landon. If you can't get him, try Ivy or Clayne. Tell them where we are and that we've stumbled on a hybrid. We need a priority airlift to get her out of here. And whatever you do, don't let LT get on the line to the battalion."

---

"Why does Thomas Thorn want to meet with Ivy and me anyway?" Landon Donovan asked.

He and his wife-slash-partner Ivy were sitting across from John Loughlin, their boss and director of the

DCO, in a small, nondescript building in a suburb of Washington, DC. After coming back from the rescue mission in Costa Rica, he and Ivy had spent weeks believing John was working with the people creating the hybrids they kept going up against. John had quickly figured out they were spying on him and told them to meet him in this building if they wanted to know what was really going on.

That was back in December. Since then, he and Ivy had been meeting with John a couple times a week, reading through the meticulous files he had on the members of the Committee that ran the DCO.

After they'd gotten a look at the files, especially those on three particular members of the Committee—Thomas Thorn, Rebecca Brannon, and Xavier Danes—it became impossible to believe John was the bad guy. All of it was circumstantial stuff that would never be allowed in a court of law, but if even half the information John had collected on these three was true, then they were some of the coldest, most ruthless people around. Landon would rather fight a hybrid bare-handed than face politically powerful monsters like them.

The files, along with proof that John's signature on a document Landon had found months ago showing the DCO had bankrolled Keegan Stutmeir's hybrid research was a forgery, was enough to convince him and Ivy that their boss was clean. It didn't hurt that John had opened up about the strange shifter Ivy had run into on the rooftops of Crystal City a while back, the one with the reptilian eyes and the disconcerting presence. Turns out, he was Adam, the first shifter the DCO had ever recruited—the one who'd supposedly gone rogue and killed his teammates.

"You should know by now you can't trust every classified file you read," John had told them months ago. "The real story about what happened to Adam and his team is a lot different than what's in that file. He's been on the run since 2003. If the people who framed him back then knew he was still alive, they'd go to any lengths to hunt him down and kill him."

In response to Landon's question, John looked up from the report he was currently perusing on the other side of the table to regard Landon over his reading glasses. "Why does Thorn want to meet you? Because I've made sure he's aware of the fantastic work you two have been doing for the DCO. And more importantly, I may have implied that you two have a habit of keeping certain…inconvenient…details out of your official reports."

Landon exchanged looks with Ivy. If John only knew.

"Why would you tell him that?" Landon asked.

"I'm hoping you two might be able to get close enough to former senator Thorn to finally have a chance to get some real intel on the man," John admitted, "because reading thousands of old classified documents I've collected over the last ten years isn't getting us anywhere."

"Where and when are we meeting Thorn?" Ivy asked. "And what do you think he'll want to talk about?"

"You're scheduled to meet him at Chadwick-Thorn's corporate offices tomorrow at nine," John said. "As far as what he'll want to talk about, your guess is as good as mine. Mostly, he'll size you up to see if you'll be receptive to working with him, though I wouldn't be surprised if he brings up what happened in Costa Rica. If we're right and someone else on the Committee was backing the hybrid experimentation going on down there, he's going to be sniffing for details."

Landon still couldn't understand how a man who had stepped down from his senate seat three years ago to take a hand in running his defense contractor company was still on the Committee. But according to John, once a person was selected for the Committee, it was a lifetime position.

Landon was about to ask how much detail he and Ivy should get into with the ex-senator when his cell rang. He pulled his phone out of his pocket and frowned when he recognized the number of the satellite phone Angelo and his team carried. There was no way in hell they'd call unless it was important.

He thumbed the button. "Angelo?"

"No, Captain. It's Derek. We're in Tajikistan and have a situation. We need your help."

Landon glanced at Ivy to see her looking at him in concern. With her feline shifter hearing, she had easily picked up the words.

"What's wrong?" he asked Derek. "Is everyone okay?"

"We're fine, Captain. But Angelo captured one of those unique individuals like we met in Costa Rica."

Derek couldn't say the word *hybrid* over the satellite phone because everything was recorded. But there was no doubt that's what the Special Forces medic was talking about. Landon was about to ask how the hell they'd stumbled across such a unique individual in the middle of Tajikistan, but Derek continued.

"Captain, Angelo thinks this is one you're going to want to see. She's kind of...special."

Landon saw Ivy's dark eyes widen. They'd never

encountered a live female hybrid before. "What do you mean...special?"

There was an uncomfortable pause. They could only say so much over the satellite phone. "Well, Captain, there's no other way to say it...she kind of reminds me of Ivy. The way she moves and behaves...it's a little eerie," Derek said. "Angelo thinks you need to come and get her."

Beside Landon, Ivy went pale. He almost reached out to take her hand but caught himself just in time. While John might have been honest with them, they hadn't come clean with him about a lot of things—like the fact that they were married.

Landon glanced at John, wishing for about the hundredth time that they'd been able to tell him about Stutmeir capturing Ivy and stealing her DNA. It would have made what he was about to ask a whole lot easier.

"Hang on, Derek." Landon lowered the cell phone. "John, Angelo and his Special Forces team have captured a hybrid in Tajikistan. They need help getting her out of the country and back here to the DCO."

Landon's gut clenched at the look of horror in his wife's eyes. He knew she was terrified of the female hybrid being brought back to the DCO, and he couldn't blame her. They needed to hide that her DNA had been taken, and he knew she felt responsible for it having been used in this way. But if Angelo had taken the thing alive, it was because he thought the creature had a chance to conquer the hybrid serum running through her veins, like Tanner had done. Ivy might be too scared to see that at the moment though, so he hoped she would just trust Angelo's judgment, like he did.

Across from him, John was already on his cell. Landon heard him saying something about a priority airlift out of Bagram Air Base.

"Derek," Landon said into the phone. "We're setting up an extraction now. Can I get in-country transport to where you are now, or do you need to move to a secure location first?"

Landon glanced at Ivy again as he wrote down the grid square location Derek gave him. She was pale as a ghost and her hands were shaking. He tried to comfort her with a look, but she wasn't paying attention. He had no doubt that, in her head, she was right back there in that lab in Washington State as Stutmeir's doctors tortured her and took her DNA. All these months and it was still like it had just happened yesterday.

He prayed that finding this hybrid wasn't going to destroy everything they'd worked so hard to keep hidden. But right then, he didn't know if God was going to answer that particular prayer.

# Chapter 2

ANGELO LOOKED OUT THE WINDOW OF THE BLACK Hawk at the rapidly approaching asphalt and concrete maze that was Bagram Air Base. Fortunately, they didn't seem to be heading for any of the main terminals. That was good. Angelo had no desire to parade this woman around a couple hundred curious people. He'd already figured out that she didn't like crowds much.

He twisted his wrist around to see his watch—something that was rather complicated since the woman was sleeping in his arms at the moment—and saw that it had been barely more than six hours since the hybrid had latched on to him and refused to let go. He had to admit, he was impressed. He knew the DCO had some serious pull, but getting a priority clearance helicopter flight all the way from southern Tajikistan to the huge airfield in northern Afghanistan complete with an in-flight refueling in that amount of time? The SOCOM commander himself didn't get that kind of service.

As the helicopter banked, the woman made a small noise of complaint and dug her fingers into his camo overshirt even more. Across from Angelo, Derek's eyes followed the move, but he didn't say anything.

Minka had been like that since leaving the little mud building back in the village, clinging to him like he was the only thing keeping her afloat in a world gone mad. Before she fell asleep, he'd gotten her to tell him her name—Minka Pajari. Looking at her now, sleeping so soundly, it was hard to think of her as anything other than a scared, beautiful young woman. She certainly didn't look like a monster.

The people back in that village would probably argue the point with him, of course. They'd been gathered around the building when Angelo had come out with Minka in his arms. They'd thought she was dead at first and had cheered him for his bravery. When they discovered she wasn't, the crowd had turned ugly fast, demanding he turn her over so they could kill her themselves. A few of the men who'd run out of the building screaming in terror after Minka had defended herself were there, much bolder with half a village of armed men behind them. They were the ones pushing hardest for Minka's blood.

Fortunately, Angelo and the rest of the guys on the team could be quite persuasive when they wanted to be. Even the LT had backed him up. But any goodwill they'd gained by repairing the clinic was gone by the time Angelo had led the way out of the village with Minka still sleeping like a baby in his arms.

Angelo thought Minka would wake up when the Black Hawk touched down, but she didn't stir. Around him, the other guys got to their feet and grabbed their gear. Derek picked up Angelo's rucksack without him having to ask, then followed the rest of the team out. Angelo waited until they'd all left before getting to his feet and carrying Minka off the helicopter.

He was a little surprised to see an armed Air Force Security Police detail waiting to meet them at the edge of the hot pad. They escorted his team to the fully prepped

C-17 Globemaster cargo aircraft a short distance away, then stood guard. The pilot, a major named Falk, and a full-bird colonel named Janzen that Angelo was pretty sure was the airbase commander were both near the cargo ramp of the plane.

Falk took one look at Minka, then frowned in confusion. "That's my classified cargo?"

Janzen lifted a bushy brow in Angelo's direction. "Sergeant?"

Angelo nodded. "Yes, sir. This is her."

Janzen was clearly curious but didn't ask. "Let's get her on board then."

After holding Minka for six hours straight, he should have been relieved to hand over the hybrid to someone else, but there was a crazy part of him that didn't want to let her go.

Aware of Janzen, Falk, and everyone else watching him, Angelo looked down at the beautiful woman in his arms. "Minka. We're here."

She blinked sleepily, gazing up at him with big, brown eyes that were full of trust. "Here?" she repeated in Tajik.

Angelo nodded and slowly set her on her feet. Holding on to one of her hands, he started to lead her into the plane. But Minka wrapped the fingers of her other hand in his overshirt and yanked him back, her eyes wide with terror.

"It's okay," he said softly. "These men are going to take you somewhere safe."

She shook her head wildly, pressing herself up against his side and wrapping her arm around his like a clamp.

"Now I know why we needed a medic on the flight,"

the pilot muttered, motioning to someone inside the plane. A big, blond guy appeared, a black bag in his hand. "Can you give her something to calm her down for the flight?" he asked the man.

"Yeah, sure."

The medic set down his bag, then dropped to one knee. At the sight of the syringe he pulled out, Minka went from a confused, frightened woman to a hissing, snarling hybrid in the blink of her glowing red eyes. Claws and fangs came out, and she lunged at the medic. If Angelo hadn't wrapped his arms around her waist and held her back, the guy would have been in big trouble.

Even with Angelo holding her, the results of her display were pretty awesome. The medic, the pilot, the colonel, and the whole Security Police detail took about five steps back really fast. The SPs recovered first, yanking out their Berettas and aiming them straight at Minka—and Angelo. That just provoked his team to do the same, and within seconds, everyone had their guns pointed at someone.

*Shit.*

Angelo ignored them and focused on Minka. "It's okay. No one is going to hurt you. I promise. You don't have to be afraid."

He hoped that would calm her down, but she didn't shift back. If anything, her eyes glowed more brightly. Okay, talking her down wasn't going to work. Wrapping one arm around her, he slipped the other under her legs and lifted her into his arms, pulling her close. Minka immediately wrapped her arms around his shoulders and buried her face in his neck, her claws and fangs disappearing.

Angelo looked at the medic. "The syringe probably isn't a good idea."

Major Falk scowled from the opposite side of the cargo ramp. "Well, we're going to have to do something. It's a long ride back to the States, and I can't have her running around the cargo hold like a lunatic. And no, my crew chief isn't going to be responsible for her. Hell, my mission didn't even say anything about a person. They told me I'd be carrying a top secret asset. What am I going to do with a psychotic two-legged saber-toothed tiger? What the hell is she anyway?"

Colonel Janzen ignored the pilot, eyeing Angelo and Minka appraisingly. "She seems to be content in your arms, Sergeant."

"Yes, sir," Angelo agreed, only then realizing he'd been slowly rocking Minka gently in his arms. "She's been like this since I picked her up six hours ago."

"Then we don't have a problem." Janzen jerked his chin at the plane. "Get on the bird."

Angelo did a double take. "Sir?"

Lieutenant Watson lowered his pistol and moved forward to stand beside Angelo. "Sir, Sergeant Rios can't just leave the country without orders. He'd be court-martialed."

The colonel narrowed his eyes at Watson. "Lieutenant, I wasn't told much about this operation, but the orders I was given were very clear: get whatever the fuck your SF team is carrying back to the States— ASAP. So it's simple. This"—he gestured at Minka— "woman is going to the States, one way or the other. Your platoon sergeant carried her all the way here, and if he has to carry her the rest of the way, he will." He pinned Angelo with a hard look. "Now, get the fuck on the plane, Sergeant."

When a colonel told you to jump, you usually said, "How high?" But leaving the area of operation? Angelo glanced at the lieutenant.

Watson shrugged. "You heard the colonel, Sergeant. Get on the bird. I'll clear it with HQ when I get back... somehow."

"Hooah, sir." Giving the other guys on the team a nod, Angelo curled his arm more tightly around Minka and climbed up the ramp.

Derek tossed Angelo's rucksack into the back of the plane, and the engines were winding up before Angelo even got situated on the nylon bench seat with Minka. Even though the engine noise grew to uncomfortable levels, she was already falling asleep, as if she couldn't care less about anything now that she was in his arms again.

—∿∿∿—

Landon and Ivy arrived at the DC offices of Chadwick-Thorn exactly at nine. The red-haired receptionist smiled and told them to have a seat in the immense lobby.

"Mr. Thorn will be with you in a few minutes."

That had been fifteen minutes ago.

Landon tossed the latest copy of *Fortune 500* on the table and looked out the expansive row of windows lining one whole side of the lobby. From there, he could not only see all the way across I-295 and the Potomac River, but he could also easily make out the shops and restaurants of Old Town, Alexandria.

"I wonder how often they have to clean these windows," Landon mused.

Ivy gave him a look. "Seriously? With everything going on right now, you're worrying about how often they clean the windows?"

That wiped the smile right off Landon's face. Ivy was still freaking out about that female hybrid his old team had captured...and with good reason.

"Hey," he said softly. "It's going to be okay."

Landon knew it was a lame thing to say, but he couldn't think of anything better, and he hated to see his wife scared.

Her expression softened. "How, Landon? You know as well as I do that the hybrid Angelo and the other guys found was almost certainly created using my DNA. And if Derek was able to recognize the link between me and this hybrid just by looking at her for a few minutes, how long do you think it will take the doctors at the DCO?"

Her normally dark eyes swirled with green like she was about to shift...or lose control. Landon moved in his chair, pressing his arm up against hers. It was nothing overt enough for someone to notice, but it was contact all the same. They'd become very adept at using subtle signs of affection like this since they'd gotten married, and the effect of the simple touch was amazing.

Even though the green glimmer faded from Ivy's eyes, Landon still glanced out the corner of his eye at the receptionist across the room, just to be sure she hadn't overheard. But the woman was on the phone not paying any attention to them.

He turned his attention back to his wife, using one finger to caress her forearm. "Zarina will do everything she can to cover it up like she did with that girl we found in Canada, the one the doctors experimented on with

your DNA. She was able to contaminate the evidence
so no one could make a connection between that girl
and you."

Ivy didn't say anything as she stared out the big windows at the wind-roughened surface of the Potomac.

The hell with whether the receptionist saw or didn't
see. Landon gently turned Ivy's chin until she was looking at him. "And hey, if the DCO does figure it out and
wants to fire us over the fact that we broke their damn
rule that said I was supposed to kill you if you were
about to get captured because we fell in love with each
other, screw them. We'll be just fine on our own."

She reached up and gave his hand a quick squeeze
before dropping her hand with a glance at the receptionist. "I know that."

"If you know, what has you so worried?"

She was silent as she looked back out at the water
again. In the distance, one of the harbor's water taxis
plowed up a white froth, and Ivy seemed transfixed by it.

"If this hybrid was made with my DNA, it will mean
I'm responsible for yet another woman being experimented on and tortured," she finally said. "Knowing
Stutmeir's doctors did it once already with that precious
teenage girl from Canada was hard enough to deal with.
But another woman, one that has almost certainly been
horribly mistreated for months? I don't know if that's
something I can go through again."

Landon remembered the weeks right after they'd
found that girl like it was yesterday. Ivy had been a
mess. He'd tried to tell her over and over that what had
happened to the girl wasn't her fault, that the blame laid
squarely on the shoulders of those sick assholes trying

to use science and medicine to create man-made shifters. But his words hadn't helped. She blamed herself for
every minute of suffering she imagined that girl endur-
ing, and nothing he said would ever change that.

He almost reached out to pull her into his arms,
then stopped himself. He finally settled for touching
her knee out of sight of the receptionist. "Ivy, I don't
know what we're going to find when we get back to
the DCO complex, but one way or another, we'll get
through it together."

Ivy nodded, but he could see in her eyes that she was
already imagining the worst.

Landon glanced at his watch. Obviously, former
senator Thorn wasn't big on punctuality. He would have
said as much to Ivy, but right then, Thomas Thorn and
another man walked into the lobby and toward them.
Landon stood and buttoned his suit jacket. Ivy rose as
well, running her hands down the jacket of her pantsuit.

According to his file, Thorn was fifty-nine years old,
but he could have easily been mistaken for a man ten
years younger. He was clean shaven and extremely fit,
with a head of dark hair that didn't even have a sprin-
kling of gray in it yet. He was impeccably dressed, too.
His suit probably cost more than Landon made in a
month. Hell, his paycheck probably couldn't cover the
man's shoes.

Thorn moved with a confident stride and a casual
smile on his unlined face. No surprise that he'd won
so many elections as a senator, all by landslides. He
exuded pure charm and charisma. But while his face and
smile were open and inviting, his eyes were as sharp
and intense as a hunter's. Thorn was studying Landon

and Ivy as he closed the distance between them, taking in every detail. Landon reminded himself again to be careful around this guy. He was dangerous.

"Agent Donovan. Agent Halliwell. Thank you for stopping by," Thorn said as he shook first Landon's hand, then Ivy's. "John has told me so much about your team's exploits that I thought I should meet you in person."

Landon smiled. "It's a privilege."

The former senator turned to the tall, blond man beside him. "This is Douglas Frasier, my head of security."

Landon didn't need an introduction. According to the file John had on forty-two-year-old Frasier, the man had been an operative for the DCO back in 2003 but had been injured in the line of duty and left due to medical reasons. The file had been sketchy on the details, but Landon got the feeling it had something to do with Adam. Landon quickly figured out what kind of injury had ended the man's career at the DCO when Frasier reached out to shake hands. He could barely lift his arm. His grip wasn't very firm, either.

"Shall we tour the facility as we talk?" Thorn asked.

"Sounds good," Landon said.

Thorn led the way while Frasier followed a good ten feet behind. While Landon was sure that at least some portion of the complex conducted serious design and engineering work, the areas of the building Thorn showed them seemed more suited to impressing visiting politicians and dignitaries. There were lots of mock-ups and models of weapons systems, advanced communication gear, and general fluffy, feel-good stuff about how much great work the company was doing for America's defense.

Thorn stopped in front of a wall mural halfway down a long hallway. It was a stylized world map with labels and pins stuck all over the place. There were half a dozen pins in the DC area, but there were ten times that many scattered across the rest of the states. Most were associated with major military installations, but some seemed to be out in the middle of nowhere. Landon couldn't think of anything of military or industrial significance in those areas, but since it wasn't like Chadwick-Thorn would show a secret hybrid facility on a map in the hallway, he muzzled his curiosity.

He took a quick glance in the area around Tajikistan though, on the off chance that Chadwick-Thorn had a pin near the place where his old team had found the female hybrid, but no such luck.

After nearly an hour of what amounted to nothing more than a dog and pony show, Landon was wondering why the hell he and Ivy were there. Other than a little personal chitchat, Thorn hadn't said anything to them he wouldn't have said to a congressional aid from Ohio.

But then Thorn took them to his fancy office on the top floor of the building with more expansive windows overlooking the river, the Pentagon, and the Washington Monument off in the distance.

Landon glanced at Ivy out the corner of his eye as they slipped into the two chairs in front of Thorn's desk. He didn't have to look over his shoulder at Frasier posted by the door to figure out that the tone of the meeting had gone from casual to intense.

Thorn stood gazing out the window for a time, his hands behind his back. "I was in the gallery in the DCO's conference room behind the one-way glass when you two were being debriefed after that mission in Washington State," he said. "While the written report of the events I read after the fact was quite impressive, hearing you two describe the operation in person was even more so. It's quite obvious that you two make a very good team."

Landon didn't say anything, and neither did Ivy. They both stared at Thorn's back, waiting to see where this was going.

"I couldn't help feeling that the situation on the ground might have been a bit messier than your report let on," Thorn added.

Landon exchanged looks with Ivy. If John was right, the former senator was sniffing around to see if they were the type who didn't mind getting their hands dirty. While he and Ivy had been forced to make the tough call more than once, it had always been because it was the right thing to do. But Thorn wasn't asking whether they knew the difference between right and wrong—he was wondering if they'd do the wrong thing if they were ordered to do it.

"Things on the ground are always messier and more complicated than most people care to hear about," Landon said carefully. "We simply focused our report on the critical facts we thought most pertinent to the people attending the debriefing."

Thorn didn't turn away from the window, but Landon expected he was smiling. "And I'd imagine that most of those listening to your briefing that day appreciated the discretion. But I'm a man who's comfortable with details that might make others cringe. In your report, I remember reading a brief line or two about you killing Keegan

Stutmeir, Agent Donovan, while Agent Halliwell dealt with Jeff Peters. However, there were no details on the exact circumstances of either death. Would you mind telling me exactly how they died?"

Landon glanced at Ivy. She smoothed an imaginary stray hair back into the neat bun at the nape of her neck. She wasn't thrilled with where this was going. Neither was he. But they'd thought the conversation might detour in this direction. As long as Thorn didn't try and bring up the subjects of Ivy's DNA, her torture, or the months they'd spent chasing after Klaus and Renard on their own, they'd be fine. If Thorn tried to dig into any of those areas, the conversation was over.

"I chased Stutmeir down as he tried to escape. When he ran out of ammo, he pulled a knife on me. I got it away from him and shoved it through his chest," Landon said with a quiet fury he didn't have to fake. The man had been the one ultimately responsible for Ivy getting tortured. A knife through the heart had been too good for him.

Thorn turned to look at him. "Stutmeir only had a knife? And there was no way you could have taken him alive?"

Landon had asked himself the same thing. "I suppose I could have tried to take him alive, but some people are too dangerous to let live. I killed Stutmeir because he needed to die."

Thorn regarded him in silence for a moment, then turned his hawklike gaze on Ivy. "And the former DCO operative Peters? How did he die, Agent Halliwell?"

Ivy's eyes flashed green as she smiled. "I ripped out his throat, though I was nice enough to let him keep his knife while I did it. I wanted him to feel like he had a chance there at the end."

Thorn didn't look away; he seemed unconcerned by the green glow rimming her irises. "If I remember correctly, Peters attacked you several years ago when you were partners. I assume that previous attack had something to do with your decision to rip out his throat instead of detaining him?"

Ivy let out a little growl. "As Captain Donovan said, he was a man who needed to die."

Thorn lifted a brow, then laughed. "Remind me never to make you angry, Agent Halliwell. I have no problem with the decisions either one of you made. We live in a difficult, complicated world. Many times, the thing most needed is decisive action taken with a clear mind and unencumbered soul. I think you two have the ability to take that decisive action at the appropriate time. It's a talent in short supply, even in the DCO."

Thorn glanced at Frasier, giving him a nod. Frasier stepped out of the office without a word and closed the door behind him.

When they were alone, Thorn stabbed Landon and Ivy with a sharp look. "Tell me what happened down in Costa Rica. And don't even start with any of that sanitized crap you put in the official report."

# Chapter 3

MINKA'S EYES FLUTTERED OPEN, BUT SHE CLOSED THEM
again and snuggled against Angelo. She smiled. His
name was fitting, considering he was her guardian angel.

She had no idea what was happening, where she was
going, or what these American military people wanted
with her. All she knew was that for the first time in a very
long time, she felt calm. The rage that had been inside
her almost every minute of her life since those doctors
had injected that red liquid into her had somehow disappeared the moment the big, handsome American soldier
had wrapped his arms around her.

She hadn't wanted to attack him back in the village.
When he'd ordered the other soldiers out of the building,
then taken his hands off his weapon and started whispering soothing words in Tajik to her, she had thought the
beast would back off and give her a chance to regain
control. His scent and voice had been so relaxing,
almost hypnotic, that her claws had immediately begun
to retract. And his face was so beautiful—honest and
sincere. With his dark, soulful eyes, wide mouth, and
silky, black hair that almost reached to his shoulders, he
was quite possibly the most attractive man she had ever
seen. She'd been ready to take his hand and let him lead
her wherever he wanted because she instinctively knew
it would be somewhere safe.

But then the cries of the angry villagers had shattered

the peaceful scene into a thousand pieces, and the beast
had come charging back, taking control and extending
her claws and teeth to their fullest.

When the beast lunged at the soldier, Minka had
fully expected him to pick up his weapon and kill her.
But he hadn't. And when he'd wrapped his muscular
arms around her and pulled her tightly against his chest,
his scent had enveloped her and a complete and total
sense of peace had settled over her. She didn't know
why being near him made the beast inside her go away,
and she didn't care. She was Minka in his arms and a
monster out of them. That was all that mattered to her.

She closed her eyes again and snuggled against him.
She thought about asking where they were going, but
then realized she didn't care. The horrible doctors were
far behind her now and she was safe in Angelo's arms.

———

Angelo couldn't remember being so exhausted. He'd
been holding Minka for the better part of their twenty-
hour flight back to the States. He'd slipped away long
enough to use the tiny restroom on the C-17 once, thank
God, but other than that, he'd held her the entire time.

He didn't understand why, but Minka only seemed
calm when she was in his arms. Every time he tried to
put her on the seat next to him, she'd dig in her claws.
And when she fell asleep deeply enough for him to
move her, she immediately woke up and climbed right
back into his lap. Finally, he just gave up. If the only
way she could sleep was in his arms, then so be it. She
looked like she needed the rest. Besides, what man
didn't enjoy a beautiful woman curled up in his lap,

even if she did treat him like a scratching post every time she woke up?

He'd gotten Minka to eat something a couple hours earlier, when the crew chief came down to the cargo section and tossed him a flight-crew box lunch and a bottle of water. Minka clearly hadn't thought much of it, but he'd done his best to get her to eat as much of the dry sandwich as he could. She felt so light and fragile in his arms, he doubted she'd eaten a full meal in weeks, maybe months.

As Minka had been eating, one of the sleeves on the camo overshirt he'd given her to wear had slipped down, revealing a series of scars along her forearm, from her wrist all the way up to her inner elbow. He clenched his jaw as he remembered seeing cut marks and puncture wounds like that before, on Ivy, after she'd been captured and tortured by Stutmeir and his doctors. It wasn't that hard to imagine it had been those same doctors who'd tortured Minka. Damn, why the hell hadn't the DCO found and killed those fucking psychos already?

After she'd finished eating, Minka had snuggled up against his chest and fallen asleep again. Angelo should have slept too, but he couldn't take his eyes off her. Even after everything she had obviously been through— exhaustion, starvation, torture—she looked like an angel. A beautiful, peaceful angel. Seeing Minka like this, it was hard to believe she was a hybrid. She looked more like the kind of girl he'd take out on a date—if he was the kind of guy who bothered with dates.

Angelo resisted the urge to push her long, dark hair back from her face, afraid he'd wake her up. Instead, he leaned his head back against the seat. But he didn't close his eyes. They'd be landing soon. Besides, his mind was spinning way too much to consider even taking a combat nap right now. So he watched Minka sleep while he tried to figure out what he was going to do when he got to the DCO.

He'd dealt with the covert organization enough in the past to be seriously worried about what some of the people there might have in mind for Minka. He and Tanner had spent a lot of time talking together down in Costa Rica, and Angelo knew the DCO hadn't treated the hybrid very well. Sure, he was alive, had a place to sleep, and food to eat. But they watched him like a hawk, and constantly poked and prodded him like a damn lab rat. Tanner had told him once that he was alive for one reason: because he was the only known hybrid with a trace of self-control.

Angelo had no doubt that some of the higher-ups in the DCO would regard Minka the same way, like she was just another lab rat to be poked, prodded, and experimented on. Others would be less concerned with what made her tick. They'd simply want to know how they could turn her into a weapon.

As Angelo gazed down at the beautiful woman in his arms, he decided right then he wasn't going to let any of that happen to Minka. She was a person, made this way against her will, then tortured and mistreated by almost everyone around her, even her own people. She needed to be protected, not turned into a science project—or a weapon. She'd gone through enough already.

He was still thinking about exactly how he was going to stop any of that from happening when the stocky crew chief came down the steep stairs from the flight deck and moved halfway into the cargo section.

"We'll be on the ground at Anacostia-Bolling in fifteen minutes. There's a security force from…well, from somewhere to take you where you need to go, wherever that is."

"Thanks," Angelo said.

The crew chief's blue gaze fell on Minka. "Hey, I hope everything works out okay with her. She looks like she's had it pretty hard."

"I hope so, too."

The crew chief did a quick inspection of the cargo section, checking panels, lights, and wires, then headed back upstairs without another word. A few minutes later, Angelo felt the cargo plane start to descend.

Minka didn't even stir when they landed, or when the C-17 taxied for what seemed like a really long time. Heck, she didn't do much more than turn her face into his chest a little more when the cargo ramp dropped down with a rumbling hydraulic groan. Typically the crew chief would have been down there already, checking the plane's status and getting the aircraft's passengers ready to disembark. Maybe the DCO had instructed the guy to stay in the cockpit.

The rear part of the plane had been towed into an aircraft hangar, and Angelo could see three black SUVs waiting for them, along with a team of ten heavily armed men in tactical gear. DCO security, he guessed. He'd hoped Landon and Ivy would be there to meet them, but no such luck.

Minka jerked awake as two of the black-clad men stepped onto the loading ramp of the plane. Angelo held up his hand, indicating for the men to stop where they were. They halted but lifted the barrels of their M4s slightly. Angelo ignored them, focusing on Minka instead. While she was eyeing the men warily, she hadn't shifted, but Angelo got the sensation that she was only a hop, skip, and a jump away from going berserk depending on what the security guards did next.

"It's okay," he whispered.

Wrapping one arm around her shoulder and slipping the other under her knees, he got to his feet. Minka relaxed against his chest, but her eyes remained alert and focused on the men the whole time. Angelo had no doubt the fangs and claws would make an appearance if anyone made a hostile movement. Angelo didn't recognize any of the men, but he knew their type—hardcore security drones who looked like they didn't take a crap without referring to a manual first. If Minka did anything out of line, every one of these Cybermen would happily shoot her dead.

Angelo walked to the end of the cargo bay and down the ramp. One of the men stepped in front of him, forcing him to come to a stop. Tall, with dark hair and eyes that seemed like they didn't miss a thing, he gave Minka an appraising look, then locked gazes with Angelo.

"Does she need to be sedated?"

Angelo shook his head. "No. She's fine as long as no one threatens her."

The man regarded Minka for a few moments, then sized up Angelo again. Finally, he must have come to some conclusion because he nodded his head curtly and pointed at the second Suburban in line.

Four of the guards got into the lead vehicle, while

another four took the back one. That left two guards—including Eagle Eye—with him and Minka. There was a heavy steel cage separating the front and backseats, so it wasn't like the two in the front seat were any braver than the rest. They'd probably just lost at rock, paper, scissors.

Angelo was relieved when Minka allowed him to put her in the seat beside him. He really didn't want to drive through DC traffic with her in his lap. Unfortunately, getting a seat belt on her turned out to be a waste of time. Three seconds after he'd clicked hers into place, the claws came out and she shredded it. Then she wiggled over, sliced through his belt as well and grabbed hold of his arm. She snuggled close, her claws retracting.

He chuckled. "Not into safety restraints, huh?"

Minka ignored him, her eyes huge as they headed out to the highway and she saw DC spread out before her. As the driver sped up and merged onto 295, Angelo really wished he had that seat belt back. He'd rather jump out of a plane with a beach umbrella for a parachute than be on the roads around the nation's capital. The people here drove like they were insane. The driver of the Suburban was a perfect example.

The vehicle headed south on 295, then onto 95 south. The DCO's training and medical complex was about an hour outside the city, near Quantico, so he guessed that's where they were heading. No surprise there—it wasn't like they'd want to have a hybrid brought to their main offices in the middle of town.

Angelo was just trying to look over the driver's shoulder to see how fast they were going when Minka's soft voice yanked his attention back to her.

"What?" he said.

She turned away from the window to regard him with big, cinnamon-brown eyes. "Are there always so many cars on the road here?"

He blinked. "You speak English?"

"Yes," she said simply.

There was a slight accent to the word, maybe Russian or Eastern European mixed in with Tajik. Something told him there had to be an interesting story there, but that would have to wait until later.

He glanced out the side window to see a small two-door Mini go zipping by even though their convoy of SUVs had to be doing over eighty. "Yeah, I guess," he said in answer to Minka's question. "Washington, DC, is a big city with millions of people. The roads are packed from before dawn until well after nightfall."

Minka stared at him for so long he wondered if maybe he'd thrown too many words at her at once. Just because she could say a few words in English, that didn't mean she was fluent. He ran into the same problem with Tajik and Farsi—talk to someone for a few seconds, and they'd start rattling off whole sentences like you were a native.

But Minka only nodded like she understood everything he'd said. "I've never seen so many cars. And they all drive so fast. Everyone here must be very good drivers." When he chuckled, she gave him a confused look. "Did I say something wrong?"

Angelo was stunned to see she actually looked embarrassed. What did she have to be embarrassed about? She spoke English far better than he did Tajik.

"No, you didn't say anything wrong," he said quickly.

"It was just that I was thinking people around here drive like they're crazy. Way too fast."

Minka nodded, accepting his answer. Then, without a word, she crawled into his lap so she could get a better look around. She did it so unabashedly that Angelo couldn't stop himself from grinning as he put a protective arm around her.

She pointed at a big building with a large number of cars parked around it. "What is that place—a mosque?"

He glanced out the window and realized they were passing the big Hoffman Center. "That's a movie theater. The number twenty-two means there are twenty-two screens."

Her eyes widened. "Twenty-two movies playing at the same time?"

He nodded as she went back to gazing out the window again. After that, the drive turned into a game of twenty questions, except it was more like a hundred. He never realized how many things he took for granted until Minka continued to ask him what they all were. Parks, malls, golf courses, carpool lanes, IKEA—the list of things that caught her attention seemed endless, and he couldn't help but smile at the awe in her eyes after each new discovery.

Even the two expressionless gargoyles in the front seat cracked a smile at some of the things she asked, especially when Minka pointed at a man on the side of the road surrounded by cops and K-9s and asked if they were helping him with car trouble.

Thanks to all the questions Minka asked, the hour-long trip to the DCO complex zipped by in a flash. She fell silent as they weaved through the gates and she

caught sight of the armed guards standing there. She
climbed off Angelo's lap but stayed close to him, the
tension returning to her body.

After they got through the gate, she relaxed a little,
but he could tell she was still on edge. When they
stopped behind one of the main buildings, the eagle-
eyed guard opened the back door for them. The moment
he and Minka stepped out, the security force surrounded
them. Two took point to lead the way, but most closed in
behind them. Angelo couldn't decide if they were being
treated like visiting dignitaries or criminals.

At first, he was a little worried Minka might be too
scared to walk on her own because she was definitely
tense as hell. He was all ready to carry her if he had
to, but she only pulled the uniform shirt he'd given her
more tightly to her chest, then latched on to his arm with
her free one and gave him a nod.

They moved through several long hallways with lots
of turns and offices. There were a few open doors, and
even some windows here and there that looked into
cubicle-filled spaces. If it wasn't for the armed security
guards, Angelo might have been lulled into thinking
this was just a normal, everyday Fortune 500 company.
Then again, he was walking beside a woman who could
turn into a snarling she-cat when things went bad. He
sure as hell wasn't walking around Microsoft.

The guards led them into a large, open room that
looked like it couldn't decide whether it wanted to be a
medical facility or a science lab. There were three men
dressed in white lab coats, a half-dozen beds, lots of
equipment that looked like it belonged in a hospital,
and the distinctive smell of antiseptic cleaners. There

were also lots of microscopes, centrifuges, and other things that were probably completely normal in a lab like this, but given the DCO's history with hybrids, Angelo couldn't help thinking it looked a little like Frankenstein's lab.

Minka stiffened the moment they walked into the room, and Angelo slowly slipped his arm down and encircled her waist. He wasn't surprised to discover she didn't think much of the lab-like room.

Angelo looked around for Landon and Ivy and was disappointed to see neither of them were anywhere to be found. Before he could ask where they were, a squirrelly looking jackass in an expensive suit walked in the room. The man took one look at Angelo and Minka and glared at the lead guard.

"Who the hell is this?" he asked, motioning to Angelo. "And why isn't the hybrid sedated and restrained?"

Angelo had never met the man, but he didn't have to be a genius to figure out it was the one and only Dick Coleman, deputy director of the DCO. Landon had said the man was the worst kind of bureaucrat and a Grade A asshole. Angelo immediately decided his friend had been too kind.

Angelo didn't miss the look of irritation that flashed across the security team leader's face at being questioned about how to do his job. "Because I didn't think it was necessary."

"You weren't hired to think. You were hired to look intimidating and occasionally shoot things," Coleman snapped. "Get rid of the soldier; then get that hybrid strapped to a table, so the doctors can tranquilize her."

Angelo knew he couldn't babysit Minka forever, but

he sure as hell wasn't going to turn her over to someone like Coleman, especially if the asshole thought he was going to stick a needle in her. Minka didn't seem interested in waiting around to see what was going to happen. She went from shy, quiet Tajik girl to snarling saber tooth in two heartbeats, lunging forward with a hiss and taking a swipe at Coleman with her claws. If Angelo hadn't tightened his arm around her waist and held her back, the jackass would have been looking for his face in the nearest corner.

But instead of realizing how incredibly fortunate he was to still be alive, Coleman motioned to one of the doctors. "Get her sedated. Now!"

Angelo wrapped his other arm around Minka's waist and yanked her close. The idiot doctor must have thought Angelo was actually going to hold her while he stuck the needle in her arm because he boldly stepped forward with the ridiculously long syringe. Bad idea. If they thought they knew what a pissed-off hybrid looked like before, they got a whole new education on the subject. Minka darted forward so fast and so forcefully she actually dragged Angelo's big-ass body with her. Minka's claws and fangs extended so far, it boggled his mind trying to figure out where they had been hidden. The scream of rage that came out of her was so loud and terrifying, people half a mile away probably pissed themselves.

Trusting Minka wouldn't turn her rage on him, Angelo dug in his heels and got a better grip on her. The move made her hesitate, and he used the opportunity to spin her around behind him. Lashing out with his foot, he kicked the doctor in the hand and sent the syringe flying. Then he planted the sole of his combat boot in the guy's stomach and shoved him back ten feet.

Angelo slipped his right arm around Minka's shoulder and yanked her tightly to him, hoping close physical contact would calm her down like it had back in Tajikistan. She kept hissing and growling, and those weapons of hers definitely didn't retract, but she didn't fight him.

Angelo glowered at the doctor. The man had his arm wrapped around his stomach where Angelo had given him a shove. "You try that again and I'll put the next syringe up your ass. She doesn't do needles. Do I make myself clear?"

The doctor looked to Coleman for guidance, but the deputy director was too busy giving orders to the security guards.

"Restrain her."

Angelo noted with interest that more than half the men didn't move, including Eagle Eye. But four of them moved forward to do Coleman's bidding.

Okay, he'd had enough of this shit. He was hungry, tired, and hadn't even seen a shower in a month. He'd brought Minka here to get some help, but if this was the way the DCO was going to act, he'd haul her right the fuck out of there and dare anybody to stop him.

Jaw tight, he pushed Minka a little farther behind him. She growled long and low but moved as he directed.

"You obviously don't know who you're dealing with, but I can guarantee you boys aren't nearly big enough or mean enough to handle me," he told the four security guards. Then he pointed at Coleman. "And when I'm done with them, you're next. Only it won't be a needle going up your ass like your doctor friend; it'll be my boot and whole fucking leg."

Coleman's face turned so red, Angelo thought he might rupture something. But the guards definitely hesitated.

"That's enough," a soft but firm voice said from the doorway.

Angelo glanced over to see John Loughlin standing there looking like he'd just walked in on a classroom full of unruly schoolkids. Angelo had met the director of the DCO briefly before heading down on that rescue mission to Costa Rica. He'd gotten a pretty good vibe off the man, but Ivy and Landon hadn't been sure they could fully trust him. Angelo had no idea if anything had changed between the director and his friends while he'd been deployed to Tajikistan, but until he knew for sure, he wouldn't put his faith in the man, either.

One thing was definite, though: John knew how to take charge of a situation. With a few words and a couple hard looks, he had the doctors and all the guards except for the team leader cleared out of the room in seconds.

When everyone had left, he turned to the remaining guard. "Jaxson, please find Zarina Sokolov and ask her to come in here."

Jaxson nodded and walked out, leaving Angelo alone with Minka and two of the most powerful men in the United States, if not the world.

"Have you completely lost your mind?" Dick demanded of John. "This is totally against security protocol. This grunt isn't even cleared to be on the complex, much less know about hybrids. And while we're talking about hybrids, leaving us alone with a dangerous one like her without guards for protection is the definition of insanity."

John fixed Coleman with a cool look. "Actually, Sergeant Rios is cleared to be here. If you check the security clearance database, you'll see that he has a top secret clearance and was granted full access to the hybrid program in mid-November of last year."

Angelo might have gone down to Costa Rica to help rescue Kendra and Declan, but he wasn't sure he liked the idea of the DCO director taking it upon himself to associate him with programs Angelo really didn't want to be part of.

Then again, he did like seeing Coleman stand there grinding his teeth together. Maybe if John kept poking him, the man's head would actually explode.

"Are you trying to tell me that you've been using active duty Department of Defense personnel to conduct sweeps for hybrids on foreign soil?" Dick spit out. "And that you've been doing it since November? Without informing the Committee or me? You know that's a direct violation of Committee protocols and that I have no choice but to make sure they know."

"I'm sure you will. Let me know how that goes," John said, appearing completely unconcerned. "Until then, you might want to leave the lab, considering there's a dangerous hybrid in here and all."

The vein in Dick's neck throbbed. Damn, he looked like he might actually take a swing at John. Minka must have thought so too, because she started hissing and yowling at the deputy director, trying to free herself from Angelo's restraining arm. Not that she was trying too hard. If she were, Angelo wouldn't have been able to stop her. But Coleman clearly decided he'd had enough because he threw a disgusted look at all of them, then turned and stormed out.

Minka calmed down the moment Coleman was gone. Her fangs and claws retracted and the red glow faded from her eyes. She still stayed close to Angelo though, and he slipped an arm around her waist again, holding her close.

A few feet away, John regarded them with interest. "You did a good thing getting this girl back here to us, Sergeant Rios."

"Did I?" Angelo asked sharply. "Because right now, I'm getting the idea she'd be safer in Tajikistan. The villagers might have been trying to kill her, but at least they weren't trying to experiment on her."

John seemed taken aback by the heat in Angelo's voice, but before he could say anything, a woman's voice interrupted him.

"And there isn't going to be anyone experimenting on her here, either."

The Russian accent immediately gave away the attractive woman with wavy, blond hair and blue eyes as Zarina Sokolov, one of the few scientists in the world who actually understood the hybrid process that Stutmeir and his team had developed. Zarina had been kidnapped from her home in Moscow by Stutmeir early on in his insane quest to create man-made shifters, and while he'd executed many of the scientists and doctors he'd taken captive, she'd proven herself smart enough to keep around. But while the Russian doctor had been forced to help Stutmeir create the first hybrid generation, she had also done a lot of good. For one thing, she'd saved Tanner's life by making it look like he had died, then slipping him out of captivity with the other bodies Stutmeir's men had been taking out for burial. She'd also tried to help Ivy escape when she'd been captured. That plan hadn't worked out as well, but not due to lack of effort.

But even more than all that, Landon and Ivy had told him that the brilliant doctor had single-handedly driven the DCO's own hybrid program completely off-course and made it impossible for anyone here to ever replicate the hybrids Stutmeir had created out in Washington State.

So while Angelo might not have known if he could trust John, he knew Zarina was okay.

"Angelo," John said as if reading his mind. "I'll never let anyone experiment on this girl again. You have my word on that." Before Angelo could point out that he didn't know John well enough for his word to mean all that much, the director motioned toward Zarina. "I think it would be better if I leave you two in Zarina's capable hands, at least until you can trust we're on the same team."

Giving Angelo a nod, John turned and walked out, leaving him and Minka with the Russian doctor. Angelo made the introductions and was surprised when Minka seemed to immediately take to the woman.

"Let's go to my office," Zarina said with a smile. "I have everything I need there to check Minka out, and I think it will be less stressful."

Angelo glanced at Minka to see what she thought of that. Minka nodded but kept one hand on his arm.

They walked down several long hallways with a few

left and right turns thrown in just to confuse him, but finally they arrived at Zarina's office. It didn't have any beds or the antiseptic smell like the lab they'd been in, but it had a microscope, carts full of medical instruments, and pieces of expensive-looking equipment just like the other room, in addition to a desk, a computer, and a printer.

Zarina was reaching for a stethoscope on one of the carts when Minka suddenly whirled around to face the door. Fearing Coleman had come back to cause trouble, Angelo turned and instinctively pushed Minka behind him but then relaxed when he saw Landon and Ivy. He couldn't remember the last time he'd seen his friend in a suit, unless you counted the tux Landon had worn at his wedding, but Angelo had to admit his friend pulled off the corporate look well. Ivy was dressed in a more feminine version of the same, her waist-length hair in a bun.

He glanced at Minka. "It's okay. They're friends."

Grinning, he stepped forward to shake his best friend's hand, engulfing him in a man hug. Landon slapped him on the back so hard Minka let out a growl. Angelo pulled away with a chuckle, then turned to introduce Minka to the two people he respected more than anyone in the world only to stop when he saw that Minka and Ivy were staring at each other in wide-eyed shock.

He guessed Minka was staring because she'd never smelled anyone remotely like her before, and Ivy was definitely like her. Having the two of them standing this close together, it was impossible not to miss the connection between the two of them. It wasn't that they looked a lot alike—no one would mistake them for sisters or anything. But there was definitely something eerily similar in the way they carried themselves.

He expected Ivy to step forward and greet Minka. The way Ivy had been treated by Stutmeir and his doctors, she understood better than anyone what it was like to be tortured and treated like something less than human. Instead, Ivy turned and walked out of the room without saying a word. Angelo looked at Landon to see that his friend was just as shocked as he was.

"Is everything okay?" Angelo asked.

"Yeah." Landon gave him a tight smile. "I have to admit, when you said you needed to get a hybrid back here, I didn't think you'd be coming with her."

Angelo shrugged. "It was the only way we could get her on the plane short of drugging her, and I wasn't going to let that happen. She really doesn't like needles, and she definitely doesn't have a problem letting people know it."

Landon gave Minka an appraising look. "Really? If it wasn't you telling me she's a hybrid, I wouldn't believe it. She looks harmless."

Angelo chuckled. "Ask Dick how harmless she is. She would have removed his face just a few minutes ago if I hadn't been holding on to her."

"She doesn't like Dick, huh? She obviously has good taste then." Landon held out his hand to her. "I'm hoping you speak English because my Tajik is rusty as hell. I'm Landon Donovan, a friend of Angelo's."

Minka stared at Landon's hand for a moment but didn't reach out and take it. Instead, she only nodded her head in his direction, then stepped closer to Angelo and took his arm again.

Angelo ignored the curious look his former A-team leader gave him. "Give her some time. She has a lot of reasons to distrust people. Minka, this is my best friend. You can trust him like you trust me, I promise. Landon, this is Minka Pajari. And yes, she speaks English."

Minka nodded at Landon again but didn't say anything.

"Now that the introductions are finally over with," Zarina said with a smile, "maybe I can check out Minka and make sure she's okay?"

Landon nodded. "Sure. Sorry to hold you up, Doc. I need to talk to Angelo for a second anyway."

Angelo was fine with that. He turned to Minka, taking her hands in his. Damn, they were so tiny in his big, rough mitts. "I'm going to talk to Landon while Zarina checks you out, okay?"

Minka shook her head. "I'm afraid."

"You don't have to be afraid," he said softly. "Zarina won't hurt you."

"It's not that. It's just…" She dropped her eyes, her voice trailing off.

Angelo slid a knuckle beneath her chin and gently tipped her face up. Even with all the dirt, she still looked beautiful. "I wouldn't let you stay here if I didn't think you'd be safe, Minka. I'll just be out in the hallway. I won't leave your sight."

She bit her lip. "Promise?"

He smiled. "I promise."

Minka's gaze went from Zarina to him. She still looked like she didn't think it was a good idea, but she finally nodded. Even then, she kept her eyes locked on him as she sat down in one of the armchairs in front of the desk and let the doctor examine her. The fear in her eyes at the thought of being just a few steps away from him made Angelo's heart squeeze as he and Landon walked into the hallway.

Landon noticed it, too. "Wow, she's really attached to you."

"Yeah," Angelo agreed as he watched Zarina shine a small light in Minka's eyes. He tensed, afraid Minka would freak out, but instead she smiled at something the Russian doctor said. Damn, Zarina was good with hybrids. "I'm not sure why, but being in immediate contact with me seems to help Minka stay calm. Strange, I know."

Landon shrugged. "Not really. Zarina has that same kind of effect on Tanner."

Regardless, Angelo kept one eye on Minka as he got Landon up to speed with what had happened in Tajikistan and the crappy initial meeting he and Minka had had with Coleman and his damn doctors.

"I'm telling you right now," he added, "I won't let anyone lock Minka up and experiment on her. If Coleman thinks he's going to try that, I'll haul her cute ass out of here and disappear with her."

Landon shook his head. "You won't have to do that. Nobody is going to hurt Minka. John will make sure of that."

Angelo gave him a sharp look. "You and Ivy trust him now?"

Landon nodded. "It's a long story that we can talk about later, but yeah, we do. He's on our side. He'll find Minka a place to stay where she's comfortable—maybe one of the dorms here on the complex, like the place Tanner stays."

Angelo wasn't so sure anyplace on the complex was going to work for Minka, not with Coleman around. "She's going to need a place she can feel safe, preferably somewhere I can stay with her until she gets settled in." He sighed. "Speaking of which, maybe John could run interference with the battalion. The new lieutenant said he'd take care of it, but you know Major Bennett. LT could use some backup."

"I'll mention it to John. I'll also talk to him about Minka and make sure he understands the situation. He'll find a safe place for her." Landon glanced at Minka. "I'm going to let you get back in there. I'll catch you later."

Angelo nodded. He wasn't too sure about John yet, but if Landon said the director would figure something out, then he would. If not, Angelo would damn well keep his promise and get Minka out of there.

He headed back into Zarina's office and was surprised when he found Minka talking with the doctor in Russian and holding a plush toy sloth of all things.

# Chapter 4

MINKA'S WORLD HAD BEEN SPINNING FROM THE moment she'd arrived at this place. There were some people she immediately felt a connection with, like the nice man in charge of the guards; the doctor, Zarina; and Angelo's friend, Landon. They all seemed nice, and the beast inside her felt no threat from them.

Then there was the woman who had come in with Landon. Minka couldn't understand what to make of her, and neither could the beast inside her. The woman's scent had been so strangely familiar. But more than that, there had been something else about her that told Minka she was incredibly important. She just didn't know why. And unfortunately, the woman had left before Minka could figure it out.

But the most unsettling aspect of this place that Angelo had brought her was the lab. It put her whole body on edge. It was like the beast was waiting just a few inches away, ready to burst back out if one more bad thing happened.

That was why she'd been so worried when Angelo had wanted to go out into the hallway to talk to his friend. In fact, she had just about panicked. What if the beast came back the moment he stepped away? Even after that doctor had come at her with the needle and she'd lost control, Angelo had brought her back from the edge simply by pulling her close. If he let her go, would the monster come back?

Minka took a deep breath, trying to calm herself the best she could as she sat down in the chair beside Zarina's desk. She couldn't keep holding on to Angelo for the rest of her life. Besides, Zarina seemed like a very nice woman—and surprisingly calm even though she was in the same room with a monster. Perhaps Zarina could help keep the beast away.

Still, as logical as that all sounded, Minka kept her eyes locked on Angelo. If the beast came charging back, she was prepared to be back on her angel's arm in an instant. But just being able to see Angelo seemed to have a calming effect. Not as much as touching him, but if she focused her attention on him, she found that the beast was content to murmur in the background.

She was so focused on Angelo that she didn't realize the female doctor had begun the examination. She stiffened, remembering all those times the other doctors had hurt her.

Zarina must have noticed how tense Minka was because she immediately stopped what she was doing and stepped back. "Minka, I just want to make sure those people who did this to you didn't do anything else." She smiled. "I promise I won't hurt you."

Minka didn't say anything. While she believed Zarina, that didn't mean she wasn't scared to death at the same time. She wrapped her arms around herself protectively, pulling the uniform overshirt Angelo had given her tighter as she looked in his direction again. Part of her wanted to call out to him while the other part wanted to run into the hallway and cling to him. But it seemed like he was having an important conversation with his friend. And she had already caused him so much trouble. She didn't want to cause more.

"Minka, do you feel like you're about to lose control?" Zarina asked suddenly.

Minka jerked her head up to stare at the doctor. She wanted to shake her head, afraid of what Zarina might do to her if she knew how close the beast was to breaking free. But instead, Minka nodded, then waited for Zarina to reach for a needle—that was what the other doctors had done.

Zarina smiled. "I understand, and it's okay. What you need is something else to focus on, something you can hold on to that will help keep the animal calm."

How was it possible for Zarina to understand what she was feeling? It was like she had dealt with people like her before. But something to hold on to was exactly what Minka needed—preferably, *someone*.

Minka watched as Zarina walked around her desk and picked up a small, furry…thing from the bookshelf behind it. Minka thought at first it was some kind of rabbit pelt. What on earth did the doctor want her to do with that?

But one sniff told her the thing had never been alive, and she was more confused than ever. It was not until Zarina came over to her that Minka realized it was some kind of child's toy, soft and furry like the animal it was supposed to represent. Minka had owned a cuddly bear when she was very little, but it had looked nothing like this one. She wasn't sure what kind of animal this was even supposed to be.

Zarina smiled. "This is Boris. He's a sloth from Central America. He is very friendly and likes to be hugged." She held out the toy to Minka. "Give him a hug and see if it helps."

Minka felt very foolish as she took the child's toy and gave it a squeeze. But she immediately realized holding the furry thing did indeed help. It felt like the beast inside was smiling. If she hadn't known better, she would have thought it was amused.

So she hugged Boris and kept an eye on Angelo standing outside the door as Zarina slowly unbuttoned Angelo's uniform overshirt enough to check her chest, stomach, and back. Minka tensed when Zarina ran gentle hands across the faded scars on her back and shoulders.

Even though Zarina wasn't hurting her, the feel of her hands there made the beast uncomfortable. Minka hugged Boris more tightly, but Zarina was too busy talking softly to herself in Russian to notice.

"Why would any human do this to another?" Zarina murmured softly.

"The doctors who made me this way tortured me to force the beast to come out," Minka answered in the same language.

Zarina looked at her in surprise. "You speak Russian?"

Minka nodded. "Yes. My father is Russian. He was serving in the Soviet Army stationed in Dushanbe when he met my mother. After the Soviet Union collapsed, he stayed and they married."

Zarina seemed delighted to have someone else to speak Russian with, and Minka couldn't help but pick up on the woman's exuberance. She smiled, automatically relaxing as the doctor continued her exam.

But no matter how distracted she was by Zarina's

words, she was aware of Angelo's return the moment he walked into the room.

"I see you've made a new friend," Angelo said, chuckling as he placed a gentle hand on her back. Minka immediately felt herself relax.

Zarina glanced at him as she wrote something down on a notepad. "There have been quite a few studies that show hugging a plush animal can help with anxiety in adults as well as children."

"This is Boris. He is helping me get through the exam," Minka said softly, hoping Angelo wouldn't laugh at her.

But he didn't. He merely reached out and ran a finger over the sloth's furry head. "If he's a friend of yours, he's a friend of mine." He glanced at Zarina. "Is this the one Tanner bought for you as a way to apologize for running off to Costa Rica?"

Zarina nodded. "Yes. He said it was your idea. Did you really think having him buy me a stuffed animal would make up for him leaving without telling me?"

Angelo shrugged and gave the doctor an innocent look that Minka decided didn't really work on him. Clearly he did not know that, though.

"Yeah," he said. "I thought it might."

Zarina shook her head as she made some notes. When she was done, she looked at Angelo again. "Physically, Minka is as fit as any other shifter or hybrid. But for me to understand what those doctors did to make her this way, I'm going to need to draw some blood."

Minka was still trying to figure out what a shifter was when she heard that, and she decided she didn't care what they were. Her fingers tingled as her claws started to lengthen.

"I don't think that's a very good idea, Doc," Angelo said. "Minka isn't really a fan of needles."

"I realize that, but I need to know exactly what was done to her and who did it."

Minka didn't understand what Zarina meant, but from the way Angelo's shoulders slumped, he obviously thought this was something they needed to do.

"If I let you take some of my blood, will it help you find a cure for this?" Minka asked, holding up a hand to show them her curved claws.

Zarina's eyes were sad as she shook her head. "I've been trying, but I've been working on it for over a year and I'm not even close. A sample of your blood might help me figure it out. If nothing else, it might stop this from happening to another person."

Minka bit her lip. She was terrified of needles, but if it might keep this from happening again, she would do it.

"Okay. You can draw my blood," she said to Zarina, then looked up at Angelo. "But I'm scared."

Angelo dropped to one knee beside her so that his soulful eyes were level with her own, then took her hand in his. "I know, but I'm right here. I promise Zarina won't hurt you or try to inject you with anything."

Minka already knew that, but it still helped to hear Angelo say it out loud.

He must have sensed her unease because he tenderly brushed her dirty hair back from her face. "Why don't I go first, so you can see exactly what Zarina is going to do?"

Minka nodded, even though she already knew what Zarina was going to do. But if it put off getting stuck for a few more minutes, she was okay with it.

Zarina explained the process of drawing blood in a

soft voice as she slowly poked the small needle into Angelo's muscular arm.

"See?" Angelo grinned at her as he rolled down his sleeve afterward. "Nothing to it."

Minka didn't think it had been nothing. She grabbed on to Angelo with her hand, squeezing Boris as Zarina tied something rubbery tightly around her upper arm. She tried to watch as the Russian doctor moved the needle toward her arm, then decided against it. Instead, she turned and looked at Angelo. He was much more pleasing to focus on.

Angelo was looking down at her arm, a grim expression on his face. For a moment, Minka thought Zarina was doing something improper, but when she looked down at her arm, she realized he wasn't focused on the needle, which Zarina had put into her arm without Minka even feeling it. Instead, Angelo's gaze was locked on the series of parallel scars running sideways across the inside of her forearm.

When Zarina pulled out the needle, there wasn't any blood. A moment later, Minka couldn't even see where the needle had gone in. She was about to pull her arm back, but Angelo stopped her, gently rubbing his long fingers across the scars.

"Zarina, I thought hybrids healed as fast as shifters. Were these scars from before Minka was changed?"

Minka almost pulled her arm away in embarrassment, not wanting Angelo to see the ugly scars, but he placed a single finger gently on her wrist.

Zarina studied the scars. "No, these are relatively fresh." She lifted her eyes to Minka's. "How badly did they cut you?"

Minka swallowed hard. She didn't want to think about it. "Very badly," she whispered. "They gave me something so I couldn't move, then strapped me down to a table and cut my arm open to the bone. They took out so much flesh, I thought they were trying to remove my arm, but I found out later they just wanted to see how severe of a wound I could recover from."

Minka heard Angelo swear, but she didn't look at him. She didn't want to see the pity she knew would be there. But she couldn't stop the tears from forming in her eyes as she remembered the pain and the terror she'd experienced. She had been so sure she would die, but the beast inside wouldn't allow that. It had healed itself, albeit more slowly than usual. In time, Minka was sure even the ugly scars would be gone.

She kept her head down, so Angelo and Zarina wouldn't see the tears. But Angelo slipped a finger under her chin and tilted her face up to look at him. She saw no pity there. Only anger so intense it turned his normally soft eyes to stone.

"Minka, I promise that nothing like that will ever happen to you again," he said hoarsely. "And if I get the opportunity to someday kill the men who did this to you, I will."

Minka nodded, cherishing the way he gently wiped away her tears with his thumb more than the promise of revenge. While she truly hated the doctors who had experimented on her, she couldn't imagine wanting another human dead on her account. Not even them.

The beast inside, however, growled in approval at Angelo's plan. It was more than willing to let Angelo kill those doctors, and even happier to help.

Minka had just wiped the last of her tears away when Angelo's friend Landon appeared in the doorway along with the man who had sent the rat-faced man away in the lab.

He walked in and extended his hand with a smile. "I didn't get a chance to introduce myself before. I'm John Loughlin, the director here."

She reached out and hesitantly took his hand with her right, then placed the other—the one with Boris in it—over her heart and bowed her head slightly in the custom of her country. "Minka Pajari."

John glanced at Zarina. "Everything check out?"

Zarina smiled. "Minka did very well. She even let me draw some blood."

"Excellent," John said. "I'm sure she could use a shower, something to eat, and a comfortable bed after what she's been through. I know that Angelo has some concerns about her staying on the complex. In your opinion, is Minka stable enough to stay somewhere else, Doctor?"

Zarina didn't answer right away, and the longer she hesitated, the more nervous Minka became. Angelo must have sensed her fear because he took her hand and gave it a reassuring squeeze.

"I think that would be fine," Zarina finally said. "As long as Angelo can stay with her."

Minka turned to look at him. She wanted to think she knew what his answer would be, but then realized she didn't know.

He smiled. "Of course I'll stay with her."

She sagged with relief. She knew Angelo couldn't stay with her forever, but for right now, at least, he would, and she was grateful.

John nodded. "In that case, Landon has volunteered to let both of you stay at his apartment. It only has one bedroom but a big couch from what he tells me, so the two of you should be able to make it work. And you'll have the place to yourselves since he's going to stay with a friend."

The director gave Landon a pointed look that Minka was sure carried some significance, although she didn't know what. But it was none of her concern. All she cared about was being with Angelo.

Minka was about to thank Landon for offering to let them stay at his apartment, and John for allowing it, when a man's voice interrupted her.

"Have you all lost your minds?"

Minka jerked around to see the rat-faced man standing in the doorway. A growl vibrated in her throat as the beast tried to claw its way out. It might have succeeded too, but Angelo got a firmer grip on her hand and tugged her closer. The beast wasn't happy, but it behaved.

"There is absolutely no way that hybrid is leaving this complex," Rat Face said. "I want her confined."

John turned to face the man, positioning himself slightly in front of Angelo. "*That hybrid* has a name, Dick. It's Minka Pajari. And Dr. Sokolov has determined she's stable enough to leave the complex as long as she stays in Sergeant Rios's care."

"*That hybrid* is dangerous, and she belongs to us."

Angelo was the one who growled this time. "No, asshole, I'm the one who's dangerous. Minka is cute and cuddly compared to me." He nudged her behind him. "And she sure as hell doesn't belong to you. She doesn't belong to anyone but herself. Got it?"

The rat-faced man—Dick—turned red, and for a moment, she thought he might try to fight Angelo, but instead, he directed his anger toward John. "If this goes sideways, you're the one taking the fall."

"That responsibility comes with the title of director," John said.

Dick muttered something under his breath that sounded like "not for long," then turned and stomped off.

John sighed. "I'm sorry about that. Dick can be somewhat irritating." He gave her and Angelo a smile. "I think Landon can take it from here. I'll see the two of you tomorrow."

Landon looked at Zarina. "Anything else you need right now, or can Angelo and Minka get out of here?"

"We're done." She smiled at Minka. "Get some rest and I'll see you in the morning, okay?"

Minka nodded and would have turned to leave when she suddenly remembered she still had Boris. She held him out to the Russian doctor. "Thank you for letting me hug him."

Zarina's smile widened. "Why don't you keep him for a little while?"

Minka looked from Zarina to Boris and back again. "Are you sure? I don't know Tanner, but he must be special to you if he brought this back all the way from Central America. I wouldn't feel right about taking something he gave you."

"Tanner won't mind if you borrow him," Zarina said. "Besides, Boris has been wanting to get out of the lab and see the sights."

Minka caressed the sloth's fur. She wasn't sure why hugging the plush toy helped keep her calm, but it did, and she was relieved to be able to take him with her. "Okay. If you're sure."

"I am," Zarina said.

Landon led her and Angelo back through the maze of hallways and offices, and outside to his pickup truck. Landon's scent permeated the interior, which wasn't surprising since it was his truck. But she also smelled the beautiful, dark-haired woman who was with him earlier. They must spend a lot of time together.

Landon took them on the same roads they had arrived by but in the opposite direction. The scenery was just as intriguing now as it had been then, and she could not resist asking what things were as they drove. Fortunately, Landon didn't drive as fast as the man who'd taken them to the complex, so she was able to see a lot more. This country was so full of new and exciting things, and she had the urge to experience all of them.

When they got to his apartment building, a four-floor multicolored brick building on what seemed like a surprisingly quiet street, Landon parked in the underground garage. He grabbed a big black bag from the backseat, then led them to the elevator and up to the fourth floor.

Having never seen an apartment outside of Tajikistan, Minka was surprised to see how huge his was. She walked through the kitchen and into the living room, holding Boris in her arms and wondering what one person could possibly do with so much space. In her home village, a full family of six or seven people would live in a place like this, but in Washington, DC, Landon lived here alone. He must work a lot though, because while his scent was present, it wasn't very strong. If she had to guess, she would say he hadn't been there in a week or two.

Landon handed Angelo a big, black bag with a shoulder strap and zipper along the top. "These are some clothes Layla had in her locker at the DCO. It's mostly workout stuff, but it's clean. She said they should fit Minka."

Minka hugged Boris close, her fingers curling into his soft fur. These people were giving her clothes to wear? She'd been wearing the same ripped and tattered blouse and skirt since being captured all those months ago. The thought that she might be able to finally throw them away and wear something else brought tears to her eyes.

"As for you, dude," Landon continued, "there's a closet and a dresser full of stuff in the bedroom." He grinned. "Have to have two of everything, so I can make it look like I still live here. Oh, and there's some food in the kitchen that should still be edible along with a whole stack of take-out menus in the drawer by the landline. Are you good on money, or do you need something to hold you over?"

Angelo shook his head. "I'm good. Get out of here. We're just going to call for a pizza or something, then head to bed. It's been a really long day."

Minka's spirits leaped at the mention of bed. She hadn't slept in one in so long that she barely remembered what it felt like.

She was still dreaming about how wonderful sleeping in a real bed again would feel as Landon left, telling Angelo he'd be back in the morning. Angelo locked the door's three locks, then joined her in the kitchen.

"You want to take a shower and change while I order

pizza?" he asked as he started digging through a drawer
full of papers.

A shower? She'd been strapped or chained to an
endless succession of dirty floors and laboratory tables
for months. Then, after escaping, she'd slept in the dirt
for weeks. She was beyond filthy and probably looked
a fright.

She nodded enthusiastically to both parts of his question. "I'd love a shower—and pizza."

She'd eaten pizza before when she was younger
and lived in Dushanbe, and it had been delicious. She
eagerly grabbed the bag of clothes and started for the
door Landon had pointed out that led to the bathroom
when they had first come in.

She was halfway there when panic struck, stopping
her cold. If she took one more step away from Angelo,
the beast would be out. She could already feel it slipping
out from between her mental fingers as she tried to hold
it in. She squeezed Boris more tightly, but it didn't help.

She was about to spin around and go back into the
kitchen. She would just wash up in the sink.

But just then, she felt Angelo's hand on her back,
gently guiding her toward the bathroom as he ordered
pizza on the phone. When they reached the bathroom,
he pushed open the door, then covered the phone with
his hand.

"I'll be right out here the whole time," he said.
"I promise."

Sighing in relief, Minka nodded her thanks and
walked into the large bathroom. Angelo closed the door
behind her, but she immediately turned around and
opened it halfway. She knew it was horribly improper

for an unmarried woman to leave a bathroom door open while she was naked within, but she didn't care. She'd already lived with the embarrassment of sleeping in his lap throughout the entire trip here, so she could live with this, too.

Setting Boris on the counter, she took off the over-shirt Angelo had given her to wear and carefully hung it on the hook on the back of the door, then stripped off her skirt and underwear, dropping them on the floor. They were much too dirty to put on the nice clean counter.

It took her a while to get the water temperature right, but when she finally got it the way she wanted, the gentle spray felt delightful on her naked skin. She didn't even hide the little growl of appreciation the beast let out as the warm water soaked her long hair and rinsed months of filth from her body.

"You okay in there?" Angelo asked from just outside the door, concern in his voice.

She laughed—God, she hadn't done that in a long time. "Yes, I'm very okay in here. This feels very wonderful. Don't worry. I'll wash fast, so there will be enough hot water for you."

He chuckled. "Take your time. You won't use up all the hot water, I promise."

She blinked water from her eyes. "Really?"

"Really. And feel free to use Landon's bodywash. I'm sure he has some in there."

She looked up at the wire cradle hanging from the shower nozzle and saw several bottles of liquid soap. She recognized some of the words, but her reading skills weren't as good as her speaking abilities. She sniffed each of the bottles until she found one she liked.

That was when she recognized a familiar scent on the bottle, and it wasn't Landon's. It was the woman who'd been with him outside Zarina's office—the one she'd smelled in his truck. The one who smelled so much like Minka herself.

As Minka lathered the scented soap into her hair, she thought about why the woman had reacted like she had when she'd first seen Minka. It was like the other woman hated her. She hoped that wasn't the case, but if the woman did, there was nothing she could do about it. She would just worry about herself—and Angelo—and try to find a way to deal with what had happened to her.

Minka rinsed off, then stepped out of the shower. She hadn't felt so clean in a very long time.

As she reached for one of the fluffy towels on the wall rack, she caught a glimpse of Angelo sitting on the floor just outside the open bathroom door. Minka blushed a little at the thought that he could easily see her naked if he turned his head and looked at her.

But he didn't do that. He simply sat there and waited patiently as she dried off, then slipped into the clothes Landon had given her. While she'd never met Layla, one sniff of her clothes made Minka realize she also smelled familiar—not quite as familiar as the dark-haired woman with Landon, but very close.

Layla was apparently a little smaller than Minka because the bra, exercise pants, and tank top would have definitely been too tight if Minka hadn't lost so much weight while in captivity. She turned and looked at herself in the bathroom mirror, almost blushing again at how the fabric of the top and pants fit snugly to her breasts and bottom. She'd never worn anything like this.

But it was all she had, so it would have to do. At least she had clothes to wear; that was the most important part. She'd have to remember to thank Layla as soon as she could.

She looked at her old bra and skirt still sitting in a pile on the floor. She was good with a needle and thread. Maybe she should try to repair them. No. There was more ripped fabric than whole fabric. Besides, no amount of washing would ever get out all the blood and dirt. Plus they'd only remind her of a time she'd much rather forget. So she rolled up the tattered pieces of clothing and shoved them in the small trash can beside the sink.

Angelo stood as she stepped out of the bathroom, and she didn't miss the way his eyes traveled up her body before locking with hers. His gaze probably should have offended her, especially since she wasn't used to men looking at her that way at home. But for reasons she didn't understand, she did not mind. If anything, she enjoyed it. Even stranger, the beast seemed to enjoy it as well. She could almost hear the animal purring.

Angelo recovered before she did, looking away to pick up a pile of clothes on the floor beside him. "Um, I didn't know what you liked on your pizza, so I ordered plain cheese. I hope that's okay?"

She nodded, aware that Angelo was trying very hard not to stare at anything below her neck. She would have found it charming if it wasn't for the amazing way his heated gaze made her feel.

"There's a twenty-dollar bill sitting on the table by the door for the pizza, but I should be done in the shower before the delivery person gets here."

Still not looking at her, he ducked into the bathroom.

Minka stood in the doorway, Boris clutched to her
chest, watching as Angelo pulled his uniform overshirt
over his head without undoing the buttons, which she
thought was a pretty impressive feat. Then she saw
what he was hiding under there and decided the view
was much more impressive. Technically, he was still
clothed, but the light tan T-shirt was really tight, and she
didn't have to use her imagination very much to figure
out there were a lot of muscles under it. Just the sight of
his big arms rippling as he moved was enough to make
Minka catch her breath.

When he reached behind his head to pull off his
T-shirt, Minka found herself licking her lips in anticipa-
tion. She felt bad for watching him like this, but she
couldn't help herself. Then she looked up and saw
Angelo regarding her with an amused expression on his
handsome face.

"I understand why you want to keep the door open,
and I'm okay with that," he said. "But you might want
to look the other way for this part."

Minka felt heat rush to her face. She nodded and
stepped out of the doorway, turning to sit down on the
floor beside the bathroom like Angelo had done. Her
fingers dug into the stuffed sloth's fur. She was glad he
couldn't see her face because it was probably bright red.
Why had she been staring like that?

She was so caught up in those thoughts, she barely
realized her claws had partially extended and her gums
were tingling, like her fangs had been trying to slip out,
too. What was happening to her?

She closed her eyes and focused on thoughts of

Angelo a few feet away. Her claws slowly retracted and her breathing slowed.

Then, her ears picked up the sound of Angelo's boots hitting the floor, quickly followed by his pants. She could tell by the distinctive sound his belt buckle made against the tile. Of course he was taking off his pants. He was going to take a shower.

As she heard him pull back the curtain, then water turning on, it suddenly hit her. There was an extremely attractive and muscular man without any clothes on only a few feet away from her. If she turned her head, she'd have seen something she had never seen in her life—a naked man. Her claws immediately popped out again, and she felt her fangs poking into her lower lip.

Minka silently rebuked herself, swearing she would never do anything as rude as that. But before she knew it, she was leaning sideways to peek around the corner. Her mind was screaming at her to stop, but her body refused to respond. This time she couldn't blame it on the beast, though. This was all her.

The shower curtain was closed, but it was so wet, she could practically see through it. And the view? Minka didn't have the words to describe it—in English, Russian, or Tajik.

Angelo was soaping his hair, and she could see the silhouette of his naked body through the shower curtain. She tried to turn away, telling herself it was very wrong. But her eyes locked on the outline of something between his legs she had definitely never seen before. Her fangs dug into her lips. Gripping Boris tightly in her hands, she rose to her feet and walked into the bathroom.

She was only a meter from the shower curtain when

a ringing sound from the front of the apartment startled her so much she jumped.

Angelo stopped moving behind the curtain, his hands over his face as he rinsed off the soap. "Was that the doorbell?" he called as if she were still outside the door. "I'll get it. Let me just get the soap out of my eyes."

He reached for the curtain, rinsing at the same time. Sure he was going to yank it open and see her standing there, staring, she spun around, darting for the front door.

"I'll get it!" she called back.

If Angelo stepped out now, all wet from the shower with soap running everywhere, she wouldn't be able to control herself.

"You sure?" Angelo asked.

She could hear him furiously trying to get out of the shower. Was the towel in there big enough to wrap around his waist?

"Yes!" she said.

Her claws were still partially out, and she would have slowed down to try to get them back in, but the delivery person was banging on the door now, and she was sure Angelo was coming.

Minka grabbed the money Angelo had left on the table, cranked the three locks open as fast as she could, then jerked open the door. The guy standing there jumped at her sudden appearance. Were her fangs showing?

But then he smiled, showing her uneven teeth behind a straggly beard and unkempt mustache. Minka suddenly felt ill at the odor that came off the man. He was attracted to her, and he was disgusting.

"Hey, babe," he said, touching the brim of the red ball cap he wore. "You're not the same hottie that's usually here. Maybe a younger sister—an equally hot, unmarried, younger sister?"

Minka had never heard a man say something so forward to a woman in a polite setting, and the impulse she felt developing was scary in its intensity. She thought she might actually kill the man. The growl was already building and she wasn't sure she could keep it in.

Before she could do something she would regret, Minka shoved the money at the man, trying her best to keep her extended claws tucked into her palm. Then she yanked the pizza box out of his hand and pushed him back into the hallway. Slamming the door, she locked all three locks. Unfortunately, the man didn't seem to get what she was trying to tell him.

"You know you only gave me a three-dollar tip, right?" he called through the door. "I normally get more, but I'll take your phone number instead."

She slapped her palm against the door so hard it shook in its frame. Just for good measure, she let out a low, dangerous growl.

There was silence on the other side of the heavy wood door for a few seconds. "That's cool. I'm okay with three dollars."

Minka stood by the door, waiting until she heard the sound of his retreating footsteps. When she finally turned around, her claws and fangs had disappeared back to where they were supposed to be. That was when she caught sight of Angelo standing there. He was wearing jeans and a T-shirt, water dripping from his long, wet hair to plaster the tight material to his skin.

He looked…amazing.

She felt her pulse start to beat faster again and tried

to look somewhere else, but it was useless. Every time she looked away, her gaze snapped right back to him.

His mouth quirked. "You sure you never lived in Washington? Or New York?"

She shook her head, confused by the question. "No, of course not."

He chuckled. "Could have fooled me because you handled that delivery guy like a pro. Remind me never to get fresh with you."

Minka had never heard that expression before, but she guessed he meant the deliveryman had been flirting with her. She would definitely not mind at all if Angelo flirted with her.

She realized she had been standing there, holding the pizza—which smelled very good—for a long time without saying anything. She blushed again, sure Angelo would know where her mind had been.

But he simply pointed at the big, white box in her hands. "You want to eat now? I'm starving."

---

Angelo grinned as Minka grabbed a third slice of pizza. When they'd sat down on the couch with a couple bottles of soda and a roll of paper towels, she had claimed she wasn't very hungry and that just a single slice of the great big, cheese-smothered pizza would do. That first slice had disappeared in less than a minute and Minka was reaching for another before he'd even opened his drink.

"This is very good," she said.

Holding the slice in one hand, she used the other to wipe the corners of her mouth with a paper towel in a gesture that was very dignified and polite. Okay, that definitely wasn't something he was used to with the people he normally ate with. The guys on his SF team would have rolled up whole slices like burritos and shoved them in their mouths at once. Of course, Minka was a hell of a lot better company than any of his guys, too. And a damn sight better looking. Even with a mouthful of pizza, she was easily the most attractive woman he'd ever laid eyes on. The funny thing was, as she sat there in those tight yoga pants and curve-hugging tank top, he got the feeling that Minka didn't have a clue how beautiful she was.

When she had stepped out of the bathroom after her shower, her long, dark hair so clean it shined, and her face free of dirt, his jaw had just about hit the floor. God, she was a knockout.

But he minded his manners. While parts of Tajikistan were very progressive due to Russian influence, others could be as conservative as any other predominantly Muslim country. Minka might be confused, embarrassed, or even offended if she thought he was behaving poorly around her.

So he kept his eyes on the appropriate parts of her anatomy and focused on the pleasant conversation.

"You've eaten pizza before?" he asked as she sprinkled Parmesan cheese on her slice and spread it around with her finger. Then she licked that same finger off in a move that was completely innocent—and incredibly sexy.

"Yes, many times when I was younger and lived in Dushanbe. Not quite as often after my parents and I moved to a small village north of Khorugh."

*Shit*. Her parents. Angelo had been so worried about

getting Minka back to the United States and the DCO, he hadn't even thought about the possibility of her having family back in Tajikistan. They probably had no idea what had happened to their daughter, or even that she was alive.

He set his half-eaten slice of pizza back in the box and wiped his hands on a paper towel. "Are your parents in Khorugh now? Is there a phone number we can call to let them know you're okay?"

It would cost Landon a butt load, but Angelo would pay him back. He was already reaching for the cordless phone on the table when he realized Minka had become very still.

"Is everything okay?" he asked.

Stupid question. She'd been held captive and turned into a hybrid. How could she be okay?

She slowly nodded, putting her pizza down, too. "Yes. It's just that I'd rather not call my parents. If they find out that I'm alive, they will want me to come home right away."

"Isn't that a good thing?" He tried not to let his confusion show. "That your parents love you and want you to come home?"

Minka shook her head, her beautiful eyes suddenly sad. "They wouldn't love me or want me in their home. Not once they see what I've become. I'm a monster now, and it's better if they think I'm dead."

Angelo was so stunned that all he could do was sit there and stare. He knew Minka had been through a lot, but he hadn't truly realized how bad it must have been. She'd rather her parents think she was dead than have them discover she was a hybrid. That was screwed up.

He reached out and took her hand. "You're not a monster, Minka. I can promise you that."

The smile she gave him was as sad as the look in her eyes. "I have claws and fangs that barely fit in my mouth, my face twists into something horrible when I'm angry—and I'm angry all the time. I've killed people, torn them apart. If that is not a monster, what is it?"

"Someone did something very bad to you," he said softly. "But that doesn't make you a monster. It makes them the monsters. We're going to find a way to get you through this, and someday, I'm going to make sure you get home to your parents."

Minka nodded but didn't reach for her pizza. He didn't either. Neither one of them had an appetite left, he guessed. He closed the lid on the box.

"We can finish the rest later," he said as he stood.

Carrying the box into the kitchen, he stuck it in the fridge, then went back to the living room. Minka was sitting with her legs crisscrossed under her, Boris clutched to her chest, and a far off look on her face. Angelo sat beside her and put what he hoped was a comforting hand on her knee.

"It's going to be okay, Minka."

She nodded but didn't look convinced.

"Zarina and the DCO know a lot about what those doctors did to you," he said. "Zarina's done some amazing work helping another hybrid like you get his rage under control."

She blinked. Damn, she had some seriously long eyelashes. "There's another…person like me at the place we were today?"

"Tanner Howland." Angelo jerked his chin at the plush sloth. "The guy who gave Boris to Zarina."

Her fingers gently caressed the stuffed animal. "Hybrid. What does that word mean?"

Angelo probably wasn't the best person to explain it, but he was the only one there right then. "It means something—or someone in the case of you and Tanner—made from combining two different parts. You and Tanner are part human, part animal, kind of like a shifter."

"Shifter?"

Now he'd gone and done it. Angelo didn't know if he was going to make any sense, but he tried to answer her question the best he could without getting too complicated.

"Remember the dark-haired woman who was with Landon when you first met him today?" he asked. "She's a shifter. Unlike you and Tanner though, she was born part animal. You and Tanner were injected with something to make you that way."

Minka considered that. "So that is why she smells different. And the woman who let me use her clothes— Layla—she's a shifter, too? She smells very much like the dark-haired woman."

Angelo nodded. "Yep. Layla and Ivy are sisters."

She fell silent, as if thinking about everything Angelo had told her. That gave him a chance to ask something he was curious about.

"How did you end up in that village where my team and I found you?"

If Minka was surprised by the change in subject, she didn't show it. Instead, she told him how she had been captured while crossing the mountain pass that led from her home to the small U.S. military compound where she worked. When she described the two doctors who had experimented on her, it wasn't hard to figure out that they were the same ones who'd hurt Ivy. Angelo knew for a fact that the DCO was going to be very interested in what Minka knew about these guys. He just hoped they cared as much about helping Minka.

"I don't know how long I was a prisoner," Minka admitted. "They captured me in midsummer, then moved me around a lot, so I lost all track of time or even where I was." She shivered. "It was just one long, horrible nightmare."

She obviously didn't want to talk about the details of what had happened while the doctors held her, and Angelo didn't push. He had dealt with the same kind of issue in Special Forces. When guys went through a rough patch, you couldn't get them to talk about it until they were ready. Minka would open up when it was the right time for her.

He smiled as she yawned. She looked exhausted. So was he, for that matter.

"You ready to go to bed?" he asked.

Minka's big, brown eyes widened.

It took him a second to figure out what he'd said, and when he finally did, he chuckled. "I meant that you get the bed. I get the couch."

She blushed. "I am a little tired."

They took turns using the bathroom; then he led her into Landon's bedroom.

"I'll be right out there on the couch," he reminded her. "We can leave the door open if you want. And if you need anything during the night, just call my name. I'm a light sleeper."

Minka nodded, then climbed into bed, Boris in hand. Angelo waited while she got the pillows and blankets situated to her liking.

"You good?" he asked.

She nodded but didn't look very sure of her answer. Well, he was going to have to go back into the living room at some point. It wasn't like he could crawl into bed with her—as much as he would like to. *Shit*. He shouldn't be having thoughts like that. She needed to feel safe and protected right then, not have some guy pawing all over her.

"Good night, Minka." He smiled as she snuggled into the blankets a little deeper. "I'll see you in the morning."

He flipped the light switch but left the door open. On the way to the living room, he stopped to snag a blanket and pillow from the linen closet in the bathroom. Man, his buddy had seriously bought into the whole wedded bliss thing. The Landon he used to know would have been satisfied with a stack of army-green wool blankets and those striped pillows that shed feathers all the time. Then again, if he and Ivy did stay there occasionally to make the place look lived in, Angelo was pretty sure she wouldn't have been down with that.

He took off his T-shirt and jeans, then flopped down on the couch in just his boxer briefs. Damn, he was beat. Before stumbling on Minka, he'd been humping through the mountains of Tajikistan for nearly two months straight. He hadn't slept on anything more comfortable than a pile of leaves, and the couch felt damn good.

He ran his hand through his long hair, then folded his

arm behind his head. Thinking about the team made him wonder when he'd join up with them. It was obvious Minka had developed an attachment to him because he made her feel safe. Angelo didn't have a problem admitting he felt a certain attachment to Minka as well. But he was Special Forces, and SF lived in the field.

Angelo muttered a curse. Where had that thought even come from? He'd known Minka for a little more than twenty-four hours. It wasn't like they were going to start dating anytime soon. Shoving that thought aside, he rolled onto his side when movement behind him made a tingle run down his neck. He instinctively reached down for his weapon, then realized he didn't have one—and that the movement behind him had to be Minka.

She stopped beside him, wordlessly gazing down at him, her eyes glowing with the slightest tinge of red. Through the dim light coming in through the window, Angelo could see her standing there in her yoga pants and tank top, clutching Boris to her chest, her face tense.

He was about to ask if she'd heard a strange noise, but then he decided that would be a stupid question. If her hearing was like Tanner's, she could probably hear people talking at the far end of the corridor. She'd probably come out here because she couldn't sleep so far away from him.

He considered offering her the couch while he settled for the floor next to it, but he instinctively knew that wasn't going to work. She needed contact, and there was really only one way to do that.

Swearing to himself that this was probably really stupid, Angelo pulled back the blanket and made room for her on the couch beside him.

Minka stared at his naked chest before her gaze slowly slid down to his boxer briefs and bare legs. With her hybrid senses, he knew she could see every little detail. But she didn't say a word. She simply climbed onto the couch and silently curled up beside him. She adjusted Boris so he wouldn't be in the way, then gently rested her cheek on Angelo's shoulder. He pulled the blanket up over both of them, and within seconds, she was completely relaxed and breathing deeply.

The soft purr of contentment she let out was so beautiful, it produced an amazing sensation inside him—a need to protect this woman stronger than anything he'd ever felt in his life.

That was when he realized he wasn't going to be able to leave Minka anytime soon—regardless of being Special Forces.

# Chapter 5

JAYSON HARMON STIRRED THE BURRITO MEAT IN THE frying pan on the stove, adjusting the temperature with his free hand, so it wouldn't burn. He didn't want to have to toss the whole thing in the garbage and call for takeout. Not tonight. Because tonight was special.

He was making dinner—and burritos were one of the few things he knew how to make besides spaghetti and meatloaf—to celebrate the end of Layla's probationary period in the covert division of the Department of Homeland Security where his former commanding officer, Landon Donovan, and Layla's sister, Ivy, also worked. Layla had been there for three months and was now considered a fully qualified psychologist for the covert organization. The status change meant Layla could work completely on her own with her patients. Jayson knew how important that was to her—hence the special dinner.

He'd met Layla Halliwell at Landon and Ivy's wedding back in June of last year, and the connection between them had been intense and instantaneous. She looked like a supermodel, but there was way more to it than that. She was a bubbly, outgoing person who was as beautiful on the inside as on the outside. It was impossible to be with her without some of her optimism rubbing off on you, and it wasn't too much of a stretch to say Layla and her optimistic outlook had turned his life around.

Jayson had been in a pretty bad place when they'd met. He'd gone through a few back surgeries, and even though most of the rocket-propelled grenade shrapnel from that ambush in Afghanistan had been removed, there was very little to be done for the severe amount of nerve, muscle, and bone damage he'd sustained. He couldn't walk without support and tremendous pain, and didn't want to think about what kind of life he was going to have in front of him.

A little voice in the back of his head had told him this was as good as it was going to get and that it wasn't good enough. He'd mentally checked out of his physical therapy, started hitting the pain meds way more than he should have, and allowed his mind to go to some dark places where he wondered why he even bothered trying.

Then, when things had been their darkest, Layla had walked into his life. He had no idea why someone as beautiful and vivacious as she was had taken an interest in him, but she had. The next thing he knew, she was coming to his room at Walter Reed every day, playing video games with him, taking him for walks around the recovery ward, even attending his physical therapy sessions with him.

Layla had pulled him out of the funk he'd been in, getting him serious about his rehab and making him think that he just might have a future. Sure, every once in a while he still found himself wallowing in self-pity, but that shit stopped the moment he saw Layla. And when it had been time to move out of Walter Reed and transition to outpatient therapy, Layla had been right there with him, helping him find this apartment and making sure he could get around it okay.

He owed her so damn much. Tonight, he was just trying to repay a little bit of his debt to her.

Jayson used a spoon to dip out a small amount of the simmering meat, blowing on it before he gave it a taste. It wasn't too bad, but it could definitely use a little more kick. He turned and reached for the red pepper in the spice rack. A sharp pain immediately shot out from his lower back, zipping down his legs and all the way up to his neck.

"Shit!"

He reached out and grabbed the counter, praying his legs wouldn't give out on him. Layla was going to be there any minute, and he sure as hell didn't want her finding him in a crumpled heap on the floor. That would just suck all.

He stood there sweating for a few minutes, torn between reaching for his cane leaning against the refrigerator in the corner or stumbling over to one of the chairs at his small kitchen table.

Finally deciding to go for the chair, he turned the heat down under the pan, put on the lid, then carefully moved over to the table. Every frigging step drove a railroad spike of agony through his lower back, but he made it. As he slowly lowered himself down into a chair, he briefly considered taking a pain pill but quickly dismissed the idea. Tonight was all about celebrating with Layla, and he didn't want to feel—and sound—doped up.

So instead, he sat there in the chair and breathed through the pain. They'd tried to teach him about dealing with it without resorting to narcotics at Walter Reed, but he hadn't been very attentive during the sessions. So Layla had taught him to do it her way, with a mix of deep breathing exercises, meditation, and visualization.

He'd thought it would never work, but it had, and now she had him doing it five days a week and also anytime he had a flare-up—like now.

It wasn't magic, but putting his mind somewhere else for a while gave the pain a chance to dull somewhat, and when he came back out of his relaxed state, he found he could manage it okay.

He was back at the stove finishing up the refried beans and the Spanish rice when the doorbell rang.

"Come on in," he called.

He heard the door open, then close. A moment later, Layla came into the kitchen, looking beautiful as always. Part Native American, she had long, dark hair and the most expressive brown eyes he'd ever seen. Sometimes, when the light caught them right, they almost looked as if they had a hint of green in them—like they did now, as she smiled and kissed his cheek.

What had he done to be worthy of this amazing woman's attention?

"Need help with anything?" she asked, her eyes sparkling as they roamed over the table he'd already set.

"Nah." He grinned. "Dinner's almost ready. Go wash up."

He had the food on the plates and was ladling extra salsa on the burritos when Layla came back in.

"Mmm, it smells delicious," she said as she sat down. "You didn't have to go to so much trouble, though."

Jayson sat down across from her. "Of course I did. Today was a big step in your career, and I want to help you celebrate it. Besides, I've wanted to do something special for you for a while, to show you how much I appreciate everything you've done for me."

She smiled. "I would normally point out I haven't done anything difficult, since you've done all the heavy lifting, but my mom always told me to accept a compliment with grace, so I'll simply sit here and accept your appreciation—and your cooking. It looks amazing."

He chuckled as he picked up his knife and fork and began cutting into his burrito. "How was work today? Anything cool happen that you can tell me about?"

Pretty much everything she worked on was classified, so if she couldn't, that wouldn't be unusual.

But while they ate, she told him about a new patient who had just been brought in from the field with what appeared to be extreme PTSD and anger control issues.

He glanced at her over the rim of his water glass. "Was she an operative who got hurt on a mission?"

Layla shook her head. "Not really. She's a person of interest that one of our part-time field agents came across. He brought her back thinking maybe we could help her out."

Jayson wanted to ask for more details, but it was obvious Layla was going out of her way to give him as much as she could without letting any classified information slip. He understood why. The work she did at the DHS was classified out the wazoo. Even though it shouldn't have bothered him, it did. It wasn't like she enjoyed not telling him—it was part of the job. But there was a time, before that RPG had filled his back full of metal fragments and nearly severed his spine, when he'd been part of all kinds of classified operations. He'd held a top secret clearance and had access to dozens of special programs that few people in the world even knew existed. Now his security clearance was just a piece of paper in his soon-to-be medically retired personnel record, and he was a broken man limping around with a cane, living vicariously through the career exploits of his girlfriend.

It was pathetic, but sometimes it felt like he was watching her move farther and farther ahead while he slowly disappeared in her dust trail.

Jayson pushed those selfish, whiny thoughts behind him. This night was about Layla, not him and his screwed-up insecurities.

"How about you?" she asked. "Anything on the job front?"

He shook his head. Jobs were kind of slim for a guy with nothing but a military history degree, a screwed-up back, and a requirement to miss work three times a week for physical therapy. Layla was doing everything she could to help, but she hadn't had much luck, either.

She reached across the small table and gave his hand a squeeze. "We'll find something soon."

Jayson hoped she was right. He was still drawing a full lieutenant's paycheck for now. But as soon as his medical retirement was finalized, his military pay would disappear and he'd be left with nothing but his VA 60 percent disability pay—barely over a thousand dollars a month. He had a pretty good amount of money in savings, most of which he'd inherited from his parents, but he couldn't depend on that. He'd need a job soon, or Layla might be visiting him in a homeless shelter.

"I had another run-in with Ivy today," Layla said suddenly.

Jayson winced at the hurt tone in her voice. Unfortunately, this was one area he definitely couldn't help her with because he didn't have a clue why Ivy had been such a jerk since Layla had started working at the DHS.

"Did she actually say anything this time or just shoot you one of those glares of hers that could melt steel?"

Most of Layla's run-ins with her sister had been of the latter variety. Ivy and Landon had been out of the country when Layla had gotten the job at the DHS, but the moment Ivy had learned her sister would be working at the same organization as she was, she'd lost it. Since then, there had been a few biting words, but mostly just of lot of glaring. The only time Ivy had been even remotely friendly to Layla was when they'd all gotten together at their parents' home for Christmas, and that was only because Ivy hadn't wanted their mom and dad to know they were fighting.

"Yeah, she said something all right." Layla sighed. "That I was wasting all the money Mom and Dad had spent sending me to college."

Even after all the crap said back and forth over the last few months, that caught Jayson by surprise. "What the hell was the purpose of that, some kind of emotional blackmail?"

Layla shrugged. "Probably. She couldn't get me to quit any other way, so I suppose she thought pulling Mom and Dad into this might help."

"I really don't understand this." Across from him, Layla was looking longingly at the other burrito in the casserole dish. "Go ahead. You can have it." He almost laughed when she eagerly transferred it to her plate. Where the heck did a woman her size put all the food she ate? "I mean, you found a job that you love, that pays well, and where you get a chance to use the skills you learned in school. Plus, you're helping people. What else does she want? It's not like you're strapping people down to a table and waterboarding them or anything. What's her problem?"

"I think she's worried I'm going to end up in the field," Layla said, "and that scares her."

Jayson lifted a brow. "You, a field operative? Seriously? You're a shrink. Why the heck would she think the DHS would put you in the field?"

Layla's head snapped up, and for a moment, he was reminded that she was indeed Ivy's sister. The look she was giving him right now could have stripped paint off a car at ten feet. But just as fast, it was gone, replaced by one of indifference.

"I don't know." She shrugged. "Maybe I'm just reading the situation wrong."

She was stonewalling. Whether it was because the subject was classified or simply because it involved her sister, Layla wasn't telling him the whole story—again.

Layla finished cutting the burrito, then pushed her plate to the center of the table, so they could share. When he gave her a curious look, she smiled. "I want to make sure I save room for dessert."

More likely, she was simply being nice. She could have easily put away the whole thing if she'd wanted. She just liked sharing food with him. As they each took turns eating bites off her plate, Jayson certainly wasn't going to complain. Sharing could definitely be fun.

Layla moved her chair closer to his, and they huddled together as they ate the *tres leches* cake with strawberries he'd been forced to buy from the bakery down the street because he knew there was no way he'd ever be able to make it himself. Every time their shoulders or arms made contact, it sent little zaps of electricity shooting across his body. Damn, he had it bad.

He was still thinking about that when Layla put down her fork, then leaned in close and planted a warm, soft kiss on his cheek. Yeah, it was only a kiss on the cheek, but it still felt damn nice.

"What was that for?" he asked.

She gave him a smile that just about stopped his heart. "No reason. Can't a girl kiss her guy after he went to so much trouble cooking a special dinner for her?"

He lifted a brow. "You realize that I bought the cake at the bakery, right?"

She whacked his arm. "Stop. It was a perfect dinner. Very romantic. And I loved it."

Without another word, Layla kissed him again, this time right on the lips. Damn, she tasted frigging amazing.

The kiss lingered for only a moment before Layla pulled back. "Why don't we toss everything in the dishwasher, so we can move this over to the couch?"

Jayson would have said the hell with the dishes, but Layla was so responsible. She did most of the work, while he took care of the stuff that had to go back in the fridge. And he was able to handle it without moving too horribly slowly or twinging his back.

Once they hit the couch—a big, comfy job that his back absolutely loved—Layla snuggled up close and gave him another kiss on the cheek. "Thanks again for dinner."

"You're welcome," he said.

Layla's lips moved from his cheek back to his mouth. He slid his fingers in her long hair and pulled her closer as he deepened the kiss. God, her kisses were like a drug he could get really addicted to.

They had made out a few times before this, but it had never been very serious—more like curious friends than lovers. But it was getting serious now, especially when Layla decided it would be easier to kiss him if she was straddling his lap. In a graceful move that would've put a cat to shame, she swung one leg over both of his and settled herself comfortably on his crotch—all without breaking their kiss.

His cock immediately took notice of the sudden warmth parked just above him, perking up enough to suggest that maybe his doctors at Walter Reed had been right and that none of the nerve damage he'd sustained during his back injury had affected his ability to have normal sex. He'd never quite believed them, since he hadn't had the opportunity to test out their claims. Hell, he couldn't even remember getting a hard-on since his accident.

But as Layla wiggled back and forth on his lap while they kissed, her skirt riding a little higher up her thighs, the heat from her panty-covered pussy engulfing his cock through his jeans, he had to admit he was starting to get a nice erection now.

Apparently Layla noticed too, because the grinding she was doing couldn't have been by accident.

Both her hands cradled the back of his head; all ten of her eager fingers weaved tightly into his hair. Jayson couldn't stop himself from letting his mouth drift sideways, following the line of her jaw until he reached her ear, then letting his tongue taste her there.

The half purr, half moan that escaped her lips was

the sexiest sound he'd ever heard, and he had a sudden desire to make her do both a whole lot more. He imagined carrying her to his bed, yanking off her clothes, and licking her all over until she went insane from the pleasure, then burying himself deep inside her and riding her hard as those beautiful, strong legs of hers wrapped themselves around his waist, urging him for even more.

The brakes slammed down on that vision real quick, and reality came crashing in with a seriously painful thud.

He couldn't do any of those things, he realized suddenly. His screwed-up back would never let him make love to Layla like that—ever.

And with that realization, all the fire and excitement he'd been feeling dissolved as if someone had dumped a bucket of cold water on him.

Layla obviously picked up on that because she drew back to look at him. "Jayson, are you okay? Did I hurt you or something?"

The question destroyed any remaining sexual tension between them. They would never be able to make love like two normal people. She would always have to hold back, out of fear that she might hurt him. What kind of woman would ever be satisfied in a relationship like that? He wanted Layla more than any woman he'd ever known, but he was never going to have her—not the way he wanted…or the way she deserved.

Whatever hard-on he'd had was gone now, and knowing that Layla was fully aware of it made looking at her one of the toughest things he'd ever had to do.

"No, you didn't hurt me. I just think we need to slow down," he said softly. "We don't have to rush into anything, you know?"

She looked at him like she was about to cry, which made him feel even worse. "But I thought maybe tonight we could make love, as part of celebrating everything that's going good for both of us."

Layla had wanted to take their relationship further for a while now. He'd known that. But if tonight had shown him anything, it was that their relationship had gone about as far as it could go.

He swallowed hard, shook his head. "I don't think that's going to work out tonight. Maybe we can try some other time."

Jayson could tell Layla was fighting to hold back the tears, and he felt like kicking himself. Why the hell didn't he just have the balls to tell her that this was never going to work, so she could find someone else to have a life with?

Probably because his balls had been damaged by that RPG as much as his back.

She bit her lip. "Do you think it would be okay if I spent the night? We can just sleep in the same bed together. We don't have to do anything."

He found it easier to shake his head this time. "You have to work tomorrow, and I have an early rehab appointment. It might be best if you headed home."

Jayson thought she was going to argue, and he didn't have a fucking clue what he would say if she did. But then as quickly and as gracefully as she'd climbed on his lap, she was off.

"Thanks for the dinner," she said softly as she grabbed her coat from the overstuffed chair. But she didn't look at him as she spoke or as she put on her coat.

Then she was gone, and he was left there on his

couch, wondering what the hell had just happened. A couple hours ago, he had been a handicapped vet with few if any job possibilities, an approaching financial crisis, and a good shot at a lifetime of pain.

But he'd had an amazing woman in his life to balance out all that shit.

Now, he was pretty sure he didn't have that woman, and he wasn't sure where his life went from here... except down.

# Chapter 6

MINKA COULDN'T BELIEVE SHE WAS HUNGRY AGAIN, especially since she and Angelo had eaten breakfast barely two hours ago, but when Zarina had brought out a plate of soft, flaky pastries for them to nibble on while they talked, she sat down and eagerly grabbed a Danish. Minka didn't know whether it was being in captivity for so long or the animal inside that made her ravenous lately. Regardless, the pastries were too delicious to pass up.

"So, the doctors injected you with this blood-like serum within a day or so of your capture?" Zarina asked as she sipped her tea.

Minka nodded. "Yes."

She didn't like to talk about it because talking about it only reminded her of how horrible those men had been to her. But before Angelo left her alone with Zarina, he'd told her it was important to tell the doctor as much as she could remember about what had happened to her.

She broke off a piece of Danish but didn't eat it. "After they injected me, there was so much pain that I didn't think I would survive, but after it subsided and I was able to open my eyes and look in the mirror they held up to me, I saw my eyes were no longer brown but green and that I had fangs." She swallowed hard. "They told me they'd made me better, but I knew right then that they'd turned me into an animal."

Yesterday, she would have said monster, but after talking to Angelo last night, she preferred to think he was right and that she wasn't a monster. But she did turn into a beast, there was no denying that.

"Did they inject you with the serum just that one time?" Zarina asked.

"Yes."

"But your eyes didn't glow red right away?"

Minka shook her head. "No. All I know is that they were green that first time; then later, the doctors told me that my eyes glowed red, especially when I was angry."

"I'm guessing the doctors made you angry on purpose to see how you would respond," Zarina said.

Minka nodded. "There was so much rage inside me, and I could never control it, no matter what I did. It wasn't very hard for them to make me angry. All they had to do was threaten to hurt me, and the beast would come out. Sometimes the beast would go away after that. Other times, it would stay in control for days, and I'd be forced into the background and have to watch the beast rage without being able to do anything."

"I know how hard that must have been for you," Zarina said. "But the rage seems to go away anytime Angelo is around, right?"

Minka couldn't help but smile. "Yes. I don't understand why it happens. It's like he is my guardian angel, watching over me and keeping the beast away. When he is near, I feel safe. Like nothing and no one can hurt me."

Zarina regarded her thoughtfully. "So he doesn't have to be touching you for you to keep the rage at bay? He just has to be close?"

"Yes."

Minka hadn't realized until last night, while she was lying in bed, that she could actually feel Angelo out in the living room. It hadn't been as comforting as having him right there beside her—which is why she'd abandoned the bedroom and moved out to the couch with him—but it had kept the beast "at bay," as Zarina said.

She slowly turned in her chair until she was facing the back wall, the one with a framed photograph of a field of snow. Minka closed her eyes and thought of Angelo. Within moments, she immediately knew where he was in the complex. Not because she could hear him talking, or pick up his delicious scent—he was too far away. But there was some sense that told her he was in one of the offices in the next building over.

Minka turned to face Zarina again. "Angelo is that way, maybe thirty or forty meters. And he is worrying about me at this very moment."

She couldn't tell the doctor how she knew either of those things. She just did. But his proximity, and the fact that he was thinking about her, were the reasons she was able to stay calm right then, even though he wasn't in the same room with her.

"That's amazing," Zarina whispered.

Minka agreed, though probably for different reasons. The fact that she knew where Angelo was standing at any given moment was certainly interesting. But she would save the word *amazing* to describe last night.

Being able to sleep on Angelo's big, muscular chest had been the closest thing to heaven she could imagine existing in this world. Hearing his strong heart beating under her ear the whole night had lulled her into the deepest and most comfortable sleep she had ever had in her life.

Then, when they'd woken up that morning, he told her that he'd make breakfast while she used the bathroom first. A man making her breakfast? That was something she'd never imagined could happen.

Truthfully, she could have stayed there on the couch with him all day. She almost blushed at the direction her mind went when she thought of cuddling up on his naked chest again, like she had last night. It had been very difficult not to run her fingers through his hair. She'd been very careful not to put her hands anywhere they weren't supposed to go, but still. Those soft, black shorts he'd been wearing did little to hide that there was something very interesting down there. And if her hip had occasionally brushed up against it while she was on the couch with him, she could hardly be blamed for being curious.

Minka quickly shoved a piece of Danish into her mouth and chewed, hoping Zarina wouldn't see her face flaming scarlet. She'd never had those kinds of thoughts about a man before. But then again, she'd never met anyone remotely like Angelo.

When Minka finally looked at Zarina, it was to find the doctor regarding her with an expression that could only be described as concerned.

"What's wrong?" she asked.

Zarina smiled. "Nothing's wrong. I'm very happy that you can be calm around Angelo." The Russian doctor hesitated, as if she wasn't sure if she should continue. "It's just that you're going to need to find a way to control the rage inside you when Angelo is not with

you. He's in the army. At some point, he has to go back
to his team, wherever they might be."

A part of Minka knew that, of course, but hearing it out
loud terrified her so badly, the control she'd had a moment
earlier started to crumble. Her breathing came faster. Then
her claws and fangs popped out. Suddenly, the urge to
tear into something was overwhelming, and it was all she
could do not to lunge at the woman across from her.

"Zarina, I cannot stop it," she growled. "Get out and
lock the door. Find Angelo. Hurry!"

Minka expected Zarina to run full speed for the door,
but the other woman stood up and immediately came
around to her side of the table and shoved Boris into
her hands. Then, as if she didn't even care that Minka
was a split second away from turning into an animal
that would shred her to pieces, Zarina knelt down by her
chair and started talking to her softly in Russian.

Minka closed her eyes and hugged Boris, desperately
trying to keep the beast in its cage. But the beast was
winning; she could feel it taking control.

Zarina stayed right beside her, telling her to relax,
telling her that it would be fine, to think about Angelo
being nearby, to think about his arms around her.

Minka wasn't sure how long it took, but when she
finally opened her eyes, Zarina was back in her seat,
writing notes on a pad. Somehow, the Russian doctor
had successfully kept the beast from getting out.

"I'm sorry," Minka said softly. "I don't know what
happened."

Zarina glanced up from her notes with a small smile.
"Yes, you do. You got scared at the thought of Angelo
not being here with you, and you lost control. All the

more reason to learn some different techniques to control your darker side."

Minka didn't say anything. She needed Angelo like she needed air. Without him, she would be an animal in a cage, just like she'd been in Tajikistan. She'd escaped but would never be free of the one thing that truly haunted her.

Tears stung her eyes, and she blinked them away.

She was about to ask what these other techniques that Zarina had mentioned were—not that she thought any of them would work—when she picked up a familiar scent that immediately put her on alert.

Zarina must have seen her tense because the doctor turned toward the doorway the same time Minka did. It was the rat-faced man from yesterday, the one she instinctively knew would always be a threat to her.

He gave her an appraising look, his gray eyes taking in the tea and the Danish and the way she was still clutching Boris to her chest.

"Is the hybrid sedated, Dr. Sokolov?" he asked.

Zarina stood up and moved closer to the door, as if to keep him from coming in. Was it her imagination, or did he actually take a step back? That was odd, considering Zarina struck Minka as one of the least intimidating and most compassionate people she'd ever met.

"Of course, I haven't sedated her, Dick. That would be unnecessary, not to mention rude."

That was his name—Dick.

From Minka's time on the base where she'd worked with the U.S. military as a translator in Tajikistan, she knew the word *dick* was slang for male genitals. It clearly fit him.

Minka was so caught up in those thoughts that she almost missed what Dick and Zarina were saying, something about where Minka had been found, how she'd become a hybrid, and why she seemed to be so much more in control than any other hybrid the DCO had found.

"Sergeant Rios found her somewhere in southeastern Tajikistan," Zarina said. "Minka escaped from a facility almost certainly run by the two doctors who were working with Stutmeir, but she very rarely saw them. She was heavily drugged when she escaped and wandered for weeks. She has no idea where the actual lab facility is."

While Zarina had technically answered the question, she was leaving out many of the more important details Minka had told her. That surprised Minka. She'd thought Zarina was a very honest person, but now she was lying so calmly and convincingly, it was hard for Minka to doubt what the doctor was saying. Zarina knowingly lying to a man who was obviously very powerful in this place told Minka how much the doctor distrusted Dick. It convinced her even more that she was right to hate him.

Dick's eyes narrowed as they fell on Minka. "That's disappointing to hear. And the improved control that she appears to exhibit? Is that a coincidence, or does she represent a new radically improved generation of hybrid?"

Zarina shrugged. "I've already looked at her DNA. There aren't any significant differences between her and the first generation hybrids we've already studied. Perhaps she's more docile simply because she's a woman."

Minka frowned. She and Zarina hadn't talked about this subject at all, and Minka wasn't really sure what some of the words they were saying meant. But even so, she could instinctively tell that Zarina was lying about this, too.

Dick snorted as if Zarina's answer amused him. "Maybe. Perhaps you'll learn more after you've had time to study her." He regarded Minka again. "She's definitely not like the others. There's something about her that's familiar, though—I just can't put my finger on what it is."

He stared at Minka for another moment, then turned and walked out without saying anything else. The moment Minka heard him reach the end of the hallway and turn the corner, Minka looked at Zarina.

"You lied to him. Many times."

Zarina nodded as she walked back over to the table and sat down. "He's a bad man and can't be trusted. The only people you can trust here are Angelo, Landon, Ivy, John, and me. There are several others too, but you haven't met them yet. I'll make sure you meet them soon though, so you know who they are."

Minka was about to ask Zarina if the other hybrid—Tanner—was one of those people when she caught another scent out in the hallway. But it wasn't Dick this time. It was Angelo.

He walked in a moment later, Landon and John right behind him. He was wearing jeans and a T-shirt, like yesterday, that showed off his well-muscled arms. He had his silky, dark hair loose instead of in a ponytail, too. She decided she liked it that way.

A feeling Minka could only call giddy coursing

through her, she jumped up and greeted him with a smile. He grinned and took her hand, and just like that, a sense of calm washed over her. As Zarina had said, it was probably not good that she was so dependent on Angelo. But what could she do? Her soul wanted what it wanted.

Beside Angelo, John smiled at her. "I just wanted to stop by and make sure you were doing okay."

She smiled back at him. "Yes, thank you. For everything."

Minka knew he was responsible for her having the freedom to leave the complex and stay with Angelo, and she appreciated that gift. It was strange how different this man was from Dick. Even though each had an air of power, John's presence was tempered with compassion, while power seemed to be the only thing Dick was interested in.

"If there's anything I can do to help you feel more comfortable here," John continued, "please just ask."

She considered that. There was only one thing she could think might help make her feel more comfortable, so she asked.

"Could you make Dick go away?"

John exchanged looks with Landon and Zarina. "We'd all like that. But unfortunately, he's difficult to get rid of."

"Dick came sniffing around right before you got here," Zarina said. "He's intrigued by Minka as much as he is afraid of her. I told him things I thought might deter him from delving too deep, but he's smart enough to know she's unique. He's going to keep poking around to see what Minka knows about those doctors and why she's so different from the other hybrids."

"Dammit," John muttered. "Unfortunately, I can't completely keep Dick away from Minka, but I can try to get in his way. He's digging for someone on the Committee, and I want to know who." He gave them a nod. "I'll see you later."

Zarina motioned to the nearly full tray of pastries on the table as John left. "Eat the rest of these. I'll just end up eating them all myself if you don't."

Minka laughed as Angelo and Landon practically attacked the tray. It looked like they hadn't eaten in days. She liked watching Angelo eat though, especially the way he licked his fingers in between each bite. She had no idea why she found it so intriguing, but she did.

"I think Dick has already noticed the similarities between Minka and Ivy on some subconscious level," Zarina said as she sipped her tea. "He's as perceptive as a fence post, so he hasn't made the connection yet. Right now, he simply thinks there's something familiar about Minka. But given time…"

Landon looked at her sharply. "So Minka was definitely changed using Ivy's DNA?"

Zarina nodded. "Yes. I did the test yesterday to confirm it."

Landon swore. "I'd better go tell Ivy. I think she already knows, but I need to tell her she's right—and let her know that Dick is probably going to figure it out soon, too."

"I'll do my best to prevent him from making a direct DNA match," Zarina told him. "I'm already tinkering with Minka's blood samples to change them just enough to hide it. But I'm not sure Dick will care about bloodwork if he gets it into his head that Ivy and Minka are somehow related."

Landon left, leaving Minka grasping to understand what she had just heard. Her English was not good when it came to science and medical terms, but she thought DNA had something to do with blood. Had Zarina meant that Ivy's blood was inside Minka? Was that why she had these horrible claws and fangs, because the doctors had tried to make her like Ivy?

Minka was still mulling over that when she realized that Zarina was telling Angelo about Minka's little loss of control a while earlier. Minka looked down at her plate, embarrassed to have him hear about her little episode.

But he didn't get upset. He simply asked how Zarina had talked Minka down and if she thought there was anything else they could be doing to help Minka stay in control.

"I definitely think there is," Zarina said. "As a matter of fact, Minka and I were just talking about that before Dick showed up." She looked at Minka. "I'd like you to talk to some of the other shifters here at the DCO, kind of like a group session. I think it would be good to get their perspective on how they deal with their animal natures. Would you be okay with that?"

"Which shifters?" Minka asked.

"Layla Halliwell. She's one of our psychologists, so I think she'll be able to help you understand what's happening inside you when the rage takes over."

"Okay. Is there anyone else?"

Zarina exchanged looks with Angelo. "Actually, there is one other person I'd like you to meet. I have a friend named Tanner Howland. He's a hybrid like you and has had to face many of the same issues you're dealing with. He has some techniques that have helped him, and I think they might help you. Would you be willing to meet with him, too?"

"Yes, I think this would be a very good thing to try." If anyone could teach her to control the animal inside, it would be another hybrid.

Zarina smiled. "I was hoping you'd say that."

"What about Ivy?" Angelo asked. "Will she be there?"

Zarina hesitated, then looked down at her notepad. "No. Ivy's busy with something else."

Angelo's mouth tightened, but he didn't say anything, which left a very uncomfortable silence in the room.

"When can I meet Layla and Tanner?" Minka asked Zarina.

"It might take me a little while to set things up," Zarina said. "Maybe tomorrow afternoon?"

Minka glanced at Angelo, who nodded.

"Great." Zarina pushed back her chair. "I'll arrange it now."

Minka watched her go, then looked at Angelo. "I think talking with Layla and Tanner will be good for me."

He smiled. "Me too."

"So, what do we do for the rest of the day? Do we just sit here?"

Angelo chuckled. "We could. Or we could do something else. Landon gave me the keys to his truck, so we can do anything we want for the rest of the day. What do you want to do?"

Minka grinned. She had no idea what she wanted to do, but whatever it was, she would be with Angelo. Beyond that, she didn't care.

They still hadn't decided on anything by the time they got to Landon's truck. When Angelo opened the door, she climbed in, then slid into the center of the seat. As soon as he got in beside her, he reached over to pull the seat belt across her lap and lock it into place.

"You have to keep the seat belt on," he said when she gave him a questioning look. "And you can't shred it with your claws."

Minka tried to take a deep breath, squirming in the seat. She felt so trapped. Why would anyone wear this? It was like some kind of torture.

"I didn't have to wear one last night. Or this morning," she complained.

"That was because Landon was driving and he didn't press the issue. Now, I'm driving, and I want you wearing a seat belt. It's safer."

She lifted up on the belt so she could take a deep breath. "But I feel trapped. I can't even breathe."

Angelo slipped on his own belt with a click, then lifted a brow. "Now you're being dramatic. You're not trapped, and you can breathe just fine. Stop panicking."

She wanted to believe him, she really did. But she felt sure she was going to suffocate. She reached over and pressed the red button that released the restraining device. The moment the belt was loose, she could breathe again.

She looked at Angelo to see him frowning. She dipped her head. "I shouldn't have done that, should I?"

"No." He sighed. "At least you didn't shred it. I appreciate that. So does Landon. But we're not going anywhere until you have your seat belt on."

They sat there, gazes locked, for a few moments.

Then he blinked. "Traffic accidents are very common, and this belt will help keep you safe in case we have one. I won't risk your life by driving without a seat belt," he said. "You're too important to me."

Knowing she was important to him made her feel warm all over. How could she argue with him now? She slowly put the belt back on and made sure the tab clicked into place. She sat very still and tried to breathe.

After a few moments, she looked at Angelo. "I think I'm okay now."

"Thank you." His mouth curved. "I understand it's difficult for you to wear anything that makes you feel confined after what happened to you, but it really is safer."

He started the truck and pulled out of the parking lot, then drove toward the main gate. As they did, Minka tried to memorize the way, but it was difficult. Even though they were going back the same way they had come that morning, the roads still seemed confusing. She was not sure she would ever find her way around this place.

As they turned off the main road—Angelo called it the interstate—she caught sight of the big building with the number twenty-two on it that she had seen yesterday.

Minka whirled around to look at Angelo. "Can we go see a movie?"

He flashed her a grin, his eyes twinkling. "Would you like that?"

She nodded, practically bouncing in the seat. Well, as much as she could bounce with her seat belt on. She hadn't been to a real movie theater in years—never one this big. And she'd never gone to one with a man. The fact that she was going with Angelo would make it even more special.

———

"What did you think of the movie?" Angelo asked.

Okay, that was probably one of the dumbest questions ever. Obviously Minka had enjoyed the movie. She'd been like a six-year-old on a sugar high since the moment the animated Disney film had started.

She smiled, her eyes sparkling. "It was absolutely the most amazing thing I've ever seen. I didn't know they even made movies like that. Can we watch it again right now?"

Angelo laughed. When she looked at him like that, it was hard saying no to anything she wanted. "How about we get something to eat first? Then we can see the movie again if you want."

Minka bit her lower lip, looking damn cute. "But they have food in the theater," she reasoned.

"Snack food. And we've already had a tub of popcorn and a box of M&M's. We need more than that if we're going to sit through another movie."

"I suppose you're right. Though the popcorn and the M&M's were delicious." She looked longingly at the theater they'd just left. "We can come back though, right?"

God, she was adorable. "Of course. In fact, we don't even have to drive anywhere. There's a nice restaurant around the corner. I saw it as we walked in."

As they walked hand in hand along the sidewalk, Minka told him about all her favorite parts of the movie they had just seen, which was pretty much the entire thing, including the previews. She slowed when they reached the restaurant, studying the outline of the bison on the logo of Ted's Montana Grill painted on the window.

"What kind of animal is that?" she asked curiously.

He smiled as he followed her through the revolving door. "That's an American bison, or buffalo. They're sort of like big cows except way tastier."

Angelo asked for a booth while Minka looked around. He had a hard time not laughing as she stared up in fascination at the big bison's head mounted on the far wall.

"She seems quite taken with our mascot."

Angelo glanced at the man who'd come up beside him. Short and heavyset, his name tag read Bryce. Underneath it was the word *Manager*. "Yeah, she's fond of animals, I think."

Bryce smiled. "You might want to take a look at this then."

The manager walked behind the bar and reached into the glass display case. A moment later, he came out with a plush bison wearing a white handkerchief around his neck sporting the name of the restaurant. "This is Ted."

Angelo grinned. Minka would love it. They needed to find a replacement for Boris—who was currently waiting in the truck for them—so they could give the sloth back to Zarina anyway. This would be perfect.

"I'll take it," he said.

Bryce handed it over with a laugh. "I'll tell your waitress to add it to your bill."

Minka had moved away from the bison and was studying the photos on the wall when the hostess led him to a booth. When she came over, he got up so she could slide in beside him.

"Did you see that bison on the wall there? He's so big. And so cute."

Angelo grinned. "I thought you might say that. That's why I got a smaller version." He took the plush animal from inside his jacket, where he'd been hiding it, and placed it on the table. "This is Ted."

Minka's eyes glistened with tears as she stared at it. Crap, what had he done wrong? He'd thought she'd love it.

But then she grabbed the toy in one hand, threw her arms around Angelo, and squeezed him so hard his ribs creaked.

"Thank you," she said against his chest. "He's perfect."

He wrapped an arm around her with a chuckle. "You're welcome. But is it okay if I breathe now?"

She gave him another squeeze, then sat back in the booth with a smile, wiping away the tears on her cheeks with her fingers. "How did you know I would like him?"

He grinned. "I just guessed."

Angelo wanted to ask why she'd been crying, but the waitress came to take their drink orders. By the time the woman left, Minka had already put Ted carefully beside her on the seat and picked up the menu. He discovered that while she spoke English very well, she had some trouble reading it. So they took their time going through all the options, even things they weren't going to order.

The waitress came and went twice, but by the third time, Minka was ready to order. They both went with bison cheeseburgers and fries.

Minka picked up Ted and looked at him closely, her slender fingers gently caressing the shaggy fur around the buffalo's head. "Thank you for helping me with the menu," she said, carefully avoiding his eyes. "You are an amazingly patient man. Your wife must feel very lucky."

Minka's eyes never left Ted's fuzzy features, but it was obvious she was fishing. Damn, who would have thought it? Minka had all the subtly of a brick to the side the head.

"I'm not married," he said. "And before you ask, I don't have a girlfriend either."

She relaxed visibly at that. Setting Ted on the seat beside her again, she gave Angelo a smile. "I wasn't asking. I was just pointing out that you're very patient. I would never be so rude as to ask something so personal of you."

With that out of the way, Minka went back to talking about the movie and how it was the most amazing film she had ever seen. Angelo hadn't seen an animated movie since he was a kid, but he didn't remember them ever being so much fun back then. Of course, he hadn't been with Minka, either. She just seemed to make everything better.

"How long have you and Landon known each other?" she asked after the waitress had brought their food. "You must be very good friends for him to let you use his apartment and his truck, not to mention his clothes."

Angelo chuckled as he handed her the bottle of ketchup. "Yeah, we're more like brothers than friends. We met in army basic training fifteen years ago, then spent over a year together going through Special Forces assessment and training. We've been together pretty much ever since. Even now that he's working here, we still keep running into each other. We both know that if either one of us is ever in trouble, all he has to do is call. Most of the guys on our team are like that."

Minka was experimenting with how much ketchup it took to completely cover one of her fries. But once she had that figured out, she looked up and smiled. "Do you have any real brothers? That you were raised with, I mean?"

He shook his head as he poured ketchup on his plate. "No, I have two sisters, Venus and Lydia. My dad was in the army when we were kids, which means he was gone a lot, so it was my job to keep them from getting into trouble." He picked up his cheeseburger. "How about you, any brothers or sisters?"

Minka ate another fry before answering. "No. I was an only child."

The words came out slowly, painfully. She was almost certainly thinking about how much her parents had to be hurting by not knowing where she was or what had happened to her. Damn, he shouldn't have brought that up.

He was still trying to figure out what to say to make it better when she smiled at him again.

"Tell me about your sisters."

That he could do. "Lydia is four years younger than me and lives out in Oklahoma. My mom's family is still out there on the Indian reservation. Venus is two years younger than Lydia and lives out in L.A.—California." He snorted. "Neither of them are married, and it seems every time I call, some jerk they're dating has gotten them mixed up in something stupid."

Thank God none of that trouble had landed them in jail—yet. Angelo didn't mention that to Minka, though. When she didn't say anything, he glanced over to see that her attention was no longer on him. Instead, her gaze was locked on the bar. He looked that way to see what was so interesting and saw two guys at the bar openly ogling her. Both were in their early twenties and had the total metrosexual thing going on—pullover sweaters, button-down shirts, and crisp khakis.

Angelo's protective instinct kicked in at the looks in their eyes—along with a healthy amount of jealousy. The two guys must have picked up on it because the moment they realized he'd caught them staring, they tossed some money on the bar and hauled ass.

Minka watched them go, then turned to look at him, confusion clear in her eyes. "Were they staring at me because I talk differently than they do?"

From outside, the guys took one more quick look at Minka before hurrying down the sidewalk.

"I doubt it," Angelo said. "There was no way they could hear what you were saying over all the noise. More likely they were staring at you because you're the most exotic, attractive woman they've ever seen."

Minka blinked, her dark eyes going wide. "You really think so?"

He grinned. "Do I think they were staring because they thought you were exotic and attractive? Or do I think you're exotic and attractive?"

She blushed but didn't look away. "I would rather know what you think."

"Then yes, I think you're the most exotic and attractive woman I've ever seen," he said. "You're beautiful."

Her face turned a deeper shade of red, the look of

wonder in her eyes making him realize she hadn't ever thought of herself that way.

"Thank you," she said softly.

"You're welcome."

Minka ducked her head and went back to drowning her poor, defenseless french fries in an ocean of ketchup. Crap, she probably had more sodium on her plate than protein.

She picked up her cheeseburger and dipped it in the ketchup covering half her plate, then took a bite and chewed thoughtfully. When she was done, she looked at him seriously.

"May I ask a question?"

He nodded. "Sure."

"Why doesn't Ivy like me?"

It took him a moment to recover from the minor case of conversational whiplash she'd given him. He'd thought for sure she was going to ask to define exactly why he thought she was beautiful—something he was all ready to do, by the way. But Minka had a point. Ivy had been suspiciously absent since she and Landon had first seen Minka in Zarina's office. And the way Zarina had refused to look at him when he'd asked if Ivy was going to meet with Minka tomorrow was weird, too.

"About a year ago, those two doctors who experimented on you captured Ivy," he said.

Minka's eyes widened.

"Yeah," he said. "You can't tell anyone, though. Only a few of us know about it. The doctors were able to get samples of her DNA before the other guys from my team and I helped Landon rescue her. Since then, they've been using that DNA to try to create hybrids."

"Like me." Minka bit her lip. "DNA…Zarina mentioned that when we were in her office earlier. I am not familiar with that word."

He gave her a rueful smile. "I'm not sure I know much more than you do about the subject—school wasn't really my thing—but I'll try to explain it. DNA is the stuff inside you that makes you who you are. It decides things like what color your eyes and hair are going to be, how tall you are, what your voice sounds like, things like that."

She nibbled thoughtfully on a fry while she considered that. "And they took Ivy's blood to get hers?"

"Among other things, yeah. They tortured her pretty bad."

She was silent for a moment. "So I have parts of Ivy in me now that make me like her?"

He nodded.

Minka's shoulders sagged. "Now I understand why she doesn't like me. I remind her of what those sadistic doctors did to her."

"Ivy'll come around. You just gotta give her some time." Angelo put his arm around Minka, barely stopping himself from pressing a kiss to her silky hair. "The next showing of the movie is starting in thirty minutes. Do you want to go see it again?"

She smiled. "I would rather go back to the apartment and relax with you. Would that be okay?"

See an animated movie or lay around on a couch with a beautiful woman? Angelo sure as hell didn't have a problem deciding which one he'd rather do. "That'd definitely be okay."

He paid the bill as soon as the waitress brought it

over; then they left the restaurant, Minka carrying Ted protectively in one hand while holding Angelo's with the other. He hadn't held a girl's hand this much since high school, but damn, it felt nice.

When they reached the truck, she introduced Ted to Boris, then gave Angelo a serious look. "I will give Boris back to Zarina tomorrow, but for tonight, would it be okay if both of them sleep on the couch with us?"

Angelo's mouth twitched. So much for any thought that Minka might actually sleep in the bed tonight. But then again, was he really complaining? He'd sure as hell enjoyed having her plastered to his chest last night, that was for sure, and if she wanted to do it again—even with Boris and Ted—no way was he going to stop her.

# Chapter 7

MINKA COULD FEEL ZARINA WATCHING HER. PENCIL IN hand, Minka looked up from the strange test Zarina had asked her to take to see the Russian eyeing her thoughtfully.

"Am I doing something wrong?" Minka asked.

"No!" Zarina said quickly. "You're fine. I didn't have time for breakfast this morning, and I was thinking about running over to the cafeteria to get something, but…"

"But you're not sure if you should leave me alone," Minka finished.

She didn't blame Zarina for worrying that she'd get upset and lose control. But Angelo was just in the next building with Landon and John, so she wasn't worried about the beast making an appearance.

"Go get something to eat," Minka said. "I'll be fine. Angelo is close by, and Boris is here if I need him."

Zarina glanced at the plush sloth back in his little nook on the shelf, then looked at Minka again. "Okay. But I promise I'll be quick. Do you want anything?"

Minka shook her head. Angelo had made a big breakfast, complete with eggs, pancakes, and bacon. While the eggs and pancakes were good, the bacon was the best part. She'd eaten it only once, when she and her parents had visited her father's native Russia, but she didn't remember it tasting quite so delicious. Angelo made the best bacon.

After Zarina left, Minka turned back to the piece

of paper on the table in front of her. The test mostly involved comparing several images and marking which ones were related somehow. Minka didn't understand the purpose of the test, but Zarina said it was something she needed to complete before meeting with Layla and Tanner this afternoon.

Minka was eager to finally have a chance to talk to the female shifter and the other hybrid. Finding Angelo had been nothing short of a miracle. But even with him near, the beast had almost slipped out a few times. She had to get better at controlling the animal those doctors put inside her if she wanted to ever have a normal life again.

She finished up the test, then sat back. Almost immediately, her mind turned to Angelo and all the fun they'd had yesterday. Between the movie, dinner, and the stuffed buffalo Angelo had bought her, she was having a hard time deciding what had been her favorite part of the date. She blushed. Angelo had never used the word *date*, but it had felt like one to her, so she was going to think of it like that.

Minka picked up the pencil again and doodled on the extra piece of paper Zarina had given her, drawing a sketch of Ted. Now that she thought about it, her favorite part had not been the movie, the dinner, or when Angelo had given her Ted. It was when he had told her she was exotic and beautiful. No one had ever said anything like that to her before, and when Angelo had complimented her, she'd thought she might float right out of her seat.

She was so distracted with thoughts of Angelo—and when he might take her back to see the movie again like he promised—she didn't realize the door to the office had opened until she picked up an unpleasant scent.

She put down the pencil, got to her feet, and spun around. Dick was standing there with two men. She didn't recognize either of them, but she immediately knew she didn't like them. She was well acquainted with their type. They were bullies, like the guards who had beaten her over and over again when she was in captivity. Both were average height with short, brown hair and cold eyes.

Dick moved closer while the two other men stayed near the door, essentially trapping her in Zarina's small office. The feeling of being held prisoner again immediately made the beast inside Minka uncurl itself from where it had been sleeping and prowl around inside her head. The fact that she could feel Angelo nearby was the only thing keeping the creature at bay at that moment. Even so, she could feel her fingers tingle, like her claws were trying to come out. She squeezed her hands into fists, praying it would make them stop.

She took an involuntary step backward. "Dr. Sokolov isn't here right now, but she will be back soon."

Minka hoped the warning would make Dick think twice about whatever he was there to do, but he took another step closer, his mouth twisting into a nasty smile that reminded her of the younger of the two doctors who had tortured her—the one who liked to laugh when he hurt her.

"That's okay," Dick said. "I came here to see you anyway."

She tensed when he reached his hand inside his suit

jacket, afraid he was going for a weapon. If he did, she wouldn't be able to stop the beast from coming out. As much as she disliked the man, she didn't want to hurt him. But it really wasn't up to her. The beast would take over and decide for both of them.

Minka took another step back but was brought up short by the lab counter behind her. She darted a glance at the door, wondering if she could make it between the two men standing there before they could catch her. In front of her, Dick slowly took his hand out of his jacket and held up two photos.

"Are these the men who kidnapped and experimented on you?" he asked.

The question caught Minka by surprise. She looked more closely at the photos and immediately recognized both of the men pictured. She nodded even as she wondered if she should be admitting anything to this man. Zarina had said he couldn't be trusted, and every instinct in Minka screamed that the doctor was right.

"Did you ever hear either man's name?" Dick asked.

"No," Minka said.

Hopefully that would be the end of his questions and he would leave.

"This is Johan Klaus," Dick said, holding up the picture of the older man. Then he held up the image of the younger man—the really mean one. "And this is Jean Renard."

Dick came closer, stopping only a few inches away and trapping her against the counter. His scent was so strong and cloying that Minka had a hard time breathing. Her control over the beast started to slip even more. She wished Angelo were there.

"When did they kidnap you, Minka?" Dick asked. "How long have you been a hybrid?"

Minka was sure she shouldn't answer that. Zarina had specifically said it wouldn't be good for Dick to know too many details about what had happened to her.

"I don't remember," she said softly. "I was drugged most of the time."

That part was true at least.

But Dick didn't like her answer and began peppering her with one question after another. What had Klaus and Renard done to her? Had they injected her with some- thing or administered the serum another way? What had it felt like when she'd turned into a hybrid? When had she started gaining control over her abilities? How many more hybrids like her were there? Where had they kept her prisoner?

The questions came so fast that she couldn't have answered them even if she wanted to.

"I don't know!" she finally shouted. "All I know is that I was held in a big building in Tajikistan."

Dick smirked. "Was that so hard? That was exactly the information I was looking for. Now, I just need you to be a little more specific about the location."

Minka shook her head, not only because she didn't want to tell him, but also because she honestly did not know.

But Dick didn't want to hear any of that. He was obviously a powerful man, and she knew from experi- ence that powerful men did not like to be told no.

"How can you not know where you were held?" he demanded. "You must have seen a landmark or a street sign. Something."

She was so tired of him pressing her that she probably would have told him if she could.

"I don't remember," she said, barely able to suppress a growl. "I was drugged and unconscious when they brought me to that place, and when I escaped, I wasn't myself."

Dick's eyes narrowed. "What do you mean, not yourself?"

Minka knew she should be quiet and not tell him any more, but the rage was starting to build—and it was getting harder and harder to keep the beast in check.

"The animal in me took over," she snapped. "It stayed in control for three days. When I am like that, it's hard for me to know what's happening. By the time I regained control, I had traveled a very long way without remembering how I got there. I cannot tell you where the horrible place was because those memories aren't mine. They belong to the beast!"

Dick actually took a step back at the vehemence in her voice. But instead of looking scared, he seemed thoughtful, as if considering her words. "That's very interesting. I didn't realize hybrids could partition their memories. But while it's certainly fascinating, it will make it hard to get the information I'm looking for."

*Good*, Minka thought. Then maybe he would finally leave.

"Perhaps we're talking to the wrong half of the hybrid," one of the men near the door said.

Minka glanced over to see that they'd closed the door without her even hearing it. One of the men was standing in front of it, like he didn't intend to let her out—or anyone else in. The other man—the one who had spoken—came to stand beside Dick.

"Perhaps we should be talking to the half that has access to the memories we're interested in?" he suggested.

Dick gave the man a sidelong glance. "Powell, that has to be one of the more out-of-the-box thoughts I think you've ever had. I'm impressed."

*Oh God.* They were talking about bringing out the beast.

Minka shook her head frantically. "Please stay away. I don't want to hurt you. I don't want to hurt anyone."

Powell grinned. "That's not going to happen."

She didn't know how he could be so sure—until he lifted his jacket and pulled out a strange-looking gun. She didn't know anything about weapons, but this one looked as dangerous and deadly as any other kind she had ever seen.

The beast reacted immediately to the implied threat. Her claws and fangs sprang out, and she felt the surge of strength that came when the beast was close to taking over. She couldn't believe Dick was so stupid as to think he'd be able to talk to the beast once it was in control.

Not that it mattered. Minka refused to give up the control she'd fought so hard to maintain the last three days, no matter how they threatened her.

She closed her eyes and shut out every sense she had. She stopped smelling, hearing, or thinking about anything except Angelo. She felt him nearby, imagined him stepping into the room and wrapping her in his big, strong arms.

The beast retreated but didn't go away.

Minka let her mind drift to last night, when she'd crawled onto his half-naked body to sleep and she'd felt his warm, hard muscles beneath her. She luxuriated in the memory, feeling the same sexual stirrings she'd had last night.

This time, the beast curled up, content to go to sleep again.

"Impressive." Dick's voice intruded on her thoughts. "I believe she's able to maintain control simply by closing her eyes and reducing outside distractions. I didn't think that was possible for a hybrid. In fact, if I hadn't seen her lose control a few days ago, I wouldn't know she's a hybrid at all."

Minka's eyes flew open. Dick and Powell were both looking at her like she was some kind of lab rat. It was the same way Klaus and Renard had looked at her.

The beast uncurled itself, urging her to leap at the men and claw the evil expressions from their faces.

"What made her lose control a few days ago?" Powell asked.

Minka felt a cold shiver pass through her. He was as bad as the doctors. He liked to have power over others — liked to see her scared.

Dick gave the man a smile. "Sometimes I forget why you got chaptered out of the army, Powell. You really are a twisted son of a bitch." He glanced at the man by the door. "Moore, you might want to have your weapon ready in case she reacts a bit more aggressively than we expect."

Moore snorted. "Shit, she barely weighs a buck twenty. What the hell is she going to do to us?"

Minka tried to take another step back, but there was nowhere to go. They were going to do something to her that she wasn't going to like. She could see it in their evil, hate-filled eyes. But even so, there was still a part of her that didn't want to hurt them.

But that part was rapidly disappearing.

Dick walked over to the built-in cabinets along the wall and opened the top drawer. A moment later, he closed it and opened the one underneath. Mouth twisting, he took out a syringe like the one Zarina had used to take some blood the other day.

"If I remember correctly, you have an issue with needles, don't you?" he said in a conversational tone as he closed the drawer. "Let's see how good your control is when faced with something you hate."

He came toward her, his eyes filled with what almost looked like amusement. The sharp tip of the syringe caught the light, glinting dangerously.

Minka's fangs came out so far she tasted blood.

"Angelo!" she screamed.

She didn't know how he could possibly hear her in the next building over, but she had to try. She would never be able to contain the beast without his help.

Her claws extended, making her fingers spasm and turning her hands into weapons that yearned to tear the men apart. Then her vision took on that extra-sharp definition, and she knew her eyes must be glowing red. Every muscle in her body tightened as the beast prepared to attack.

*Please don't hurt them!* she screamed in her head. But Minka's wants and desires were shoved roughly to the side, no matter how hard she fought to retain control. The beast reveled in the look of terror that crossed the men's faces, feeding on it and wanting more.

Powell and Moore lifted their weapons, but it was too late for that. The beast was free. There was no way to stop it now.

Angelo glanced at his watch as he headed over to the building where Zarina's office was. He hadn't wanted to make Minka nervous while she was taking the cognitive test Zarina had given her, so after making sure she was okay with him stepping out for a little bit, he'd spent the last hour with Landon and John in the director's office, talking about things that had left him conflicted and more than a little worried.

"I'd like you to stay until Minka gets a little more settled in and starts feeling comfortable on her own," John had told him.

Angelo certainly didn't mind staying to help, but he wasn't quite sure Special Operations Command would be pleased.

"Don't worry," John said as if reading his mind. "I've already cleared it with SOCOM and the 5th Special Forces Group. As far as they're concerned, you've been temporarily attached to the Department of Homeland Security for a classified project. They're completely on board with it. I've also made sure your records will be marked in a manner that will indicate impressive performance without actually saying what you're doing. It should only be for a few weeks."

Angelo wasn't thrilled with the director of the DCO mucking around in his personnel records. The guy had yanked Landon out of a Special Forces A-team commander position last year like it was nothing, and now he was temporarily attaching Angelo to the DHS without even bothering to consult him first. And that was on top of adding his name and security clearance information to the DCO's database months ago. People didn't casually make entries into the performance records of Special Forces soldiers. Angelo was all about helping Minka, but it was scary as hell being on the DCO's radar. John could end his military career as fast as he'd ended Landon's.

That wasn't a very comforting thought.

As Angelo crossed the well-tended courtyard between the buildings, a cold wind kicked up, and he stuck his hands in the pocket of the lightweight jacket he'd borrowed from Landon's closet.

While John might think Minka was making amazing strides when it came to controlling her hybrid nature, Angelo wasn't so sure. She seemed fine now, but that was because he was the only thing keeping her from crashing and burning completely. He didn't like to think about how bad and how far she was going to fall when he got yanked out from under her. Even if things worked out and he stayed longer than even John wanted him to, at some point, he'd go back to Special Forces. He was terrified at the thought of how Minka would handle that.

A herd of office drones were wandering out of Zarina's building when Angelo got there. As he waited for them to file past him, he was struck by how closely his relationship with Minka was beginning to mirror that of his mom and dad's in some ways. He and Minka weren't married, but there was a strong connection between them he didn't quite understand.

The irony of the situation wasn't lost on him. He'd spent his whole adult life avoiding getting involved with a woman who might come to depend on him. Now, he'd stumbled across one in the middle of nowhere, and suddenly he was hip deep in the very situation he'd been trying to avoid. He only prayed his relationship with Minka—whatever it was—wouldn't end the way his parents' had.

God, anything but that.

He blinked back tears as he entered the building, telling himself it was the wind. As he weaved through the maze of hallways, he forced himself to think of something less depressing. Like how much fun he and Minka had had last night.

He'd let Minka shower first, then sat outside the door, chatting with her about the movie. He'd tried his best not to look, but the lure of Minka being so close, knowing she was naked and wet on the other side of the shower curtain, was hard to resist.

He'd only taken a quick peek, or so he told himself. When he saw her silhouette against the wet curtain, it was stunning—all curves and high peaks—and if Minka hadn't suddenly bent to turn off the water, he wasn't sure he could have stopped himself from joining her. Forcing himself to look away from that rounded bottom was one of the more difficult things he'd ever attempted. Even through the shower curtain, he could see her ass was spectacular.

Minka had eyed him curiously when she'd walked out of the bathroom brushing her long hair. Probably because she could hear his heart thumping like a runaway elephant. But she hadn't commented on it.

His shower had been much shorter—and colder—than Minka's. He didn't even want to imagine how embarrassed they'd both be if she curled up on top of him to sleep only to find a hard-on in place of the comfy human mattress she expected.

Even so, Minka had crawled around on him for a few minutes, kneading his chest with her slender fingers until she found a position she liked. Then she'd gracefully coiled herself alongside him, her left leg bent and resting casually across his cock, which was barely contained by his boxer briefs. Her tank-top-covered breasts—without the confines of a bra like earlier in the day—had pressed lovingly against his abs, her cheek and flower-scented hair resting on his chest right below his chin.

His cock had hardened of its own accord, but Minka only nuzzled even closer to him, pressing her thigh against his erection and dropping off to sleep. He, on the other hand, hadn't fallen asleep for a long time, but he wasn't complaining.

Angelo was so immersed in his erotic daydream he didn't realize he was lost until he almost walked into a women's restroom. Swearing softly, he turned around to retrace his steps, hoping to find something that looked familiar. He was just about to break down and ask somebody for directions to Zarina's office when he heard Minka scream his name.

# Chapter 8

I<small>F THE SOUND OF</small> M<small>INKA SHOUTING HIS NAME HADN'T</small> propelled Angelo into instant combat mode, the feral growl that immediately followed sure as hell did. He took off running. *Shit.* That growl meant Minka had completely shifted into her hybrid form, and if he didn't get to her fast, she was going to get hurt or hurt someone else. He didn't want either to happen.

Angelo mentally kicked himself in the ass for being so stupid. He should never have left her alone. It was too soon for that.

As he sped down the hallway toward Zarina's office, he spotted Minka disappearing around the far corner, a man he didn't recognize chasing her. Another man stood outside Zarina's office, a pistol in his hand. Angelo didn't even hesitate. He didn't care if the guy was packing a freaking M4, he wasn't keeping Angelo away from Minka. But the barrel of the pistol was too round and too thin to be a normal gun. It was a tranquilizer gun. And Angelo had a pretty good idea what it was for.

How the hell had this guy gotten here before him?

Then Angelo saw Coleman step out of Zarina's office, his face a little pale, the front of his suit jacket shredded. Coleman must have somehow gotten Minka alone and done something to scare the hell out of her. Angelo didn't know what Coleman had been up to, but since the man was an asshole, it was probably something worth kicking his ass over. Angelo sorely wanted to stop and beat the shit out of the man right then, but he didn't have time. He had to catch up to Minka before she got out of the building—or someone shot her.

At Angelo's approach, the man with the dart gun turned and lifted his hand in the universal symbol for "back off." The three parallel scratches across the guy's face weren't serious, but they were deep enough to show that he'd tried to get in Minka's way.

"Stand down," the guy ordered. "We have this under control."

Angelo lowered his shoulder and put it right in the middle of the man's chest, sending him flying. The guy hit the linoleum floor, thumping his head so hard he was probably out cold before he finished sliding down the hall. The dart gun went flying, bouncing and skipping along until it came to a stop in a corner.

Coleman shouted something, but Angelo only slowed enough to turn down the hallway where Minka and the guy chasing her had gone; then he put on speed, frantic to catch up to her.

While he couldn't see either of them, it wasn't hard to figure out which direction they'd gone. Minka's growls and snarls, mixed with shouting as workers realized there was a hybrid loose in the building, was better than a tracking beacon.

The corridor he was running down abruptly opened into a wide-open office space filled to the max with those fabric-covered cubicle dividers. He scanned the area, trying to find Minka.

A blur of movement to the right caught his attention, and he raced in that direction, passing several members of

the DCO's security team herding people out of the building. Beyond them, the guy who'd been chasing Minka was
sneaking around the cubicle walls, a tranquilizer gun in his
hand. Angelo had no idea what was in those darts, but he
had no intention of letting that jackass put one in Minka.

Angelo caught up with the guy just as he entered
a small, open area. The man must have sensed him
coming because he spun, trying to get the dart gun up
and pointed in his direction. Angelo blocked his arm,
intending to strip the weapon out of his hands and end
the altercation quickly, but the other guy was faster than
he expected. He immediately disengaged and shoved
Angelo back with a palm strike to the chest, then brought
the weapon up to shoot him. Angelo jerked aside just as
the gun released a hiss of pressurized air and sent a dart
zipping over his shoulder.

*Fuck.*

When the guy brought the weapon up this time,
Angelo grabbed his wrist and twisted. Knowing the man
would almost certainly go for another strike to the chest
with his other hand, Angelo braced for it. The blow hurt,
but more importantly, the dirtbag had left himself open
to a counterattack. Angelo threw a good, old-fashioned
haymaker, aiming for the sweet spot on the left side of
the guy's jaw, then ripped the dart gun from his hand,
tossing it aside and driving his fist solidly into the man's
gut. To make sure the guy wouldn't be getting up anytime soon, Angelo lifted him and heaved him over the
nearest cubicle-dividing wall. The asshole landed with
a crash that probably meant someone was going to need
a visit from IT.

Angelo spun around, searching for Minka.

He didn't have to look far. She stood on the far side of the open area, her eyes glowing bright red, claws and fangs out, looking pissed off as all hell. Had the sounds of fighting attracted her, or had she smelled him and come running? Angelo hoped it was the latter.

"Hey, Minka," he said softly. "Remember me?"

She tilted her head sideways, like she didn't even recognize him. That worried him. Had Coleman pushed Minka so far that she couldn't find her way back? The stab of pain that came with that thought almost brought him to his knees. He'd pull her back, no matter how far gone she was.

"Minka, I'm going to walk around the table now, okay?" he said. "Just relax. I'm here now. Everything is going to be okay."

Moving slowly, he stepped around the side of the table and cautiously made his way toward her. Around them, the building was quiet. DCO security must have gotten everyone out.

Minka growled as he got closer, her body tensing and her hands coming up, those sharp, curved claws ready to rip into him.

He stopped and held his hands up in a placating gesture. "I'm just going to stand here and talk to you, okay?"

She let out another growl.

"It's me. Angelo. I know you're in there, Minka, and I know you can hear me. I need you to fight for control. You don't want to hurt anyone. I know you don't."

The red glow in her eyes dimmed, and for a moment, he thought the Minka he knew had gained control of the animal. But a split second later, her eyes blazed bright, and she leaped at him.

Angelo's self-preservation instinct shouted at him to jump to the side or lunge forward and take her down before she could do some major damage. But he resisted the urge just like he had in Tajikistan and braced for her attack.

But instead of trying to claw him to shreds or sinking her fangs into him, she wrapped her arms around his neck and held on for dear life, her face buried in his shoulder. Her claws had retracted, and so had her fangs.

Angelo put his arms around her, smoothing her silky hair with his hand as he made gentle shushing sounds he hoped would calm her. That seemed to work, but then she started crying. He didn't know what the hell to do after that. So he simply stood there and held her as she sobbed against his shoulder. His eyes burned. Hearing her cry tore him apart. He'd rather shoot himself a dozen times over than hear her sobs.

Movement behind Minka startled him, and he looked up to see Zarina standing there with a look of anguish on her face. Behind her stood several guards, including Jaxson, the head of the security team who'd escorted them into the DCO the other day. They looked uncomfortable, like they were interrupting something.

Jaxson gave Angelo a nod, then signaled the other guards to leave. They turned and walked out, hesitating only long enough to stop and pick up the asshole passed out in the next cubicle.

"Let's get her back to my office," Zarina said softly.

Angelo nodded. Yeah, that would be a good idea. And then he needed to find Coleman and make sure the man was crystal clear on the fact that this was never, *ever* going to happen again.

He didn't have to wait long to confront the deputy director. The jackass was waiting for them in the hallway outside the cubicle area, four men, including the one Angelo had laid out near Zarina's office, with him as backup. Angelo would have preferred to stay with Minka, but he was so pissed, he couldn't stop himself.

He paused, then slipped his arm from around her, gently turning her to face him. "Minka, will you be okay with Zarina for a few minutes? I need to take care of something."

Minka gave Coleman a nervous glance. Her eyes filled with tears again, but she nodded. Angelo had to fight the urge to take her in his arms and just walk the hell right out of the DCO and never look back. But he knew he couldn't. She needed help that only the people here could give her—if they would stop fucking around long enough to do it.

He nodded at Zarina, watching as the Russian doctor put an arm around Minka's shoulders and led her down the hallway. The moment they were out of sight, Angelo turned and strode over to Coleman.

"What the fuck did you do to her?" he demanded, ignoring the four men who moved to get in his way. If they thought they could stop him, they were dead wrong.

He expected Coleman to go on the offensive, saying he wanted Minka locked up—or worse. But instead, the deputy director held up his hands in surrender.

"Sergeant Rios, you have every right to be angry," Coleman said. "What happened was all my fault. I thought Minka would be able to tell us where Klaus and Renard were hiding, and I must have pushed too hard. I hope you'll accept my apologies and let her know how terribly sorry I am."

Angelo snorted. He didn't buy that crap for a second. "Coleman, you're so full of shit, it's coming out your ears. I don't know what the fuck you did to her, but if you or any of your men ever come within twenty feet of Minka again, you won't have to worry about her ripping you apart because I will."

Turning on his heel, Angelo jogged the rest of the way to Zarina's office, desperate to make sure Minka was okay.

When he got there, he found Minka sitting at the table with the Russian doctor, Boris on the table in front of her. He pulled up a chair and sat down beside her. She leaned her head on his shoulder as he pulled her close.

"Hey," he said. "You doing okay?"

She sniffed and reached up to wipe a tear from her cheek. "I've been working so hard to keep the beast away, but then Dick threatened me with that needle, and it came out anyway. It always comes out. It always wins."

Angelo had never heard Minka refer to the animal inside her as if it were a separate entity. It practically tore out his heart to hear her say that it would always be in charge. He wished there were something he could do—someone or something he could fight for her—but in this battle, he was little more than a spectator. The fact was, he had no idea how to help get her hybrid nature under control.

He couldn't believe how much that hurt him. He'd met her less than a week ago, and he already cared about her more than he'd ever cared for anyone in his life.

Whatever he was starting to feel for her scared the hell out of him.

They sat in silence, Minka's head on his shoulder, Zarina watching sadly from the chair on the other side of the table, until a movement outside the door caught his eye. He turned his head, half expecting to see that asshole Coleman, but instead he found Ivy standing there. The sight of the feline shifter pissed him off almost as much as if it had been the deputy director.

*Ivy should be the one in here helping Minka, dammit.* She'd been tortured by those doctors just like Minka. She might even be able to teach Minka how to contain her animal half. But for whatever reason, Ivy preferred to pretend Minka didn't exist.

Anger suddenly burned hot in the pit of his stomach, and before he realized what he was doing, he tipped Minka's chin up and told her that he'd be right back, then got up and walked out of the room.

"I heard about what happened," Ivy said. "How's she doing?"

Angelo folded his arms over his chest. "What, you suddenly care now?"

Ivy's eyes narrowed at his tone, but the fire went out of them just as quickly. "I care. I really do. But it's…complicated."

"No, it's really not." He pointed at Zarina's office. "There's a young woman in that room confused as hell and scared to death. Minka is terrified of what she is and even more afraid that someone like Coleman is going to put her in a cage—or worse." Ivy opened her mouth to say something, but he cut her off. "You could help her if you wanted to. Hell, you have more in common with her than anyone else in this world. But for whatever reason, you'd rather stand on the sidelines and watch her suffer. That isn't complicated. It's selfish."

Ivy looked down at the floor. "I can't help her. I'm sorry."

"Why the hell not?" he demanded. "Is it because you're worried everyone will figure out your little secret about breaking the rules and marrying your partner? If it is, I'll tell them right now. Then maybe you can stop worrying about yourself long enough to finally care about a scared young woman who never asked for any of this shit to happen to her."

Ivy's eyes flared green, and she took a step toward him. To do what, Angelo wasn't sure. But he didn't move. Ivy could have torn him to pieces if she wanted to, but for the first time, she seemed like she was finally engaged in the issue.

"That's not it at all," she growled. "I couldn't care less if the DCO finds out that Landon and I are married. The worst they'd do is fire both of us."

"Then what the hell is it?" he asked. "Look, I know you don't want to have to face what those doctors did to you out in Washington, but maybe it's time you did."

Ivy's fangs came out, the tips a flash of white against her lips. She put a hand on his chest and shoved him back against the wall like it was nothing—and he had at least a hundred pounds on her, probably more.

She jabbed a single, clawed finger into his pecs. "You don't have a clue what it was like having those doctors experiment on me," she growled.

He glared back at her. "No, I don't know what it was like. But Minka does."

Ivy bared her teeth in a snarl, then turned and walked away.

Angelo stared after her, stunned. He hadn't thought Ivy was the type to run away from anything, but that's what she was doing. And for the love of God, he had no idea why.

---

Minka frowned at the iPod sitting in the docking station in Landon's apartment. It shouldn't have been so difficult to figure out how to turn it on. She'd seen American soldiers use them before at the base where she worked. She would have asked Angelo how to do it, but he was already in the bathroom, taking a shower, and she wasn't going to get anywhere near that door until he was finished and fully dressed. She had almost walked in on him the past two nights, and she didn't want to risk it happening again. Just thinking about it made her mind go places it shouldn't, like wondering what would happen if she slipped into the shower with him.

Feeling her face heat up, she returned her attention to the iPod. After the day she'd been through, listening to music would be nice—if she could turn it on. She moved the button on the side back and forth, but nothing happened. Maybe the thing was broken.

She stared at it, replaying the day's events as she tried to figure out how to make the iPod work. She and Angelo had been in Zarina's office the whole day, with them trying to convince her that she wasn't a rabid animal who belonged in a cage. She wasn't so sure. If Angelo hadn't been there, she wasn't sure what would have happened.

"Minka, I'm not going to sit here and let you beat yourself up over this," Angelo had told her firmly. "You didn't hurt anyone, even though Coleman gave you every excuse in the world to do it. The animal inside you was more interested in running away than hurting them. You wouldn't have done that a few days ago."

Part of Minka knew he was right, but that didn't keep her from worrying anyway. "If I continue to have these violent outbursts, sooner or later, someone like Dick will lock me away," she'd told him. The thought had broken her heart. "I couldn't live like that, especially if it means being kept away from you."

Angelo had cupped her face in his big hand, his dark eyes fierce. "That is never going to happen. I won't let anyone do that to you. I promise."

Minka wasn't sure if that was a promise Angelo could even keep, but it had made her feel better anyway.

"Angelo is right," Zarina had added. "I've been helping Tanner for almost a year now, and he still has bad days, when he loses control, too. And nobody is trying to lock him in a cage. You're doing much better than he did when he first got here, but you have to accept that this is going to be a long process. Learning to control the animal inside you is kind of like eating an elephant—you have to do it one little bite at a time."

Minka was laughing to herself at the idea of eating a whole elephant as she ran her thumb over the front of the iPod. Music suddenly filled the apartment, making her jump.

It was American music, of course, but even though she'd never heard the song before, she decided she liked the beat. It was very rhythmic and made her want to move her feet. That was exactly what she'd been looking for—something to help put this bad day completely behind her.

She spun in a circle, lifting her hands to the side and clapping lightly before spinning back in the other direction. She hadn't danced since she was a teen back in Dushanbe, but as she started moving around the room, she found herself naturally falling into the traditional Tajik dance steps and combining them with the more modern movements she'd picked up while living in Tajikistan's capital.

Suddenly remembering where she was, she glanced over her shoulder at the bathroom, to make sure Angelo was still in the shower. She liked dancing, but she'd be embarrassed if he saw her. Just because she enjoyed dancing didn't mean she was good at it.

But the water was still running, so he would probably be a few more minutes. She would hear him long before he came out.

She made a circuit around the couch, spinning and twirling, clapping her hands and even putting a little wiggle into her hips as she went. She laughed. It was impossible to dance and not be happy.

She was just starting her third lap around the living room when a tingling sensation along the back of her neck made her whirl around. Angelo was standing right behind her wearing a fresh pair of jeans and a black T-shirt, a big smile on his face.

Minka stopped so suddenly she almost fell over. She was considering making a dash for the bedroom when Angelo took her hands in his.

"Why'd you stop?" he asked, tugging her a little closer. "You looked like you were having fun."

Before she realized what he was doing, Angelo started moving in time to the music. She automatically moved with him. She wasn't feeling nearly as embarrassed to have him see her dance as she'd expected. In fact, being this close to his big, muscular body made her almost completely forget about everything except how amazing he was.

She laughed as he spun her in a circle, then wrapped one arm around her waist and moved her around the floor in a dance step that she'd never seen before but picked up quickly. He was very graceful for such a big man.

"I love your laugh," he said softly. "It's very beautiful—like you."

She ducked her head at that, not necessarily embarrassed by his compliment, but definitely feeling her face grow warmer. "Thank you."

She glanced up at him from under her lashes and felt her tummy flutter at the way he was looking at her—as if he were seeing her for the first time and liking what he saw.

Minka moved a little closer to him. While she was having a hard time paying attention to anything but the way Angelo was looking at her, some part of her realized that the music had changed. The rhythm was noticeably slower, deeper, more insistent, and her movements became less playful and more suggestive. She'd never danced with a man like this before, but with Angelo, it felt…right.

He spun her in another circle, but this time he stopped her before she came all the way around, and she found herself with her back to him, looking at him over her shoulder as he slid his hands down to her hips and danced behind her. She instinctively moved in time with him, almost moaning at how the heat of his body felt against her back.

She took a step closer, seeking more of that warmth. That was when her bottom brushed up against him. She should have moved away, but she couldn't. It felt too good. She could hear his heartbeat quicken as the thin material of her yoga pants came into contact with something very firm under his jeans. She was inexperienced, but not naive. She knew exactly what that bulge was. The thought that she aroused Angelo made her feel very…powerful.

Minka realized that her heart was beating just as fast as his. She tried to tell herself it was simply because she was dancing, but that was silly. She'd been dancing much faster earlier and her heart hadn't been racing anything like it was now. No, her heart was pounding because she was so close to Angelo. She'd never felt arousal like that, and for a moment, she wondered if it was the animal inside her that was making her feel it.

Then Angelo spun her around and pulled her into his arms, and she stopped caring why she felt it. It felt good. That was all that mattered. Smiling, she wrapped one arm around him. She wanted to feel his body pressed against hers, wanted to touch all of him.

She wasn't sure how long they stood there, gazing at each other before Angelo bent his head and kissed her. A delightful little shiver ran through her body. It was almost the same thing she felt when the beast was about to take over. But instead of feeling scary, this was...exhilarating.

He buried one hand in her hair, holding her gently as his mouth opened a bit and his tongue ventured out to explore. She parted her lips in invitation, almost growling at how delicious he tasted.

She hadn't realized she was kissing him back until he groaned. That was when she discovered that now her tongue was in his mouth, exploring all on its own. She was surprised at how aggressive she was. She was normally not like that in any situation. Then again, she was a different person now.

Minka had never kissed a man in her life. The right situation—and the right man—had never come along. Even though she had nothing to compare them to, something told her Angelo's kisses were special.

As changes went, this was one she could definitely live with.

She moaned as Angelo slipped one hand down to the curve of her bottom and pulled her tightly against him. She could feel his hardness press against her even through his jeans. She actually trembled a little at the thought of what was hidden in there.

Minka slipped her hand into his long, silky hair, kissing him with a passion she'd never realized a person could feel. Maybe it was the beast inside her, or maybe it was just being with Angelo. Either way, right then, she was much more aware of her body than she'd ever been before. There were little sparks of electricity running all along her skin. Her fingernails and teeth were tingling like mad, like they were just on the edge of coming out but didn't want to for fear of ruining the moment. And more than anything else, she felt an insistent pulsing between her legs.

She slid her other hand down his stomach, not sure where she was going to let it wander, when Angelo suddenly caught her wrist and pulled away with a groan.

The move was jarring and so frustrating that she thought for a moment the beast would respond like it did when threatened, and attack Angelo. But she closed her eyes and took a few deep breaths, savoring Angelo's taste on her lips. When she opened her eyes again, it was to see him gazing down at her with something that could only be hunger in his dark eyes. That confused her even more. If he enjoyed what they were doing, then…

"Why did you stop kissing me?" she asked. "Did I do something wrong?"

He let out a breathless laugh and shook his head. "You didn't do anything wrong, trust me. But if we don't stop now, things might go a little further than we intend."

Minka smiled, pleased that she'd been right about him being just as excited as she was. "Would that be bad—if things went further?"

He cupped her face, caressing her cheek with his thumb, his eyes soft. "No—God no. But there's no need to rush. Things are always better when you take your time."

Minka supposed she could agree with that, though there was a part of her that was more than ready to take it as far as Angelo wanted to go. But she could wait—as long as she didn't have to wait too long.

"Should we just go to bed instead?" she asked. She was looking forward to curling up with him on the couch. Perhaps they could even kiss a little more.

He smiled. "In a little while. We might want to watch TV first to…you know, calm down. Although, right now, I think I might need to take another shower—a cold one, this time."

Minka wasn't sure why he'd need to take another shower, especially a cold one, until she remembered the very large bulge in his jeans. Then a cold shower made complete sense. She had to bite her tongue to keep from admitting she didn't mind if he was hard down there when they went to bed. Then again, if he was that aroused, she doubted either of them would get much sleep—not that she would have complained, of course.

# Chapter 9

"Do you want me to stay?" Angelo asked. "I can hang out in the hallway, make sure Coleman and his morons don't bother you again."

She and Angelo had gotten to Layla Halliwell's office for her first session with the DCO's psychologist a few minutes ago, and now Angelo was standing in the doorway looking like he was more than ready to camp outside all day if she asked him to.

"Thank you, but I don't think that will be necessary," she told him. "I doubt Dick is going to bother me while I am with Layla."

Angelo didn't seem convinced. "Maybe I'll just wait until Tanner gets here."

Minka couldn't help smiling. It would be silly for him to wait in the hallway, not to mention very boring.

"I will likely be with Layla for hours and would feel terrible knowing you were sitting on the floor in the hallway with nothing to do," she said. "Go find Landon and spend some time with him."

When Angelo hesitated, Minka thought she might have to say something else to convince him, but then he leaned closer—close enough that his scent filled her nose and did crazy things to her pulse—and kissed her on the cheek. "Okay. But if you need me, tell Layla to call Landon on his cell phone and I'll come running."

While the chaste kiss hardly compared to last night's

fiery ones, it still sent a little charge of electricity zipping through her. She almost reached up to pull him in
for a real kiss but caught herself. Even though she knew
Americans were less reserved when it came to public
displays of affection, it might have been a bit wrong to
kiss him in front of Layla.

So she satisfied herself with reaching up to casually
caress his slightly scruffy jawline with her finger. "I will
call if there is a problem. Promise."

Angelo gazed down at her for a moment, then nodded in
Layla's direction. "See you later. Tell Tanner I said hey."

Then he was gone, and Minka found herself closing
her eyes so she could hold on to his scent and the feel of
his lips on her cheek for a few moments longer. When
she finally turned back to where Layla was sitting on the
big U-shaped couch in the corner of her office, it was to
see the psychologist smiling at her.

"What?" Minka asked.

She couldn't keep from blushing as she walked over
to join Layla on the couch. Tall and slender with long,
dark hair and brown eyes, Layla was a younger version
of her sister Ivy. Only nicer.

"Nothing," Layla said. "Zarina said there's a serious connection between you and Angelo. She wasn't
kidding. How did you and Angelo meet anyway?" She
picked up her mug from the low table and took a sip.
"Zarina said it was in Tajikistan but didn't give me any
of the details."

Minka reached for the mug of coffee Layla had been
kind enough to pour for her earlier and sipped the hot
beverage, letting its warmth seep into her as she told
Layla the story about how Angelo had saved her in that

village, then carried her in his arms for miles to a helicopter before getting on a plane with her and cradling
her on his lap the whole flight to the United States.

She hadn't intended to reveal more than that, but
Layla was extremely adept at getting her to open up, and
before she knew it, Minka was telling her about kissing
Angelo last night. The experience was so vivid in her
mind, she could practically taste him on her lips.

"I've never felt that way before," she added. "Is it
normal to be so...excited by a man? Or am I feeling that
way because of what those doctors did to me?"

Layla regarded her thoughtfully. "Before I answer
that, do you mind if I ask how much experience you
have with men?"

Minka looked down at her hands. "None. I know that
must sound strange to you since I am twenty-six, but
though the town I lived in—Khorugh—is very beautiful, it is also very small. Most of the younger men leave
to find work elsewhere and do not return until they are
older. My parents didn't think any of them would make
a suitable husband, so instead of getting married, I spent
my time working, either as a translator at the military
base nearby or in my father's business."

"That's not strange at all," Layla said. "But since you
don't have any basis for comparison, you're going to
have to trust me when I say what I'm about to tell you."

Minka lifted her head to meet Layla's gaze. "Okay."

Layla leaned close, as if she was about to reveal a big
secret. Minka leaned closer, too. "What you're experiencing is very normal, especially for a shifter."

"But I'm a hybrid."

"Which is just another way of saying a man-made

shifter," Layla said. "Shifters like you and I have better eyesight, better hearing, and a better sense of smell than humans. Well, the same goes for sexual arousal. It's stronger and more intense for us."

Minka was relieved to hear what she was feeling was normal for a hybrid. She probably would have been attracted to Angelo regardless of what those doctors had done to her. It simply made that attraction stronger.

"So it isn't strange that I feel like this about a man I just met?" she asked. "I've known Angelo for only a few days."

Layla smiled. "That's something else about us. When we meet the right person, we fall for him really fast."

*The right person.* As in the man Minka was meant to be with. It seemed unbelievable that he would be an American soldier, but what else explained why she was so comfortable with him? She couldn't deny that she could see herself being with Angelo permanently. But he was in the army and would almost certainly leave soon. The thought not only hurt somewhere in her chest, but also made the beast restless.

"Is there someone special in your life?" Minka asked, changing the subject.

Layla's smiled faltered. "There is, but I'm not sure he feels the same way."

Minka was about to ask Layla what made her think so, but a knock on the open door interrupted her. She looked up to see a big man with a wild mane of dark blond hair and a scruffy jaw coming into the room. Even if Minka didn't know he was a hybrid by his scent, she almost would have certainly been able to figure it out by the way he carried himself. Like a caged animal—a very big caged animal.

"Sorry I'm late," he said as he closed the door.

Layla smiled. "You're right on time." She glanced at Minka. "Minka Pajari, meet Tanner Howland."

Tanner stepped forward and held out his hand, his movements slow and careful, as if he was afraid he would scare her. But while his appearance might have been wild, one look in his eyes told her that he wouldn't hurt a soul.

"Do you want some coffee before we get started?" Layla asked him.

He shook his head as he lowered himself into one of the chairs opposite the couch. "I had a cup before I came over."

Layla picked up her notepad from the table and rested it on her knee, pen poised in her right hand. Taking that as a signal they were about to get started, Minka sat up straighter and eyed her expectantly. But before Layla could say anything, someone knocked on the door, then opened it and poked their head in.

Minka stiffened when she saw it was Ivy. After overhearing the argument Angelo and Ivy had had in the hallway yesterday, she hadn't expected to see the other shifter again. Had Layla convinced her sister to join them? Minka gave Layla a sidelong glance, but the psychologist looked as surprised to see Ivy as she was.

"Ivy," Layla said. "I didn't know you were joining us."

Ivy glanced at Minka, then turned back to Layla. "It was kind of a last-minute thing. I'd like to sit in if you don't mind."

"No, of course not." Layla gave Minka a reassuring nod, then gestured to the other chair. "Come in and sit down."

Minka didn't know the two sisters, but she sensed there was a rift between them. Tanner must have thought so too, because he suddenly looked like he'd have rather been anywhere else than in the room with them.

When Ivy was seated, Layla said, "Let's get started, then." She looked at Minka. "You already know Tanner is a hybrid like you, right, Minka?"

"Yes." Minka frowned. "However, I am curious about why he wasn't made from Ivy's DNA like I am."

When Angelo had told her about Tanner, she'd assumed he was made from Ivy's DNA too, but he didn't smell anything like Ivy or Layla—or even her. She didn't think the question was an odd one, but from the shocked expressions on everyone's face, Minka wondered if maybe she shouldn't have asked.

"What do you mean, you were made with Ivy's DNA?" Layla said carefully, like she was using words Minka didn't understand. "Ivy, what is she talking about?"

Minka looked from one sister to the other. Ivy stared down at her hands clasped in her lap but didn't answer.

"I thought Layla knew, Ivy," Minka said softly. When Angelo told her not to tell anyone, she hadn't realized that included Ivy's sister. And now she'd given Ivy another reason to hate her. "I'm sorry. I didn't realize you hadn't told her. I thought…"

Ivy shook her head. "It's okay, Minka. You couldn't have known. I should have told Layla before this."

"Ivy, you're not making sense," Layla said. "How did someone get your DNA, and what does it have to do with Minka?"

Tanner cleared his throat. "Maybe I should leave."

"Stay. Please," Ivy said. "I've been keeping this secret for too long. There are people I should have trusted with this information a long time ago, and you're one of them."

Tanner looked unsure but settled back in his chair.

Minka waited for Ivy to continue, but she didn't say anything. Minka could see the turmoil in her eyes, though—like there was some kind of battle going on inside her, one that involved facing memories Ivy would probably have rather forgotten. Minka could relate.

Finally, Ivy took a deep breath. "Remember when Landon and I went on that mission in Washington State last year?" Layla nodded and Ivy continued. "Well, we were there to do recon on a man named Stutmeir. He'd kidnapped several doctors and scientists, and we thought he was making a bioweapon. But instead, he was turning humans into hybrids.

"I don't want to get into the details of how it happened, but I was captured. They held me prisoner and experimented on me, taking DNA and tissue samples from every part of my body in the most painful, humiliating, and horrible ways they could come up with. They thought that if they used DNA from a shifter instead of an animal, they could create the perfect hybrid."

Layla's eyes glistened with tears. "Where was Landon when this was happening?"

"Trying to rescue me," Ivy said. "I didn't know that, though. I thought he was dead, and I wanted to die, too. But Stutmeir wouldn't kill me. In the end, Landon, Clayne, Kendra, Angelo, and some of the guys from Landon's former Special Forces team got me out. But not before the doctors escaped with my DNA."

A tear trickled down Layla's cheek. Minka wanted to cry, too—for the torture Ivy had gone through then and the torture her sister was going through at that moment.

Ivy stood and walked over to stand in front of the window. "Landon and I spent months scouring the world looking for the two doctors, but all we found were the horribly twisted bodies of people they'd experimented on using my DNA. When the trail went cold a little while ago, I hoped they'd stopped the experiments because they hadn't worked." She took a breath. "But then, Minka showed up."

Minka felt the tears that had threatened earlier burn her eyes. She blinked, hoping no one would see.

But Ivy turned and looked straight at her. "I'm sorry for how I've been acting, Minka. It was just that every time I looked at you, I remembered all the things I'd been trying so hard to forget. Even more than that though, I'm sorry for being the cause of all the pain and suffering you went through."

Minka did a double take. She could understand Ivy wanting to forget being tortured—she did as well. But she didn't understand why Ivy was apologizing for what had happened to her.

"You aren't responsible for what those doctors did to me, Ivy," she said.

"Yes, I am. If I hadn't gotten captured and they hadn't gotten my DNA, you wouldn't have been turned into…"

Ivy choked on a sob, the words trailing off as tears rolled down her face. Minka stood and crossed the room to put her arm around Ivy even as Layla did the same.

"You didn't turn me into a hybrid," Minka said

softly. "Klaus and Renard did that. They would have experimented on me whether they had your DNA or not. And if they hadn't used it, I'd probably be dead like the other people they experimented on. But for whatever reason, your DNA worked on me, making me strong enough to survive and escape. If it weren't for you, I would never have met Angelo." She smiled. "Your DNA saved me, and for that, I owe you a debt of gratitude."

Ivy wiped the tears from her cheeks, her dark eyes filled with awe as she looked at Minka. "I don't know if anyone has ever told you this, but you're an amazing person."

Minka didn't know what to say to a compliment like that, so she just hugged Ivy again.

On the other side of the room, Tanner cleared his throat. "So, should I come over and join the group hug or what?"

Minka laughed along with Ivy and Layla. Tanner eyed them in confusion, which made Minka laugh even harder. But then, her mother always had said that men never understood women.

With Layla guiding the conversation, Minka, Ivy, and Tanner spent the next two hours talking about what happened to them while they had been held captive. At first, Minka hadn't been convinced it was a good idea reliving all of that, but it turned out to be very cathartic. Minka hadn't realized she'd been carrying such a heavy weight on her shoulders until she told them about how she'd been mistreated. Minka had no way to know for sure, but she suspected it was the same for Ivy.

"Now you know why I was so against you working at the DCO," Ivy told Layla. "Every time I thought about it, I imagined you getting kidnapped and tortured like I had been. It was hard to be happy for you with thoughts like that. I'm sorry."

Layla leaned over and squeezed her sister's hand. "It's okay. But you don't have to worry about anything like that happening to me because I'm not a field agent and I promise I never will be."

Tanner seemed to benefit from talking about what the doctors had done to him, too. Even though he had been turned into a hybrid months before Minka, in a whole different part of the world and with a different source of DNA, he experienced the same rage she did. But it seemed like he'd learned how to contain it. Minka hoped he would be able to teach her how to do it, too.

"How did you finally learn to control the beast?" Minka asked when he'd finished.

"At first, I depended on Zarina a lot—probably the same way you depend on Angelo," Tanner said. "Her voice, her scent, her presence—they were the only things that could keep me from losing it, and the only things that could bring me back if I did. Now, other techniques work for me, too. I could teach them to you, if you want?"

She nodded. "I'd like that. I want to get rid of the beast once and for all."

Tanner exchanged looks with Layla before turning his blue eyes back on her. "The beast won't ever go away, not completely. It's part of you now. But you can coexist with it and learn to keep it in the background except for those rare occasions when you need it to come out."

Minka's heart sank. She thought she'd be free of the beast entirely eventually—and she couldn't imagine why she'd ever want it to come out.

"Can you teach me how to do that now?" she asked Tanner.

Layla switched places with Tanner, letting him sit beside Minka.

"Can you feel the beast right now?" he asked.

"Yes," Minka said. "It's always there, waiting to come out."

Tanner nodded. "First, I want you to close your eyes and relax." He waited until she did, then continued. "Now, imagine that you're in a dark room, standing in front of a door. It can be any kind of door you want. Just make sure it's something you can hold firmly in your mind."

Minka pictured a solid wood door like the kind in Landon's apartment.

"Do you see the door?" Tanner asked.

"Yes."

"Good. On your side of the door, you have a handle that you can open or close. On the other side, there is no handle. That's where the beast is. It can't get through the door unless you open it."

When Minka realized the door would lead to a room where the beast was held captive, she immediately changed the door to a set of metal bars, like the ones that had been on the cell she'd been held prisoner in. It seemed the best way to keep the beast contained.

As Tanner continued to talk in his calm, steady voice about keeping the door securely locked at all times, Minka could feel the metal bars between her and the beast solidify. She imagined the beast pushing at the bars, trying to escape, but the door wouldn't open and the beast couldn't come out.

"Now, I want you to open the door just a little," Tanner said, "just enough for the beast to put one foot out."

She frowned but didn't open her eyes. "I'm not sure I should do that. What if it comes out all the way?"

"Then you'll think of Angelo and the beast will go back in," Tanner said. "Trust me, Minka. You can do this."

She wasn't as convinced. But in her mind, she pictured herself unlocking the door of the cage and opening it just enough for the beast to put one paw out. She immediately felt the beast's presence moving through her and tightened her mental grip on the cage, refusing to let it out all the way.

"Does the beast have one foot out?" Tanner asked.

"Yes," she said.

"Good. Now I'm going to teach you how to make your claws come out—and just your claws."

Minka tensed but nodded. If she wanted to control the beast, she was going to have to learn to take charge of it. Ivy's soft voice joined Tanner's, and together, they taught her how to make the claws on her right hand come out. Then Tanner had her close the door on the beast, and the claws retracted.

She opened her eyes with a laugh. "That was amazing! The beast came out and I was able to make it go back into its cage."

She could still feel it there, behind the metal bars, watching and waiting. But it didn't try to get out.

She smiled at Tanner, then at Ivy and Layla. "Thank you so much. All of you."

Tanner grinned. "You're welcome. But you did all the work."

She wasn't sure about that. "Can we do it again?"

Layla laughed. "Maybe after lunch. You've been working with Tanner for almost two hours already. We can get together afterward, if everyone is okay with that?"

Minka couldn't believe it was lunchtime already. But now that she thought about it, she was hungry. And when Ivy suggested meeting up with Angelo and Landon in the cafeteria, she eagerly agreed.

"You aren't coming to lunch with us?" Minka asked Layla as the rest of them made their way to the door.

Layla shook her head. "I wish I could, but I have to go see someone. All this talk about secrets and the damage they do has reminded me that I've been keeping some secrets of my own I need to come clean about. I'll see you guys after lunch."

Minka was disappointed Layla wasn't joining them, but she could tell it was important to the psychologist. She gave Layla a wave, then joined Ivy and Tanner. She couldn't wait to see Angelo and tell him how well she had controlled the beast.

———⁓———

Jayson was doing one of his physical therapy workouts, sweating and grunting through his core and ab exercises when the doorbell rang. He fell back on the floor and stared up at the ceiling, breathing hard. If he ignored whoever it was, maybe they'd go away.

The doorbell rang again.

"Jayson?" Layla called. "Are you home?"

Where the hell else would he be? He muttered a curse. Okay, that was uncalled for. Layla of all people didn't deserve it.

"I'll be right there!" he called back.

He rolled to his knees, then slowly pushed himself to his feet. His back had been feeling pretty good today, at least until he'd started doing the core-strengthening exercises. Now there were sharp tingles running down both legs. That usually meant he was in for some pain later. Then again, he was always in some level of pain. Why should today be any different?

He grabbed the towel he'd put on the arm of the couch and wiped his face, then opened the door. Layla stood there looking seriously hot in a slim skirt, silk blouse, and pumps.

"Hey," he said. "You get the rest of the day off or something?"

She smiled. "No. I just thought I'd stop by for lunch. Can't a girl take a break during the day to spend time with her guy?"

Jayson might have been nodding his head as he stepped back to let her in, but inside, his mind was spinning at a hundred miles an hour. Layla got an hour and a half for lunch as one of the perks of a cushy government job, but her office wasn't exactly a hop, skip, and a jump from his apartment. If she'd driven all that way, it was for a specific reason, and something told him it wasn't gonna be good.

But he went through the motions of helping her make sandwiches as she chatted.

Jayson chewed his ham and cheese sandwich mechanically, but it was impossible not to notice she had something on her mind. It also wasn't hard to figure out what it was. Layla had finally realized this thing going on between them was never going to work. She was moving upward at warp speed while he was lying around this damn apartment like lost luggage.

He swallowed hard, ignoring the stab of pain. It had been obvious from the beginning that a relationship with her was never going to work. Still, it hurt like hell.

Layla took a sip of iced tea, set down her glass, and took a deep breath. "I have something to tell you."

*Shit.* Here it comes. "Okay."

Jayson braced himself, waiting for her to politely kick his ass to the curb, but she just stared down at her half-eaten sandwich.

"It's okay," he said. "I know what you're going to say."

She lifted her head to look at him, her dark eyes filled with confusion. "You do?"

"Yeah. And I get it." Man, did he ever. "I knew we were heading here for weeks, and I don't blame you."

She frowned. "What the heck are you talking about?"

Now it was his turn to be confused. "You're here to tell me you're breaking up with me, right?" he asked.

Her eyes widened, then narrowed in irritation. Now not only was she going to dump him, but she was pissed at him, too. *Fucking great.*

"Are you stupid?" she demanded. "I'm not here to break up with you! Do you think I would come to your apartment and have a ham and cheese sandwich, then break up with you?"

Apparently, Layla wasn't here to dump his ass. He had to admit, part of him was relieved. The other part was confused.

"Okay. So if you're not here to break up with me, why did you drive all the way up here during your lunch break?"

"I came here to tell you something that would get me in a load of trouble if anyone ever found out," she snapped. "It might even send me to prison."

"Layla, if this is secret info, you shouldn't tell me," he said.

When she didn't say anything, Jayson suddenly had a horrible vision of her stumbling across deep, dark government secrets that involved assassins, political cover-ups, and unauthorized covert operations.

"I know I shouldn't be telling you," she said. "But I spent all morning talking to Ivy and came to realize that we let a secret come close to destroying our relationship. I almost lost my sister over something she refused to share with me, and I don't want that happening to us. I want to be a part of your life, and that won't happen if you find out I've been lying to you the whole time. And at some point, you'd figure it out."

"Figure what out?" God, he was so frigging confused. He felt like he needed a translation guide for this conversation.

Layla didn't seem to notice the fact that he was drowning, though. "That I'm not exactly what you think I am."

Could she be any more cryptic?

"I don't really work for the Department of Homeland Security," she said softly. "I work for an organization called the Department of Covert Operations, or DCO for short. It's buried so deep inside the bureaucracy of the DHS that they don't even know we exist."

Jayson almost laughed. "That's your big secret? That

you work for a secret organization within the U.S. government? If it is, that's not really a secret. There are probably dozens of organizations in the United States like that. And it certainly isn't going to come between us."

"No, that's not my big secret," she said. "The secret part is about how the DCO operates. They field teams of trained operatives from military, law enforcement, and covert backgrounds with those who possess…special abilities."

"Okay," he said slowly.

"Maybe it would be best if I just show you," she said. "But you have to promise to not freak out—or hate me."

He scowled at her. "Now who's being stupid? You know I could never hate you. And I'm former Special Forces. I don't freak out."

Layla gave him a small smile that was a little bit sad but didn't say anything. After a moment, she shook her head, then picked up their plates and carried them over to the sink.

"This isn't as easy as I thought."

Jayson stood and followed after her. Luckily the kitchen was small, so he didn't have to go far.

He gently put his hand on her arm and turned her to face him. "Hey. Whatever it is, you can tell me."

Layla didn't smile this time. "Just remember you said that."

She took a deep breath, then slowly held up her hands, palms facing her. As he watched, her oval-shaped nails extended and turned into claws that had to be an inch and a half long. If that wasn't crazy enough, her eyes became a vivid green, and the tips of two really sharp fangs poked over her lower lip.

Jayson tried not to freak, he really did, but he failed. He took a step back so fast he had to grab the counter to keep from falling on his ass. A split second later, the claws, fangs, and green eyes were gone, and he had a hard time believing he hadn't imagined them.

"What did I just see?" he asked.

Her eyes filled with tears. "I was right. You're disgusted, aren't you?"

"No, I'm not!"

*Shit*. He told her he wouldn't freak out. Layla looked so scared and vulnerable right then that it made his chest hurt. He pulled her into his arm, hugging her close.

"Layla, you didn't disgust me. You could never do that—even if you sprouted horns and a tail." He pressed a kiss to her silky hair. "I'm just not sure of what I saw, that's all."

Layla nodded against his chest. Then she told him that she was a shifter—a genetic mutation of a normal human who possessed certain animal traits. It sounded too insane to be real, but he'd seen the claws and fangs, not to mention the brilliant-green eyes, so she wasn't making it up.

"Are the physical changes I saw the sum total of what you do when you shift, or are there other things that make you different?" he asked.

She didn't answer right away. "I can run faster and farther, and jump higher than a normal person. My senses are keener, too. I can smell, see, and hear better."

*Wow*. "Are there others like you?"

She hesitated. "That's not something I can talk about because that would lead to secrets that aren't mine to tell."

He could understand that.

Layla bit her lip. "I know that finding out that I'm a shifter is a lot to take in, and that it might take a while to wrap your head around it, but I couldn't keep it from you any longer. I could feel us drifting apart lately, and I know it was because I was hiding things from you. Maybe you don't even realize you're doing it, but I can see you tune out sometimes when we talk. I think you were subconsciously picking up on the fact that I was keeping this huge secret from you." She sighed. "I want you to know the real me, even if that means you walk away from me because of it. That's better than letting us fall apart slowly—or having you hate me when you stumbled over my secret on your own."

Damn. He hadn't realized he'd been tuning out during some of their conversations, but if he had, it sure as hell wasn't because of anything Layla did. It was because he was a worthless piece of handicapped crap who didn't deserve her and wasn't man enough to let her go.

He opened his mouth to tell Layla that when she leaned forward and kissed him…then kissed him some more. He kissed her back, forgetting all about the fangs he'd seen earlier. She was the same Layla he'd been half in love with since they'd met.

Layla pulled away with a rueful smile. "I'm sorry to spring all this on you and then bail, but I really do have to get back to work. I have another session right after lunch. We can talk about this later as much as you want. Or if you decide you don't want to have anything else to do with me, I get it. Just text me, and I won't bother you again. I only hope you'll keep my secret if for no other reason than I'm asking you to."

She gave him a quick kiss, then picked up her purse from where she'd left it on the couch and practically ran for the door. It took a little work on his part, but he caught up and grabbed her hand. Then he turned her to face him and kissed her again—like he meant it.

He rested his forehead against hers. "Thank you for telling me. I know how hard it was for you. Nobody will ever hear about your secret from me. That's a promise."

She nodded, her eyes shimmering with tears. She turned to open the door, but he stopped her again.

"You want to come over tonight? I could order pizza," he added.

Layla smiled, the tension visibly fading. "I'd like that."

After she left, Jayson wandered into the living room and collapsed on the couch. Damn, he'd had a hard enough time trying to see how a relationship with Layla could work when he'd thought she was this amazing woman with beautiful eyes, silky hair, and a body that wouldn't quit. Now that he knew she was some kind of superhero, he didn't see how they had a chance in hell of making it.

# Chapter 10

ANGELO CRINGED AS HE WATCHED MINKA WAVE THE knife she was using to dice the tomatoes for the fajitas. She was going to cut off a finger. She'd been bouncing off the walls since he'd met up with her at Layla's office a few hours ago; she couldn't stop talking about how well things had gone with Ivy and Tanner. The only time she'd slowed down was when they'd taken a detour to the grocery store on the way to the apartment, and that was only because she'd never been in a store with so much food before.

"I couldn't believe it when Tanner showed me how to put the beast behind a door and keep it locked away," she said excitedly as she reached for another tomato. "I was even more amazed when he showed me how to open the door a little so I could get my claws to come out. I can't imagine why I'd ever want them to come out, of course, but it was very impressive anyway. Oh, and did I tell you that I'm part cat? That's why I have curved claws."

Angelo held one hand above the grill to see how hot it was while stirring the peppers and onions with the other, then gave her a quick look. "Part cat, huh?"

He had to really force himself to pay attention to the vegetables he was sautéing, or he was going to burn them. The secret to good Mexican food was the right blend of peppers, spices, and patience. But right now,

Minka was being damn distracting—especially dressed in the long boho-print skirt and tank top Layla had given her to wear. What man could think of cooking when he had such a gorgeous woman in front of him?

"Ivy is a feline shifter, and I have her DNA in me, so that means I am part cat, too," Minka said.

Angelo already knew that Ivy was a feline shifter but didn't mention it. Not that Minka gave him the chance anyway. She was telling him again how she'd learned to make her claws extend and retract. She'd already told him at lunch, but he didn't mind hearing it again. He was thrilled she was learning how to control her hybrid side. He hated the idea of leaving her, but at some point, he'd have to, and he'd feel a lot better doing so knowing she could keep the beast at bay.

But then Minka told him that Tanner and Ivy had encouraged her to use him as an anchor to help her stay in control. It was merely another reminder that no matter how many tricks Minka learned, she still depended on him. She had a much longer road in front of her than she imagined, and he was afraid he'd have to leave before she even got started.

"Did your mother teach you how to cook like this?" Minka asked from beside him, watching him work the grill to get the meat perfectly cooked.

"Nah. My dad grew up in Mexico before moving to Texas and becoming a U.S. citizen. He taught me everything I know about making Mexican food. He still makes it ten times better than I ever will."

After everything was cooked, he and Minka brought it over to the table; then, Angelo showed her how to put together a fajita.

"Careful," he warned. "It's going to be hot. And spicy."

Minka piled on the ingredients and took a big bite as if he hadn't spoken. Angelo held his breath, waiting for her to reach for her glass of water. But instead, she groaned. "This is so good. I could eat this every night."

Angelo chuckled and bit into his own fajita, feeling absurdly happy that she liked the meal he'd made. It was crazy really, especially after spending the past fourteen years becoming an expert at keeping the women he got involved with at arm's length. But that strategy wasn't working with Minka. She was slipping her way inside his defenses faster than he would have ever believed possible. He was falling for her—hard.

He'd said as much to Landon when his friend had shown him around the DCO training complex earlier that afternoon. "One second, she's sweet and innocent. The next, she's smoking hot and more sensual than any woman I've ever met. No matter how many times I tell myself not to fall for her, I keep doing it."

Landon chuckled. "Man, who ever said you have a say in anything when it comes to who you fall for? Trust me, one day, you wake up, and bam, you're so in love you can barely remember your own name. And when that happens? You just hang on tight and go with it."

His former commander made it sound so easy—and maybe it was simple for Landon and Ivy, despite having to hide their relationship. But Angelo had a job to go back to that didn't leave room for Minka.

"So what did you and Landon do this afternoon?" Minka asked, her soft voice dragging him back to the present.

Angelo looked up to see that Minka had already

polished off two fajitas. Damn, the girl could eat. "Landon gave me a tour of the DCO complex. I did some target shooting and blew up a few things. He even let me play with the expensive surveillance toys. I swear, it felt more like a recruiting pitch to get me to work there than anything."

Minka's eyes flashed green, her full lips curving slightly. Damn, why the hell had he said it like that? Now she probably thought he was going to come work for the DCO. Even if he wanted to, he couldn't, not after just reenlisting for another five years. The army wasn't the kind of job where you could walk into the boss's office and say, "I quit."

Thinking it would be a good idea to steer the conversation back to safer ground, he reached for another fajita and asked Minka a question instead. "What do you think you'll work on next with Ivy and Tanner? You going to practice with the claws for a while or move on to something else?"

Angelo felt a little crappy about changing the subject, but if Minka noticed, she didn't seem to mind. And it wasn't like he had to fake interest in what she was saying. Anything that involved Minka was important to him. Besides, he didn't know much about shifters or hybrids, so the whole thing was pretty damn fascinating.

"What do you visualize when you see the beast in your mind?" he asked.

"Before today, I thought of it as a giant, blurry monster. But after learning that the beast is a cat, that's how I picture it now." She smiled. "Not a little house cat, of course. They aren't scary enough. More like a big cat that roams the mountains."

"Makes sense," he said.

Minka set the other half of her fourth fajita on her plate and gave him a curious look. "Would you mind if I ask you a personal question?"

His mouth twitched as he prepared another fajita. He wasn't used to Minka being so reserved. She usually said whatever was on her mind, regardless of whether it was personal or not.

"Go ahead," he said.

"The first time we met, I had claws, fangs, glowing red eyes, and I tried to kill you. Since then, I've spent most of the time telling you about an imaginary creature that lives inside my head and makes me act like a monster. How are you so calm about that? Most people would have run away already."

Angelo chuckled. Not exactly the personal question he'd expected, but then again Minka rarely did the expected.

"Well, my mom was full-blooded Cherokee, and I grew up around all kinds of Indian folktales and legends. My dad was in the army, and whenever he was deployed, Mom would take my sisters and me back to the reservation where she grew up in Oklahoma. I'd stay up half the night listening to the old men tell stories about shape-shifters, animal spirits, skin-walkers, and trickster spirits." He grinned. "I'm not saying I necessarily believed in all that stuff back then, but after meeting Ivy, Tanner, and the other shifters at the DCO, it just didn't faze me that much."

Minka looked at him with wide eyes. "You're a real American Indian? Like in the movies? With horses and everything?"

He laughed again. The expression of wonder on her

face was adorable. "First, I'm only half-Indian. My dad is Mexican, so there's that. And second, Native Americans are almost nothing like you see in the movies. We don't all live in tepees and ride horses. In fact, I don't even own a horse."

Minka was a little disappointed about the no-horse thing, but she was fascinated with what it was like growing up on an Indian reservation and being surrounded by all those legends. She immediately asked him to tell her some Indian stories. It had been a long time since he'd thought about them, but to make her happy, he dug through his head and tried to remember every tale he'd heard as a kid.

He was halfway through a story about a Cherokee man who could turn into a bear when he realized they'd demolished the entire tray of fajitas. He finished telling the tale as they cleared the table and loaded the dishwasher. Then, Minka cuddled up close to him on the couch while he told her some more stories. Sometimes, she mentioned a similar myth or legend from her culture, but mostly she listened to him talk. He sure as hell didn't mind. He hadn't had so much fun talking to a woman ever.

Angelo didn't intend for the cuddling to go anywhere, but Minka was sitting there with one leg casually draped across his lap, and his hand found its way onto her thigh. He couldn't help himself. She'd been wearing a skirt when he'd found her in Tajikistan, but he hadn't exactly been focusing on her body at the time—he'd been more worried about the claws and fangs. Since then, she'd worn yoga pants. Even though they showed off the fact that Minka had nice legs, they simply didn't do them the same justice as the skirt she now wore.

Because Minka didn't just have nice legs—she had amazing legs. Long, toned, and touchable. It didn't hurt that, with her leg across his lap, the skirt slid up to show off more than half her thigh. He didn't even realize he was gliding his fingers up and down her leg until he heard her purr in the middle of a story about the redbird. It had to be the sexiest thing he'd ever heard.

He told himself to cool it, that it was crazy to let this go any further, but when Minka reached up and tugged his face down for a kiss, he didn't try to stop her. And as the kiss deepened and the taste of her lips overpowered his senses, he knew the night wasn't going to end with a make-out session on the couch.

Angelo had been seriously attracted to Minka from the moment they'd met, and every minute they spent together had moved both of them further in this direction. He might not have known how long he'd be able to stay here with her, but did he want to look back later and kick himself in the ass for being too scared to go to a place they both obviously wanted to be?

But it wasn't as simple as that. Minka might be more than willing to sleep with him, but he knew she was inexperienced with men. Was it right for him to take her to bed knowing he could get sent back to his A-team at any time? No matter what she thought she wanted, she'd be devastated.

Even though it was as hard as hell, he dragged his mouth away from hers. Minka looked lost and confused for a moment; then she frowned.

"I was right," she said softly. "You're worried about taking me to bed because I am a virgin."

"What? No!" he said.

Then he realized that, in a way, he was.

Angelo sat back. Thinking would be a lot easier if Minka moved her thigh off his lap. It was hard to concentrate with her warm, soft skin so close to his cock.

"Okay, maybe that is it—a little," he said. "But I don't care that you're inexperienced. I just don't want you to get hurt."

She laughed and ran a hand down his chest. "You're big, but I don't think you'll hurt me if we make love."

He gently brushed her hair back from her face, a smile tugging on the corner of his mouth. "I didn't mean I would hurt you that way. I meant that if we sleep together, it might make it harder on you when I have to leave. I'd rather not put you through that."

Minka was silent, considering that. "Angelo, you are the kindest, most honorable man I have ever met. I want very much to make love to you. And not sleeping with you won't make it hurt any less if you leave."

Angelo didn't miss the fact that she said "if" and not "when," but he didn't correct her. He couldn't have even if he'd wanted to because Minka swung her leg over his lap, her bare thighs against his and her panty-covered pussy directly on top of his cock. Her warmth seeped through his jeans, making his shaft harden painfully.

Talk? He could barely think straight.

Minka leaned forward and kissed him. Groaning, he buried his hand in her hair and pulled her tighter to him, surrendering to the need to be with her. Who the hell was he fooling? It wasn't like he'd ever had a chance to resist.

Her taste made him drunk, and he ran his other hand

up her bare thigh, sliding under her skirt. The feel of her taut muscles quivering under his fingers was so damn sexy that he found it hard to go slowly, but he knew he had to. For all her passion, Minka was still new at this. He was damn well going to take his time and make sure this was the most amazing night of her life.

When he reached the top of her thigh, he teased the silken skin at the edge of her panties with his finger. She moaned and rotated her hips, grinding against him rhythmically, in counterpoint to what he was doing with his fingers. The urge to slide underneath her underwear was powerful, but instead, he moved his hand around to her ass, caressing her perfect, womanly curves. Minka started breathing harder, but he kept his mouth on hers, continuing to kiss her no matter how aroused she became.

But it must have been too much for her because she broke the kiss as he slipped his fingers into the back of her panties and tickled his way down from the base of her spine to the cleft between her ass cheeks.

She let out a soft sound halfway between a purr and a growl. "I think you're teasing me."

Angelo chuckled and moved his hand around to slide a few fingers underneath her panties, playing in the damp curls there. Her breath hitched as he reached her clit, and he swore he caught a little flash of color in her eyes, though if it was red or green he couldn't say.

"Maybe a little," he admitted, making tiny circles right there on her most sensitive spot.

Minka closed her eyes, her lips parting as she gasped. She pressed her clit against him urgently, grinding her hips in tight circles and making the sexiest sounds he'd ever heard. She was so wet and hot, her breathing so ragged, that he had no doubt he could make her come if he wanted to.

But it was too soon for that. He wasn't intentionally trying to tease her. It was just that the first time he made her come, he wanted her to be completely and gloriously naked—and preferably writhing all over his equally naked body.

Angelo eased his fingers out of her panties and urged her off his lap, then stood and swept her into his arms. Minka rested her head on his shoulder as he started for the bedroom, a purr of approval escaping her lips.

When he reached the bed, he placed her gently on her feet, then gazed down at her. "You sure about this?"

She nodded, a smile curving her lips. "Very sure."

He slid his hands up her hips until he got to the edge of her tank top, then slowly pushed it up and over her head. She had on a simple satin bra with delicate lace trimming the cups, and he wondered briefly if they matched her panties. He'd find out soon enough.

Thumbs skimming the underside of her bra, he slid his hands around to unclasp it, then took it off, leaving her bare to the waist, her beautiful breasts rising and falling in her excitement. Her nipples had already hardened into firm peaks, and he gently cupped her breasts, teasing their rose-red tips between his thumbs and forefingers.

"Do you have any idea how beautiful you are?" he asked hoarsely.

Minka didn't answer. She simply reached up and tangled her fingers in his hair, urging him down for a searing kiss.

—◦∿◦—

The whole day had been like a dream.

Minka had known that kiss a few minutes ago was leading here the moment their lips had met. There was an urgency and intensity that hadn't been there the night before. She knew Angelo had felt it, too. And yet, he'd still been hesitant to make love to her. She understood his reluctance, but that was part of the reason she wanted to be with him so much. He was the kind of man who would always worry more about her than himself. She might not have much experience with men—okay, she had none—but she knew men as amazing as he was didn't come along very often. She wasn't going to waste the chance to be with him.

Still, her heart was beating like crazy. She wanted to be with Angelo more than anything in the whole world, but she was still nervous about the act itself. There were so many things she didn't know about men. What if she was so inept at making love that he was disappointed in her?

But when he'd stripped off her top and removed her bra, the awe-filled look on his face had taken her breath away. Then he was cupping her breasts and teasing the stiff peaks, and tingles rushed through her body like she'd been struck by lightning. He said something about her being beautiful, but she was too consumed by the need to kiss him again to be sure.

His strong arms wrapped around her naked back, and she shivered at the feel of the rough texture of his shirt rubbing against her nipples. She would have much preferred to press her bare breasts against his naked chest, but she wasn't bold enough to pull off his shirt like he'd done hers. And she certainly couldn't tell him what she wanted, either. Her face flamed at the thought.

So she lost herself in his kiss, moaning as his hands slid over her back and shoulders, occasionally moving around to squeeze and tease her breasts. She clung to him, afraid she'd fall if she didn't. Her whole body felt like it was on fire, and there was a pulsing need between her legs she'd never experienced before.

She was so focused on the sensation, she didn't realize Angelo had unzipped her skirt until the fabric hit the floor. Then he was kneeling down in front of her, slipping his fingers in the waistband of her panties and pulling them down. The move was so sudden she had no time to even consider trying to cover her nakedness.

But for some crazy reason, she had no desire to hide her body from Angelo's gaze. After saving her life so many times, it was like he'd already seen into her soul. Why would she worry about him seeing her like this, too?

So she stood there while he kneeled before her, devouring her with his hungry gaze. He was mere inches from that secret place on her body that no man had ever seen before. Did he think she was as beautiful there as he claimed the rest of her to be?

Angelo put his big hands on her hips and leaned forward to press his warm, soft lips on the sensitive skin of her stomach, kissing her. She grabbed hold of his shoulders to steady herself. She'd never felt anything so amazing.

As his lips traced back and forth across her quivering stomach, his hands did the same to her bottom, caressing and squeezing, holding her firmly as his mouth wandered ever lower. Just when she was sure the sensations could not get any more incredible, he moved his mouth or hands somewhere else, proving her wrong.

When his tongue teased the skin just above the curls at the juncture of her thighs, she couldn't help but wonder how much lower his mouth would go. Would he lick her *there*? The thought alone was enough to make her legs go weak. She remembered talking with her girlfriends back in Tajikistan about men doing that to women. She'd never imagined wanting a man to do that to her, but now she found herself silently begging Angelo to do that as well as many other things.

Just when she was sure Angelo would put his mouth on that most secret part, his hands tightened on her hips and he spun her around so that her bottom was facing him. She almost asked what he intended to do...until she imagined him kissing this part of her body like he'd done to her front. A whole new kind of tremor ran through her.

But instead of experiencing the pleasure of his mouth on her backside, she felt him tense. She had only to look over her shoulder to understand what had given him pause. He was staring at her back and the scar that ran from her right shoulder blade down to her opposite hip.

Minka opened her mouth to tell him that the younger doctor, Renard, had sliced her to the bone with one of the guard's knives out of anger a few days before she escaped. The cut had been severe and terribly painful at the time, but now it was barely even discernible and no longer hurt at all. But the words came out as nothing more than a sigh as Angelo began to softly kiss every single millimeter of that scar. The tender reverence he showed as he did it brought tears to her eyes, reminding her again that he was like no man she had ever met.

When he'd kissed away every bad memory of what had happened, Angelo stood and turned her around, then kissed her tenderly on the lips again before stepping back to gaze at her nude body. It felt very strange to be completely naked in front of him while he was still fully dressed—strange but not bad. Earlier, he had said she was beautiful, but now she felt the truth of his words in the way he looked at her.

Angelo reached over his shoulder and grabbed his shirt, yanking it off in one smooth motion. His boots and jeans quickly followed, leaving him standing there in nothing but a pair of very tight underwear straining to contain his arousal. He moved to take them off, and while she desperately wished to know what was hidden under there, she stepped forward to stop him. She suddenly wanted to take her time and explore first.

Minka had seen Angelo like this the previous nights they had slept together on the couch, but now it was different. Now she had permission to touch anywhere she pleased.

She placed her hands first on the thick, strong muscles of his chest, feeling his heart beat fast and rhythmically under her fingers. Her nose had already told her that he was excited—the scent was unmistakable. But it was still good to feel his heart pounding like it was.

She slowly moved her hands lower, feeling his muscles flex under her touch. He inhaled sharply as she lightly grazed the hardness pushing to escape his underwear. She smiled even as she felt her face heat at her boldness. She couldn't believe what she was doing.

She went even lower, massaging his powerful thighs before going back to trace the hardness hidden beneath the thin material of his underwear.

Angelo was the one who finally shoved them down. That was fortunate, since she didn't think she could have done it.

Minka tried not to gasp as his hard shaft sprang out. It was…huge. At least, she assumed it was—she had nothing to compare it to. Regardless, the throbbing between her legs doubled in intensity at the sight of him.

She boldly ran her hand down his stomach until it came to rest on the base of his shaft. Then she moved even slower, carefully letting her hand encircle his thickness, squeezing softly. It was so hard and pulsed in time with his heartbeat. She wanted to explore his shaft more, eager to move her fingers all the way to the tip and the bead of glistening clear fluid, as if waiting for her. But Angelo caught her hand with a groan, and before Minka knew what was happening, he lifted her up and set her on the bed. Taking one ankle in his hand, he kissed his way down the inside of her thigh. She would have complained about him interrupting her exploration, but the feel of his hot mouth on her skin made talking impossible.

Angelo pushed her legs wider, and she clutched the blanket, instinctively knowing where he was heading. Having her legs pushed so far apart—with Angelo able to see *everything*—was amazing.

Eyes smoldering, he nipped at her inner thigh, his perfect white teeth gently sinking into skin that she'd never realized was so sensitive. Her fingers twisted into the blankets, and she could feel her claws trying to slip out. But she was too focused on what Angelo was doing to worry about whether they did or not.

When Angelo reached the center of her secret place, she thought her claws really did come out and dig into the blankets, but she couldn't be sure. She dropped her head back, moaning long and loud as his tongue glided up and down her wet folds.

Her whole body trembled, and she knew she'd never in her life experienced a feeling as wonderful. The bliss as the tip of his tongue came into contact with the sensitive core at the top of her cleft was beyond simple pleasure. It was almost transcendent.

Minka heard a familiar sound in the distance, and it took her a moment to realize it was her—or maybe the beast inside her—purring as she writhed against Angelo's mouth. Her breathing came faster and faster.

She arched up on the bed as Angelo gripped her bottom in his hands and lapped at her wetness with his tongue. The waves of pleasure continued to grow until she was sure she would explode.

But she didn't. Instead, she continued to orgasm until her body was so wrung out she could barely move. Only then, when she knew she could take no more, did Angelo move his mouth away.

Minka fell back against the bed, gasping and panting to catch her breath as small tremors of pleasure wracked her body. She didn't even realize Angelo had left the room until she heard movement over by the door. She lifted her head just in time to see him walking back into the bedroom, slowly rolling a stretchy, translucent material down his long, hard shaft. She knew what it was, but yet again, it was something she had no actual experience with. She was gaining a lot of that tonight.

When he finished getting the condom rolled into place, he walked over to her, his eyes hungry. His heavy erection swayed as he climbed in bed with her, and she moved back a little to give him room between her thighs.

Her heart started racing all over again, both from the scent of her essence all over his face and the thought of what it would feel like to have that thickness buried deep inside her. For such a big, muscular man, Angelo was extremely careful as he moved between her thighs and leaned over her. He made sure to support all his weight with one arm as he kissed his way from her belly button, up past her breasts, until he finally reached her mouth.

Kissing him after he'd been down there was different, but his flavor mixed with hers wasn't displeasing. She was so focused on how delicious the combination was that she almost jumped when the head of his erection nudged against her wet, aroused opening.

Angelo must have taken her surprise for fear, because he broke the kiss and started to back off. She quickly wrapped both legs around his waist, pulling him back in. Then she reached up and buried her fingers in his silky hair, tugging him back down for another kiss. He must have gotten the message because he repositioned the tip of his shaft at her opening and slowly moved it up and down.

Minka gasped against his mouth again, not in surprise, but at the tingles that shot through her when his hardness touched that sensitive little bud at the top of her opening. She was about to complain about his endless teasing again, but then, as if he instinctively knew she was ready, he moved his shaft lower and slowly pushed it inside her.

She was right—he was huge. But definitely not more than she could take. As he slid deeper, she held her breath a little, expecting it to hurt. She'd heard before that a woman's first time could be painful. But then she realized that few women had the opportunity of being with someone like Angelo for their first time.

No matter how much she urged him to go faster, either by grinding her hips against him or pulling him tighter with her legs, he refused to rush it. He kept his thrusts slow and gentle, going deeper a fraction of an inch at a time. It never hurt, but just kept getting better and better.

Minka couldn't pinpoint when the sensation changed from extremely pleasurable to *oh my God, I am going to die if you don't thrust faster*. One moment she was moaning softly, and the next she was yowling and screaming, yanking him in with her legs as hard as she could and begging for him to take her harder and faster.

She looked up to see him gazing into her eyes as she felt her orgasm approaching. Maybe it was the intensity in his eyes as she writhed and panted under him, or maybe it was just the fact that he was buried in her as deeply as he could be. Either way, she knew this climax would be very different than her first one.

She wrapped her arms tightly around his neck, pulling him closer. She wanted him to see the pleasure he was giving her, and she wanted to see his in return.

Somehow, he knew exactly when the waves of ecstasy hit her. She knew because he started thrusting even harder. If she'd thought the cresting wave was going to be powerful before, it was nothing compared to what it felt like washing over her as Angelo took her completely. She made a feline yowl as she went crazy under him, and when the bliss became too intense, she buried her face in his strong neck and screamed his name. Then, just as she was coming down from the heavens, she felt him thrust deep and stay there, letting out a hoarse groan as he found his release inside her.

Minka cried a little then, her face hidden in his neck. There could not be anything more beautiful in the whole world than this…and Angelo had just given it to her.

It was not until well after her orgasm and after Angelo had rolled beside her and pulled her into his arms that she realized her eyes had changed during the most intense heights of her pleasure. She knew because everything around her was now bright in the dim light.

She bolted upright, making Angelo groan.

"What's wrong?" he asked.

She couldn't look at him. "My eyes changed. Oh God, I'm so sorry."

He sat up beside her, gently cupping her cheek and turning her face to his. "Why would you be sorry about something like that?"

Minka tried to look away again, but he held her still. "Because it must have been uncomfortable for you. Seeing my eyes go red like that…in the middle of what we were doing."

He chuckled. "They didn't turn red. They glowed green—the most amazing, brilliant green I've ever seen."

Green. Like a shifter's eyes. Not like a hybrid's. "It didn't make me look…ugly?"

"God no," he said. "It made you look even more beautiful."

Minka sighed with relief. If Angelo said they made her look beautiful, then they did. He would never lie to her.

She smiled. "I can't imagine ever getting tired of hearing you say that."

Angelo laughed again, a warm, soft sound that made her feel good all over. Then he leaned in close to her ear. "Good. Because I'm never going to get tired of saying it. You're beautiful."

He said it again…and again…and again. Then he kissed her, and she knew her amazing day was not over yet.

# Chapter 11

"What are you so happy about?" Landon asked.

Angelo gave him a sidelong glance as they walked down the hallway to John's office. The director had called Landon a few minutes ago, saying he wanted to meet with them. John hadn't said what it was about, but after last night, Angelo sure as hell hoped it was to tell him that they needed him to hang around for a few more weeks—or longer.

"Who says I'm happy about anything?" Angelo asked, trying to conceal the smile he knew had been pasted on his face since he'd woken up that morning exhausted but frigging stoked as all hell.

Landon looked at his wife, who was walking between him and Angelo. "You were right, weren't you?"

Ivy laughed. "Yeah, I was."

"Right about what?" Angelo asked.

She glanced at him. "That you and Minka spent the night together."

Angelo stopped walking. Ivy and Landon stopped, too.

"How did you—?" he began.

"How did I know?" Ivy smiled. "Well, the silly grin you're wearing was the first clue. But the dead giveaway is the fact that you have her scent all over you—and she's covered in yours. I got a good sniff of her in the cafeteria. It's obvious what you two were up to last night. You probably should have showered this morning. By now, every shifter in the DCO knows you two are sleeping together."

Angelo groaned as he started walking again—not in embarrassment but because he and Minka *had* showered this morning. Unfortunately, they'd decided to shower together, which had led to a quickie right there in the bathroom. After that, they'd been running a little late, so they hadn't been able to get cleaned up again before they left.

He smiled to himself. Last night had been beyond amazing. What Minka lacked in experience, she more than made up for in passion. He'd never been with a woman like her in his life. He only prayed they got to spend a lot more time together.

"You might want to wipe that goofy grin off your face before we go in to see John," Landon said as they neared the director's office. "He'll probably think you're on something."

"I think he looks good with a smile." Ivy glanced at her husband as they walked into John's office. "You should try it sometime."

John's secretary looked up from her computer as they walked in. Older, with graying hair and reading glasses perched on her nose, she reminded Angelo of his teacher in the third grade.

"Hey, Olivia," Ivy said. "John have you out here full-time now?"

Olivia nodded. "Most of the time. He's been spending more time out here at the complex lately, so it makes sense. I certainly don't mind. Cuts my commute time by half." She motioned toward the closed door that led to John's office. "He's waiting for you. And he's not alone."

Angelo didn't like the way the woman darted a disdainful glance at the door as she said the words. She obviously didn't think much of whoever was in there with her boss. He glanced at Landon and saw his friend mouth *Dick*.

Coleman was definitely with John, but there was a sharp-dressed middle-aged man there, too. Angelo didn't know who the man was, but he recognized a shark when he saw one. That probably meant the guy was a lawyer, a powerful CEO, or a politician.

John glanced at the man. "Thomas, you remember Agents Halliwell and Donovan."

"Of course. They made quite an impression." The man moved forward to shake hands with Ivy and Landon. "Nice seeing you again."

Then he turned to Angelo and offered his hand. The guy had a firm grip and looked him straight in the eye. People said a handshake could tell you something about a man's character, but in Angelo's experience, it could just as likely mean the guy was really good at playing people.

"And you must be Sergeant Rios. I'm Thomas Thorn, one of the members of the Committee that provides oversight to the DCO. It's a privilege to meet you. John and Dick have been telling me about you. You did an outstanding job of getting the hybrid back here so quickly."

The way the man had said *hybrid*, as if Minka were some kind of thing that wasn't even worth having a name, got under Angelo's skin. Combined with the way Thorn had dropped that little hint about him being in charge of the DCO, it told Angelo he wasn't going to get along with the man.

"Let's sit," John said, gesturing to the small conference table that occupied one side of his office. "We have quite a bit to talk about."

Angelo pulled out the chair beside Landon, already sure he wasn't going to like where this was going.

"I'll get right to the point," Thorn said after they were all seated. "Dick told me he spoke with the hybrid and that she was able to positively identify the men holding her in southern Tajikistan as Johan Klaus and Jean Renard, the doctors we've been trying to find for almost a year. The way she described the facility has us thinking it's permanent."

"The Committee believes the hybrid represents our best chance of finally catching Klaus and Renard, and they want to send in a team immediately," Coleman added. "They want the doctors brought back alive."

Angelo's gut twisted. Oh yeah, he definitely didn't like where this was going.

"Correct me if I'm wrong, Dick, but I thought Minka was unaware of the facility's exact location," John said. "She's not even sure how long she wandered before Sergeant Rios found her."

Coleman nodded. "Minka can't. But she told me the hybrid inside her has access to memories she doesn't. We think it can tell us. We just have to get her to let it out."

Angelo frowned. "That isn't going to work. Even if she was willing to give up control to the thing inside her, it's an animal. It's not going to draw you a map to where these doctors are, no matter how nicely you ask."

"We're aware of that," Thorn said. "But if we could put the hybrid on the ground in the general area of the facility, it could likely lead our team in from there."

Angelo jumped to his feet so fast he practically knocked over his chair. He leaned across the table to get in Thorn's face. "The hybrid has a name—it's Minka Pajari. She barely survived what those doctors did to her the first time. There's no way in hell I'm going to let you send her back there on the off chance she might be able to find those psychos."

Thorn's eyes narrowed. "You're not going to *let* us send her, Sergeant Rios? I don't remember asking for your permission. Minka is currently in this country on a political asylum visa that the rest of the Committee and I arranged. One word from me and that visa will be revoked. Keep that in mind before you start deciding what you will and will not allow."

Angelo tensed, ready to launch himself across the table and punch the asshole right in the face. He probably would have too, if Landon hadn't put a restraining hand on his shoulder.

"The ultimatums and threats aren't helping the situation," John said firmly. "Sit down, Angelo."

Angelo didn't like the idea of letting Thorn think he'd won, but John was right. Punching the guy wouldn't make the problem go away, so he sat down, then allowed himself to envision all the different ways he could have killed Thorn right then.

"Thomas, Minka's control is extremely tenuous at this point. Even if you could get her hybrid side to come out, there's no guarantee that it would do what you want," John said. "She's as likely to try to kill you as help you."

Thorn nodded. "Dick mentioned that. But he also said Sergeant Rios seems to have a knack for keeping her calm."

"So, it's your intent to send them in as a team, then?" John asked. "Even though Minka obviously has no field training and Sergeant Rios isn't a member of the DCO?"

"They wouldn't be part of the actual team going in," Coleman said. "Her job will simply be to guide them to the facility. His will be to keep Minka calm and in control. She wouldn't be in any danger." He gave Angelo a pointed look. "Besides, I'm sure Sergeant Rios wouldn't mind a free ride back to Tajikistan. It's about time he rejoined his A-team, isn't it?"

Angelo's heart dropped. This was worse than just taking Minka back to Tajikistan. For whatever reason, Coleman was using this mission as a way to get Angelo out of his hair and back to his team. Angelo had woken up this morning assuming he and Minka would have at least another week together, hopefully more. Now it looked like their remaining time together was going to be measured in hours.

Angelo could barely breathe as the rest of them discussed how fast the mission could be pulled together. Thorn was pushing for them to move ASAP and already wanted to set up a mission briefing for that afternoon. It was insane to go into something like this so fast and with so little planning, but Angelo got the feeling that what Thomas Thorn wanted, he got.

Thorn and Coleman left a little while later, the deputy director saying he'd get the ball rolling on the mission briefing. Angelo stared down at the conference table, wondering how in the hell he was going to break it to Minka. She'd be terrified about going anywhere near those doctors, not to mention devastated that he probably wouldn't be coming back with her after the mission.

"What if I just refuse to go?" he asked suddenly, searching for something—anything—to stop this from happening.

John shook his head. "I wouldn't recommend it. Thorn will call your bluff and send some other operative out to try to control her. Are you willing to let anyone but you protect Minka?"

"No." Angelo ground his jaw. "I'm just pissed at being manipulated by that prick." He looked at Landon. "I thought you said Thorn was the one bankrolling these doctors. If that's the case, why the hell does he want us to track them down? Shouldn't he know where they are? And why does he want us to capture them? Won't they lead back to him?"

Landon shook his head. "I wish I knew."

"It's possible this is all a charade and Thorn is only acting gung ho about tracking down the doctors because he already knows they aren't still at this facility—if we find it at all," John said.

Angelo frowned. "That makes no sense. Who's he trying to impress? It sure as hell can't be us."

John shrugged. "I agree. I doubt he's doing this for anyone in the DCO. This has something to do with the Committee, but with both houses of Congress out of session and no one even in town, I couldn't tell you what it is. All I can assume is that there's a game going on here that we can't see yet."

"Do you think there's a chance we've been wrong about Thorn all along?" Ivy asked. "What if someone else on the Committee is funding the hybrid research and Thorn is actually trying to stop these doctors?"

John didn't have an answer to that.

Damn, Angelo hated all this cloak-and-dagger shit. If he had wanted to play games like this, he would have joined the CIA instead of Army Special Forces.

"Can Minka do what Thorn is asking, Angelo?" John asked. "Can she access her hybrid memories and find the facility she escaped from?"

Angelo thought about it. He remembered her describing how she'd gotten her claws to extend by letting the beast out in a controlled manner. Then there was the way her eyes had stayed completely green last night while they'd been making love. That told him she'd been subconsciously keeping the beast in check even while she'd screamed in orgasm.

"My first instinct is to say no, but that would just be me trying to protect her," he admitted. "In reality, she probably can. She still has a long way to go, and there will be setbacks along the way, but right now, she's gaining control of her hybrid side more and more every day. I don't think there's anything she can't do if she really wants to do it."

John was silent as he considered that. "That's amazing. Tanner has been working on controlling his rage for almost a year, and he's only started making headway these past couple months. Zarina said Minka is the same kind of hybrid that Tanner is, but Klaus and Renard have obviously improved the serum since leaving Washington State."

Angelo saw Ivy and Landon exchange looks.

John must have seen it, too. "What?" When Ivy and Landon didn't answer, the director scowled. "If there's something I need to know, I'd rather hear it now than wait for it to come out at the wrong time. So spill it."

Ivy hesitated, looking at Landon again. Her husband nodded.

She sighed as she turned back to John. "I guess it's time we told you anyway. Minka wasn't made using the same serum Klaus and Renard used to turn Tanner. She was made from serum with my DNA."

John's eyes narrowed. "Run that by me again."

Ivy swallowed hard. "When Landon and I went to Washington State to find Stutmeir, Stutmeir captured and tortured me. Klaus and Renard were thrilled to get their hands on a shifter, so they took samples of my DNA, hoping it would accelerate their research."

John didn't say anything for a long time, but it didn't take a genius to figure out he was steamed. "Klaus and Renard have had access to your DNA for nearly a year, and you just decided to fill me in now? Why the hell didn't you tell me when it happened?"

"We were worried you'd figure out that I'd violated DCO orders and let Ivy's shifter identity be compromised because I refused to kill her," Landon said.

John swore. "Do you think I give a shit about that? That's a stupid directive put in place by Thorn and the Committee after what happened with Adam. I never expected you to carry it out. Besides, you made it clear the first time we met that you'd never turn against your partner, no matter what. Hell, that was a big part of the reason I wanted you with her. After all the shitty partners she'd had, Ivy deserved someone who would have her back." He shook his head. "No, what pisses me off is that you forced me to operate in the dark for almost a year when I could have been helping you."

Ivy gave him a sheepish look. "Landon would have

told you a couple months ago, once we realized you were really on our side, but I wouldn't let him. I was hoping against hope that he and I could find the doctors ourselves. Then, no one would ever have to know what Stutmeir and his doctors had done to me, and Landon and I would never have to explain anything."

John's expression softened. "You should have told me, Ivy. You're like family to me. I had a right to know. But I understand why you didn't."

Angelo wondered if Ivy and Landon were going to mention the part he and the other members of his A-team had played in rescuing her out in Washington. He sure as hell wasn't going to say anything about it if they didn't. There was no need to put the rest of his team on the DCO radar, too.

"So you think Minka's rage issues are being tempered by your DNA, huh?" John asked.

Ivy shrugged. "Maybe. Tanner seems to think so, but Zarina says there's no way to tell."

John frowned. "I guess I shouldn't be surprised that Zarina knows about what happened to you. She's obviously been hiding stuff from me for a while. But Tanner, too? Is there anyone else involved in this that I should know about?"

"The only other person who knows about Stutmeir getting my DNA is Kendra," Ivy said. "But that's only because she's my best friend. And Layla, of course."

John sighed. "I know we can trust them not to say anything. As for Minka, we're going to need her to get as close as we can to where you found her, Angelo, then ask her to lead you the rest of the way." He gave Angelo a small smile. "I think it might be best if you tell Minka we're sending her back to Tajikistan to find Klaus and Renard. She'll take it better from you."

Angelo nodded. He still didn't know how the hell he was going to do it, though.

Beside him, Ivy and Landon were exchanging another of those looks again, like they were trying to decide if they should say something else.

"Is there anything else you want to tell me?" John asked.

Landon waited until Ivy gave him a nod; then, he reached out and took her hand in his before looking at John. "Ivy and I are married. We have been since June."

John stared at them, disbelief clear on his face. "Married?"

"We wanted to tell you," Ivy said. "Heck, Landon wanted you to be there. But in your capacity as director, we were worried you'd be forced to split us up as a team if you knew we were violating DCO policy."

John's mouth tightened. "I wouldn't have, but you had no way of knowing that. Who else knows?"

"Layla, of course. And the rest of Ivy's family," Landon said. "Kendra, Declan, Clayne, Danica, and Angelo, as well as some of the guys on my former A-team."

John laughed. "So half of the DCO."

"You're not mad?" Ivy asked.

"Mad? Hell no. I've known you two were romantically involved for a while now. And you're obviously good at hiding the fact that you're married, so just keep doing that and everything will be fine. Not everyone at the DCO thinks the no-fraternization policy is as stupid as I do."

Then John looked at Angelo, his eyes suddenly knowing. "No one mentioned it, but I assume you were in Washington State, too? Any chance the rest of your A-team was out there with you?"

Angelo swore silently. So much for keeping the rest of the guys off the DCO's radar.

———～～～———

Minka tightened her grip on Angelo's hand as they sat down in the big conference room. She'd been relieved to see Ivy, Landon, and John when she and Angelo had walked in a few minutes ago. But Dick was there too, along with the two men who had come to Zarina's office the day they scared her into letting the beast out. There was a man deep in conversation with John, too. She didn't recognize him, but he made the beast restless, and she had to force herself not to growl.

She ignored the man and focused on Angelo's presence beside her as she studied the map of southern Tajikistan and northern Afghanistan in the front of the room. She recognized the markers for the cities and territorial boundaries but understood little beyond that, especially the various circles and lines drawn on it. But since the whole purpose of this meeting was about going back to Tajikistan to find the doctors who had hurt her, she supposed the markings must have something to do with where the DCO thought the doctors were located.

When Angelo had come into Layla's office a little while ago and told her they would be going back to Tajikistan to find Klaus and Renard, she had almost hyperventilated. She knew Angelo would be with her and would keep her safe, but the thought of the doctors had nearly brought out the beast.

At the front of the room, John moved to stand behind

the podium. He started the meeting by introducing the man who made the beast uneasy as Thomas Thorn, then said something about the classification of the briefing and other security protocols, most of which went completely over her head. She was still trying to understand what he was saying—all the acronyms made it very hard—when a picture flashed up on the big television screen over his left shoulder. It was the older doctor, Klaus. Minka only half listened as John gave them details about where the man was born, where he went to school, and his connection to the hybrid program. Klaus looked just as smug in the picture as he had when he'd tormented her.

Then another picture flashed on the screen, this time of Renard. She squeezed Angelo's hand more tightly, digging in her nails. In the photo, Renard was smiling—just as he had during the experiments he'd conducted on her. Even now, she could hear him laughing as she begged him to stop one of the hundreds of painful things he had done to her.

Angelo leaned over to put his mouth close to her ear. "Hey. You okay?"

She nodded. "I do not like that man. They are both evil, but he was the worse of the two."

Angelo traced the barely discernible scars on her arm. "Is he the one who did this?"

"Yes," she whispered.

When Angelo didn't say anything, she looked over to see him staring at the picture of Renard intently, as if he were trying to burn the image into his mind.

She turned back as John mentioned the autonomous region, which was where Angelo had found her. He

pointed at the region on a map and indicated how far
the DCO believed she had walked. He described different circles on the map, calling some of them "objective
points" and others "rally points" or "primary" and "sec-
ondary landing zones." Minka couldn't follow all of the
jargon, but she understood that was where they would
be starting their search.

"Minka will lead the team in from there," John
announced after going over the map for a few more
minutes. "In addition to Minka and Sergeant Rios, who
is Army Special Forces, the team will include Agents
Donovan and Halliwell. They both have personal experience with the doctors, which will be invaluable on
this mission."

Minka had assumed Ivy and Landon would be going,
but she was still relieved to hear John say their names.
She and Ivy had made a connection the day before that
was unlike anything Minka had ever felt with even her
closest girlfriend.

With a nod, John stepped away from the podium and
Dick took his place. Minka stiffened.

"Powell and Moore will round out the team," Dick
said. "That should be more than sufficient for an op
like this."

The beast inside Minka growled at the mention of
Powell's name. He was the guard who'd suggested Dick
should threaten her with the needle. She didn't have to
look to know that Moore was almost certainly the other
guard. Minka was no expert on military operations, but
the two men seemed like strange choices.

Landon leaned over Ivy and whispered to Minka
and Angelo, "Powell and Moore aren't typically used

for anything more than corporate security. I don't think I've ever seen them on a tactical operation. If they're going, it's more to spy for Dick or Thorn than to do any fighting. We'll need to keep an eye on them."

Dick stepped away from the podium and John took his place. "Minka, Angelo, could you please come up here? A few members of the team have some questions they'd like to ask."

Minka's pulse raced as Angelo led her up to the front of the room, but she tried not to let her nervousness show. She was going to spend quite a bit of time with these people over the next few days, so she was going to have to get used to talking to them.

Most of their questions revolved around the place where she'd been held captive. She told them as much as she could, saying she'd been chained to a wall most of the time and hadn't seen anyone except for the two doctors and the guards.

"How many guards?" Powell asked.

"Usually three." She refused to mention that there had only been two after she'd killed one of them with a rock. She tried to remember all the different faces and scents, but those memories belonged to the animal inside, and the beast wasn't talking to her at the moment. So she gave the best answer she could. "But I saw others as they passed my cell, and I smelled at least ten different men."

"Were the guards locals?" Moore asked.

"Some of them were," she said. "But most were foreign."

"What about weapons?" Powell wanted to know.

Minka didn't know much about weapons. "They carried handguns and longer rifles like soldiers carry. Some of them carried grenades."

That answer didn't seem to make anyone very happy, including Angelo.

"Were there any other hybrids like you at this facility?" Landon asked.

"Sometimes the doctors would bring in other people they experimented on," Minka said. "They'd lock them in the cells near mine, but they rarely survived very long. I occasionally heard screams in one of the other buildings, but when I escaped, there was only silence, so I assume they died, too."

Powell and Moore asked about the rotation schedule for the guards, where they slept, and, most importantly, where the doctors were located. Minka tried to answer the best she could, but she didn't know very much.

"It doesn't seem like we have to worry about hybrids. That's something, at least," Landon said. "But we could be facing as many as twenty guards. Maybe we should consider going in with a larger force, one with a few more shifters."

John opened his mouth to answer, but Thorn cut him off.

"The goal of this mission isn't to go in and get into a knock-down, drag-out fight with the guards. The objective is to get in, grab the doctors, and get out—that's all. You have the element of surprise on your side, so this job should be a piece of cake for a team with your level of training."

Minka doubted the guards were just going to stand around politely and let a team of people come in and apprehend the doctors. But no one seemed willing to challenge Thorn on his assertion.

The meeting came to a close soon after that. John

and Dick left, along with Powell and Moore. Minka had hoped Thorn would go too, but he pulled Ivy and Landon aside, leaving her and Angelo alone. Minka didn't mean to eavesdrop, but with her keen hearing, it was difficult not to.

"Hey," Angelo whispered. "Are you listening in on their conversation with Thorn?"

Minka gave him an embarrassed look. "I know it's rude, but yes I was." She frowned as a thought occurred to her. "Can you hear them, too?"

He chuckled softly. "From fifty feet away? No, I can't. What are they saying?"

"Something about not letting Klaus and Renard get captured alive, not with everything they know," she whispered. "He said there are people on the Committee who would be more than happy to use the doctors' hybrid research for their own purposes. He told Ivy and Landon they can't let that happen."

Giving Ivy and Landon a nod, Thorn glanced once in Minka and Angelo's direction, then left the room.

Minka frowned at Ivy and Landon as the couple walked over to join her and Angelo. "I don't understand. Did he just say that he wanted you to kill those doctors?"

Ivy smiled. "You heard that, huh?"

Minka nodded. "But why would he tell us during the briefing that we're supposed to capture the doctors alive, then tell you to kill them?"

"I've stopped trying to figure out what kind of games the people around here are playing," Landon said. "Either Thorn is actually a good guy who's worried about another member of the Committee getting their hands on the hybrid research and doing something with it, or he's a complete piece of crap and wants Ivy and me to clean up the mess he made."

Minka didn't know what Landon was talking about, but either way, she didn't have a good feeling about it.

---

Minka and Angelo stayed at the DCO complex for another hour, picking up clothing and equipment they would supposedly need for the mission. Angelo was unusually quiet as they drove home. He didn't say much after they got there either. Instead, he went into the kitchen to make sandwiches for dinner while she packed a few pieces of clothes and some toiletries. Then they sat together on the couch and ate while the silence grew heavy.

Finally, she couldn't stand it any longer. She put down her half-eaten sandwich and turned to face him. "Is everything okay? You're very quiet."

At first she wasn't sure if he'd heard her because he didn't answer. She was just about to ask again when he spoke.

"Everything's fine," he said. "I talked to John right before the briefing and he promised that no matter what happens on the mission—whether we find these doctors or not—you'll be welcome at the DCO. There'll be no strings attached, and he said you can keep working with Layla, Ivy, and Tanner, so you can get better at control-ling your abilities. He'll make sure you have a place to live. You'll have lots of people to help you get settled. You won't be abandoned, okay?"

Minka's throat tightened so much she could barely breathe. Angelo had said nothing about him coming back after the mission. That was why he was being so quiet. He would be rejoining his team in Tajikistan afterward.

Questions flooded her mind as she fought to hold back tears. How long would he be gone? Would he come back to her after he finished in Tajikistan? What kind of work would he be doing? Would he be safe? Would he be able to call her to let her know he was okay?

But she didn't ask any of those questions because she feared what the answers would be. Instead, she stood up and held out her hand to him. "Can we go to bed now?"

He put down what was left of his sandwich and took her hand, then led her to the bedroom without a word.

Neither one of them spoke, but this time, she didn't wait patiently for him to undress them both. She reached out and began to loosen his belt even as he started taking off her clothes. When they were both naked, she moved closer and put her arms around him, pressing her face against his smooth chest and breathing in his scent. He wrapped her in his arms, and for a little while, she could almost believe that nothing could ever hurt her with Angelo there to protect her. But then it hit her, and she couldn't stop the tears that sprang to her eyes. The pain in her chest was stronger than anything she'd ever felt. Soon, Angelo wouldn't be there to protect her, and she would be all alone. After learning what it was like to be with him, she didn't know how she could go on by herself.

Angelo's fingers slipped under her chin, lifting her face up to his. Then he leaned forward and began to gently kiss away her tears.

She almost broke down then but stopped herself, knowing how much it would hurt him to see her like that. So she pushed the bad thoughts away, enclosing them in the same cage as the beast. Then she buried her fingers in Angelo's hair and pulled him down for a kiss. Minka was terrified it might be the last time they could be together. But if it was, she didn't want it to be sad. She wanted it to be amazing. She focused on the feel of his lips on her, thinking only of his taste, the heat pouring off his body, the tantalizing sensation of his growing hardness pressing against her stomach.

By the time Angelo picked her up and set her carefully on the bed, her tears were gone and her fear was replaced with arousal. While he rolled the condom down his shaft, she slid over, leaving room for him in the center of the bed. He looked a little confused for a moment, until she grabbed his hand and pulled him down with her, urging him onto his back. Then a smile curved his sensuous mouth as she climbed on top of him. She hadn't been bold enough to do so last night, but now there was no time to worry about embarrassment. She wanted to make love to her angel this way, and if that meant she had to learn as she went, then she was more than ready.

It took a bit of fumbling, since she didn't know exactly where to put her hands and knees, but then Angelo's hands were on her hips, guiding her to the right position. And when she finally eased herself down on him, the groans that escaped them both made the momentary confusion worth it.

She leaned forward and placed her hands on his chest, carefully lifting herself up a few centimeters, then letting her bottom come down on his strong thighs in one slow, steady motion. She let out a purr as tingles spread out from her core to every part of her body. Every time she rode up and down on him, she felt a little jolt of electricity. The urge to speed up was intense, but she took her time, wanting to make the moment last forever.

But Angelo seemed to have other ideas. He got a firm grip on her hips and started moving slowly under her, thrusting in perfect rhythm with her movements. *Mmm*, that felt amazing.

Minka put more of her weight on his chest as he began pumping faster. One of his hands glided from her hip to grasp her bottom, squeezing tightly and completely taking over control of their pace. It was crazy. She was on top, but he was the one in control.

The sound of their bodies coming together as he thrust into her was so sexy, it was hard not to close her eyes and get lost in the rhythm. But she kept her eyes open, so she could look at his beautiful face. As she got closer to orgasm, that became impossible, and she collapsed forward, burying her face in his neck as he thrust hard into her and pushed her further toward her climax.

The pleasure kept building until Minka was sure she was going to scream…or shift into her hybrid form. But she wasn't worried about the beast at that moment. All that mattered was Angelo and her—their bodies becoming one, their hearts pounding together.

When she orgasmed, she screamed against Angelo's neck, unconcerned about the feline sounds she let out.

Angelo kept thrusting all the way through her orgasm, making her whole body shake uncontrollably against his. It was only as she was sliding down the backside of her climax that she felt him start to come with her.

Minka lifted her head, looking deep into his eyes as he buried himself inside her warmth. She felt him buck under her, and her heart sang as he groaned and found his release.

As his movements slowed, she dropped her face back into the crook of his shoulder, kissing him there and enjoying the pleasant tremors that continued to ripple through her body. After a few minutes, when both of their heartbeats had returned to something close to normal, she lifted her head and gazed down at him again.

He looked so beautiful lying there, a smile curving his lips, passion still darkening his eyes. One of his hands came up and traced a finger along her jaw to her chin. It was amazing how just that simple touch brought her unbelievable pleasure.

She opened her mouth, ready to say the words flooding her heart—*I love you*.

But she stopped herself. She couldn't tell him that. It would be unfair when they both knew he'd be leaving her in a day or two. Worse, while she knew he cared for her, the fact was, he'd never promised anything more than this short time together. If anything, everything he'd said about not wanting to hurt her told her that he never intended it to be more than this.

He frowned. "What's wrong?"

Minka struggled for a moment to focus on anything other than the sudden pain in her chest. She fought to push the feeling down, not wanting him to see it.

"You are very bad," she told him.

His frown disappeared to be replaced by a look of mock surprise. "Why do you say that?"

She took the finger he had been tracing across her

jaw in her hand and kissed the tip. "I was planning to go slow and make this evening last awhile longer."

He gave her a smoldering smile. "We can go slow this time if you want."

That was when Minka realized Angelo was still aroused. Actually, he was still very aroused.

It was difficult for her to change gears so suddenly, to forget her emotions and focus on the physical. But she loved Angelo so much that she'd take whatever she could get of her angel and be happy—for that night at least.

So she leaned forward and kissed him. "I'd like that very much."

# Chapter 12

"I KNOW IT'S SCARY TO THINK ABOUT GIVING UP control," Tanner said. "And I pray that you never have to do it. But if you have no other choice, I want you to be ready."

Minka was in Layla's office for one more training session with the DCO psychologist and Tanner while Angelo and the others were doing last-minute checks on equipment and loading everything up in the trucks for the trip to the airport. The plan was to leave before sunrise.

With the tight schedule they were on, the training session had been short, but it was still informative. Tanner had taught her how to make her eyes shift, so she could see better in the dark, then explained how she might be able to gain access to the hybrid parts of her memory. Both techniques involved letting the beast out of its cage in a controlled fashion, much like she had when she let her claws out.

But now Tanner was talking about letting the beast out completely.

"Why would I ever want to do that?" Minka asked.

She'd just learned how to lock the beast away in a cage and could never imagine willingly letting it out.

Tanner regarded her thoughtfully. "What if Angelo were in danger, Minka? Would you let the beast come out if you knew it was the only way to protect him? Or

Ivy, or Landon? Which is worse—letting the beast take over or watching the people you care about get hurt?"

Minka didn't answer. Tanner already knew she'd do anything for Angelo and her new friends.

"That's what I thought," he said.

She listened carefully as Tanner described the process of unlocking the door of the cage that existed in her mind and opening it wide. Thankfully, Tanner didn't ask her to actually attempt what he was proposing, because that would have been much too dangerous. But he did spend a long time explaining how to regain control afterward.

"Think about Angelo. He's your anchor. Remember what he means to you," he said. "It won't be easy, but you can fight your way back to him no matter how far into the background the beast pushes you."

Minka nodded. It would be hard, but she'd do anything to get back to Angelo, even if that meant fighting the beast tooth and nail.

Layla looked like she wanted to say something, but a knock on the open door interrupted her. Minka glanced up and saw John standing there, an apologetic smile on his face.

"Sorry to interrupt," he said. "Minka, the team will be ready to leave in about fifteen minutes. And, Tanner, if you have the time, Angelo asked if he could speak with you."

Tanner nodded. "Yeah, sure." He gave Minka a smile as he stood. "Be careful over there, okay? And don't forget who you are."

"I won't," she promised. "Thank you for all the help."

John gave her and Layla a nod, then turned to follow

Tanner down the hall, but the psychologist jumped to her feet.

"John, can I speak to you?" She glanced at Minka. "I'll be right back."

Layla and John moved a little farther down the hallway, leaving Minka alone with her thoughts. They immediately went to Angelo and how much she was going to miss him.

She'd awakened before Angelo that morning, then lay there in the dark, her head propped up on her hand as she watched him sleep. He looked so precious and vulnerable that it almost made her cry.

She'd spent a long time wondering if she was making a mistake, not telling him how she felt. But then she reminded herself it was for the best. It would only make a difficult situation worse if she poured out her heart to him now. He needed to concentrate on this mission, and be just as focused when he went back to his team.

Forcing herself to think about anything other than Angelo and their approaching separation, Minka turned her attention to the only nearby distraction—Layla and John talking softly out in the hallway.

She was finding it easier and easier to pick up on conversations, even when they were far away. She didn't even have to consciously involve the beast at all. She felt a little guilty about listening in on a friend's private conversation with her boss but reminded herself that the alternative was thinking about Angelo, and that, she didn't want to do. Besides, Layla had told her to practice her hybrid abilities whenever she could.

"If you hire Jayson, I'll take you up on the offer you

made when you first interviewed me," Layla was saying. "I'll start doing field work."

Minka didn't know who Jayson was, but he must be someone very important to Layla for her to agree to be an agent after she'd promised Ivy she would never go into the field.

"That's very generous of you, Layla, but I can't take you up on it," John said.

"Is it because Jayson was wounded?" Layla asked, her voice sharp.

"It has nothing to do with Jayson being wounded. This is about a promise I made to someone."

"My sister."

"I didn't say that."

"John, when you hired me, you told me that if I ever wanted to become a field agent, all I had to do was say the word. This is me doing that—provided you give Jayson a job." Layla sighed. "Jayson is at a crossroads right now. If he doesn't get a job, one he can be proud of doing, he might end up in a very bad place. Please, John."

John didn't answer for a moment. Then, finally, he spoke again. "Okay. And while I'm not ready to send you out in the field yet, I'll let you spend half of your time training for it."

"Thank you," Layla said. "One more thing—Jayson can never know I had anything to do with him getting the job. He would never take it if he knew I was involved. He's too proud for that."

Layla came back into the office a few moments later. Minka tried to pretend she hadn't been eavesdropping, but Layla figured it out anyway.

"You heard all that didn't you?"

Minka nodded sheepishly. "Is Jayson your boyfriend?"

Layla sat down on the couch beside her. "I'm not sure you could call Jayson my boyfriend. I wish he was, but it's…complicated."

Minka knew all about complicated. "Does the fact that Jayson can't seem to get a job have anything to do with you not being sure if he is your boyfriend?"

Layla looked at her in surprise. "Wow. How did you know that?"

Minka shrugged. "Men are very proud. If they can't get good jobs, it makes them very difficult to be around."

"That pretty much describes Jayson to a T," Layla said. "He used to be in Army Special Forces with Landon and Angelo, but he got seriously injured on a mission and wasn't able to stay on the team. He was doing well for a while, but now it seems like he's starting to give up again. Lately he's getting more depressed, and I'm worried that he's going to hurt himself." Her eyes glistened with tears and she took a deep breath. "He's home alone a lot, and he just sits around and thinks about all he's lost. That's why I asked John to offer him a job. He needs something to give him purpose and a reason to keep going. I'm not sure it will be enough, but it's all I can think of right now."

Minka knew a thing or two about coming close to giving up. She had gotten near that point many times while she'd been held captive. But then she'd found Angelo, and he'd given her hope. It sounded like Jayson needed something to hold on to long enough to see that things could get better. She suspected Layla had been that thing for Jayson for a time, but now he was getting lost again. He needed something else for now—a new anchor—to help hold him steady until he realized that Layla was there for him.

"Maybe you should get him a puppy," she suggested.

"What?" Layla said with a laugh.

Minka shrugged. "It's hard to be unhappy if you have a dog to take care of. They have a way of making people see the brighter side of things. And maybe the responsibility of taking care of a dog would help Jayson focus on something else."

Layla thought about that. "You know, that might actually be a good idea. A therapy dog sounds like just what he needs."

Minka glanced at the watch John had given her yesterday with her new uniform. It was probably time to go. She stood. "I should leave. Angelo is waiting for me."

Layla got to her feet. "Before you go, there's something I wanted to ask you. Ivy mentioned that she thought Angelo might be staying in Tajikistan after the mission was over. You and he talked about that, right? I mean, about him coming to DC after he gets back from deployment?"

Minka had been doing her best not to think about Angelo and what it would be like if she never saw him again, and having Layla come right out and ask her that very question made it hard to hold back tears.

Layla frowned. "He's not coming back, is he?"

Hearing the anguish in Layla's voice was enough to almost push Minka completely over the edge. She wiped a stray tear from her cheek. "I don't know what he's going to do."

"How can you not know? The two of you are in love." Layla gave her a curious look. "You do love him, right?"

Minka couldn't see why she would need to hide that from Layla, especially since it seemed obvious her friend already knew.

"Yes," she whispered.

"And he loves you?"

Minka felt fresh tears spring to her eyes. "I don't know. He hasn't told me how he feels. He tried to tell me that he would have to leave soon and that he didn't want me to be hurt when he did," she said. Then, at the flash of anger in Layla's eyes, she quickly added, "But I let myself fall in love anyway. It's all my fault. I can't and won't blame him."

Layla regarded her in silence for a long time, then pulled Minka in for a hug, wrapping her arms around her and squeezing tight. Minka hugged her back.

"What are you going to do, Minka?" Layla asked when she stepped back.

Unfortunately, while Minka had been giving that question a lot of thought, she'd yet to come up with an answer.

"I don't know," she said honestly. "Sometimes it seems like there is no place for me in this world if Angelo is not there with me."

---

At least the C-17 they were heading to Tajikistan on had real seats instead of those fold-down jobs like the plane that had transported him and Minka to the States. It didn't matter though, Angelo thought. Minka had spent a good portion of the trip sleeping on his shoulder. Not that he was complaining.

At the moment, however, she was leaning over the

other way, against the interior of the cabin wall, hugging his uniform jacket to her chest. She was dressed in the nonmilitary uniform typically worn by private contract security or embedded reporters, but she made it look good. Gazing at her beautiful face, he couldn't help thinking about how his outlook on everything had changed since she had come into his life.

He was still sitting there watching her sleep when Landon walked by, two cups of coffee in his hands. Landon motioned with his head toward the back of the cargo section. Angelo hesitated. He didn't like the idea of her waking up and finding him gone, but she seemed to be sleeping deeply. He quietly released his seat belt to follow his friend to the back of the plane where a pallet of equipment was secured under a cargo net.

Landon handed Angelo one of the cups, then leaned back against the gear. Angelo took a grateful swallow.

"Thanks," he said. "I always did like caffeine on a long flight in one of these loud tin cans."

"I remember," Landon said, pitching his voice to be heard above the constant drone of the jet engines. "I would have brought some for Minka, but she's been sleeping for most of the trip."

Angelo looked back at Minka, wanting to make sure she was still okay. She'd gotten better about not freaking out whenever there was some space between them, but he still worried about her.

Angelo leaned back against the stack of gear beside Landon, so he could keep an eye on her. "I think the stress of the last few days has finally caught up with her."

Landon sipped his coffee. "Does she know you'll be staying in Tajikistan with the team?"

Angelo stared down into his cup. "Yeah. We talked about it some last night. I made sure she knows she can stay in the States and will be able to keep working with Tanner."

In all honesty, he was worried as hell about leaving her to the mercy of the DCO, but John had assured him that they wouldn't use or abuse her—or turn her into a field agent.

Landon snorted. "Like I'm sure she gives a crap about that stuff."

Angelo slanted him a look. "What does that mean?"

"You're joking, right?" Landon asked. "Dude, the only thing Minka cares about is knowing how you feel about her and when you're coming back. As long as you two covered those topics, she'll be okay." When Angelo didn't say anything, he frowned. "You told her, right?"

Angelo knew damn well where Landon was going with this, but he asked anyway. "Told her what?"

"That you've fallen for her."

Angelo shrugged and swigged more coffee. "Not in so many words. She knows I care about her, though."

"You *care* about her?" Landon echoed. "Well, I care about my truck. I have a really good fitting pair of boots I'm even kind of fond of. I'm not asking if you care about her. I'm asking if you love her."

"You can't fall in love with someone in a week," Angelo protested.

Even he winced at how lame that sounded.

"That's not an answer," Landon said. "It's an excuse, and a shitty one at that. I knew I had it bad for Ivy the first time we met. Within a week, I was so in love with her, I couldn't think straight. Are you honestly going to try to convince me that what I've been seeing between you and Minka isn't love?"

Angelo clenched his jaw. This conversation was getting too real, too fast. Hell yes, he was in love with her. He had been since she'd curled up and fallen asleep in his arms on the long flight from Tajikistan. He just hadn't had the balls to admit it to himself because he'd been scared to think about what came next.

"Yeah," he said hoarsely. "I love her. But it doesn't matter."

Landon frowned. "Doesn't matter? What the fuck are you talking about? I'm pretty damn sure it matters to Minka. And it should matter to you."

"It does matter," Angelo snapped. If Landon hadn't been his best friend, he'd have punched him right then. "Fuck! It matters, okay? I just don't know what the hell to do about it. How fair is it to tell her something like that, then disappear on a string of deployments for the next five years?"

"You don't think she'd be willing to wait for you?"

He closed his eyes for a moment before answering. "Landon, we're talking about five years."

"So you spend every minute you can with her. Make sure she knows how important she is to you. And you make it through the rest of your enlistment the best you can—together."

Angelo shook his head. Landon made it sound so easy. But his friend knew it wasn't. "I don't know if Minka can do that. You've seen how she is. She needs me so much. I'm worried that when we're apart, she might lose control—or worse, just give up."

"Like your mom did?" Landon asked softly.

Angelo's chest tightened so much he wouldn't have been surprised if it had stopped beating. He'd tried to convince himself Minka was stronger than that. But the truth was, while Minka could be so strong in so many ways, she was still fragile in others, just like his mom had been.

"Yeah, like my mom," he said. "That's why I can't tell Minka how I feel. I would do anything to save her from the pain and loneliness that Mom went through."

"You can't do that, Angelo," Landon said. "You can't keep Minka from falling in love with you, and you can't keep her from being lonely and in pain when you're deployed. All you can do is love her and pray it's enough."

Angelo looked at his friend. "How the hell did you get so smart about all this shit?"

"Ivy, of course." Landon grinned. "Fortunately, I was smart enough to realize that women like her—and Minka—don't fall into the laps of guys like us very often. When they do, you need to hold on tight and not let go." His smile faded. "Dude, I don't know how to make this work between you and Minka, but I'm telling you that you need to find a fucking way."

Landon was right. But telling Minka he loved her was only half of it. The rest was about figuring out how to help the woman he loved get through the days until he could be with her again.

When Angelo went back to his seat and buckled himself in, Minka must have sensed his presence because she immediately turned in her sleep and snuggled against his shoulder. He wrapped an arm around her and put his head back, praying she would be strong enough to handle being in love with an army guy.

# Chapter 13

ANGELO DIDN'T REALIZE HE'D FALLEN ASLEEP until the thud of the plane touching down on the runway at Bagram jerked him awake. Minka was sitting beside him, looking around with wide eyes. Dammit, he could have killed Thorn for making her come back here.

He sat up straighter and took her hand, lacing their fingers together. Then he leaned over to kiss her—screw whoever didn't like it.

When the plane finally came to a stop, he stood up with everyone else. They were just getting on their rucksacks when the plane's crew chief dropped the rear cargo ramp. It settled to the asphalt with a thud, letting in bright sunlight. Angelo saw Diaz, Derek, and Lieutenant Watson waiting for them.

Laughing, Angelo took Minka's hand and headed down the ramp to meet them. He noticed Powell and Moore didn't look pleased. For some reason, that made Angelo even happier.

"You didn't think we'd let you come back here and handle this situation on your own, did you?" the lieutenant asked, sticking out his hand in greeting.

Angelo grabbed Watson's hand, but instead of shaking it, he yanked his lieutenant forward and gave him a man hug. Then he did the same to Derek and Diaz. By the time he was done, they were all laughing, asking him how the hell he'd been and what the fuck he'd done to get them pulled into this mission.

In the interest of full disclosure, he had to admit he wasn't the one responsible for bringing them in. "But I'm damn glad to see you guys anyway."

Before they could ask him anything more about the mission, Angelo took Minka's hand again and led her forward.

"You guys might not recognize her, but this is Minka Pajari, the woman we rescued in Tajikistan," he said softly, smiling as she eyed the guys shyly. "She'll be joining us on this mission."

Derek extended his hand. "I'm glad to see you're doing okay. When you and Angelo got on that C-17, I wasn't too sure how it was going to turn out."

Minka shook his hand with a smile and would have replied, but a sharp voice interrupted her.

"These people aren't cleared to be on this operation," Powell said as he glared at Derek and the other guys. "Who the hell called them?"

"I did," Landon said as he shouldered past Powell to greet Derek and the other guys. "And don't get your panties in a bunch, Powell. They've all been briefed and cleared on both the shifter and hybrid programs."

"Damn, Diaz, are you getting taller?" Landon asked as he man-hugged the smallest member of his former A-team. "I swear it seems like you've grown two or three inches since I saw you last."

Diaz chuckled. "Sorry, Captain. I hate to tell you this, but I think you're shrinking. I've heard that happens when you get old."

As everyone laughed, Angelo took the opportunity to introduce his new lieutenant to Landon.

"I've heard a lot about you, Captain Donovan," Watson said as they shook hands. "I'm looking forward to working with you."

Landon grinned. "Same here. And call me Landon. My army rank is sitting on my uniforms back in DC."

Angelo snorted. Like people were going to forget Landon was an officer. As soon as the shit started flying, he'd be shouting orders, and no one would care if he were wearing a pink tutu. Soldiers followed the person who knew what the hell he was doing.

"I'm guessing the guys have told you about the things you're probably going to see when we get there?" Landon asked Watson.

"Yes, sir." Watson shook his head. "I have to tell you, I was pretty sure they were pulling my leg, even after seeing Minka back in that village—until one of those shifters showed up and convinced me."

Angelo was about to ask what the lieutenant meant by that when Watson jerked his head at something behind him. Angelo turned to see a wiry guy with short, black hair casually leaning against one of the Humvees parked near the edge of the runway. He was dressed in a military-style uniform similar to what all the other DCO operatives were wearing.

"Trevor! I thought I picked up your scent," Ivy said with a big smile. "What are you doing here?"

Trevor gave Ivy a cocky grin. Maybe Angelo had been hanging out at the DCO for too long because he would have known Trevor was a shifter even if Watson hadn't told him. Angelo couldn't put his finger on what tipped him off. There was just something about the guy.

"My team and I were working in Jakarta and finished

up our mission early," Trevor said. "John called and asked if I could stop by and help out. It sounded like fun, so I hopped on the first flight over. I've been hanging out with the lieutenant and his team since this morning."

Beside Angelo, Powell swore under his breath. "This mission doesn't have anything to do with industrial espionage or looking for spies, so I don't know what use you're going to be on this op."

Trevor gave Powell an *eat shit and die* smile. "This job doesn't involve sitting on your ass, eating donuts, and brownnosing your way to another pay raise either, yet here you and Moore are."

Powell's face darkened and he took a step forward. Trevor pushed away from the Humvee, his eyes flashing yellow-green, long, sharp canines extending. Angelo had seen this same kind of display before, but while Trevor had the same doglike fangs and squared-off claws as the DCO's resident wolf shifter Clayne Buchanan, he didn't have the same bulky muscles and his teeth weren't nearly as long. That said, he was clearly just as dangerous.

Powell must have thought so too, because he stopped midstep. He and Trevor stared at each other for so long that Angelo wondered if things were about to get violent. Guys in military units got into it all the time. But it was obvious there was more than a little dislike brewing between Trevor and Powell. If they came to blows, it was going to get ugly.

Landon stepped between the two men and pushed them apart with a hand on each of their chests.

"Knock this shit off," he ordered. "We have a lot of gear to unload and prep before we head out, so stop your bitching."

Trevor and Powell stared at each other for a few more moments before they finally took a step back from each other and moved away. But Angelo noticed that while Trevor headed toward the cargo ramp of the plane to start grabbing gear, Powell stormed off in the opposite direction. No way in hell this wasn't going to end badly.

"I thought we were all supposed to be on the same side?" Minka's voice was soft beside Angelo.

He turned to see her standing there with a worried look on her face. He gave her hand a reassuring squeeze. "Don't worry about them. I'm guessing they're here for reasons of their own. You just stick close to me, Landon, and Ivy. We'll make sure you're okay."

—✦—

"The place where I was held should be right over that mountain ridge," Minka said with more confidence than she felt as she placed her hands on the rough boulder by her side and strained her eyes to see even farther through the gathering gloom of approaching evening.

Minka hadn't realized the land where she'd grown up had such a distinctive smell and feel to it until she'd left Tajikistan and come back. But now, the scent of sunbaked rock and dirt and the feel of the mountain breeze on her face reminded her that this place was her homeland.

Angelo stood at her side, silent but supportive as everyone else farther down the hill unloaded the gear from the strange plane that had brought them here. They couldn't fly any closer to the facility, not without someone hearing the plane. So they'd have to hike the rest of the way in from there.

Angelo had told her the plane was called an Osprey, and she'd been amazed to learn that it could land and take off like a helicopter, or it could fly like a normal plane. That had come in really useful, as they'd been leapfrogging across this particular part of southern Tajikistan for most of the day, landing every few dozen kilometers so she could get out of the tight confines of the plane and look around.

No one could understand why she couldn't guide them from the air, but she simply couldn't. The only way she was able to know for sure that they were on the route she'd used to escape the lab was to get out and walk around so she could smell the air and feel the rocks under her boots. When she did that, it almost seemed like she could remember running and walking this way—maybe.

"What if this isn't the right mountain ridge?" she asked Angelo softly. "What if we shouldn't be unloading the plane here?" She knew Ivy and the new shifter, Trevor, would still hear her, but they weren't the ones who'd been complaining.

Angelo gently turned her around to face him. "What are your instincts telling you right now? Do you think we're going the right way?"

It was such a simple question, but the answer was so complicated.

"I don't know," she said. "It was dark when I went through so many of these places, and I don't remember what everything looked like. I could be leading us completely in the wrong direction."

Angelo lifted a finger to her temple. "Don't worry about what you remember up here. I want you to tell me what the other part of you, the hybrid part, is saying. What does it remember in here?" He moved his finger down and placed the tip just above her heart.

Even though she and Tanner had talked about doing this, Minka was terrified at the idea of letting the monster out long enough to learn what it remembered. She'd been working so hard to keep the doors inside her locked tight, desperately hoping the beast would never break its way out again. Now Angelo was asking her to willingly open the door and invite the thing out. This was far more than simply letting out her claws or listening in on a conversation that was too far away for a normal person to hear.

Angelo put his hands on her shoulders and moved closer. As his scent wrapped her in its warm embrace, the fear that threatened to overwhelm her disappeared.

Minka took a deep breath. With her angel here next to her, she could do it.

She closed her eyes and relaxed like Ivy and Tanner had taught her, then focused on Angelo's hands on her shoulders. They felt so warm, so strong. She let that heat and strength envelop her.

When she was completely calm, she reached into that place inside her where the beast sat caged and waiting, ready to rip and tear into anything and everything around her, and slowly opened the door. Instead of stopping after a few centimeters, like before, she let it swing almost halfway open.

She knew the image of the beast inside a cage existed only in her head. That beast, that rage, was a part of her. The rage hit her fast and hard, like she hadn't felt since she'd gone a little crazy at the DCO, when Dick had come at her with that needle. Her claws and fangs extended so suddenly it hurt, and she winced. Just when she thought she might have let her control slip too far, she felt Angelo take her small hands in his bigger, more powerful ones. She latched on to the comfort and strength of his touch, using it as an anchor as the beast raged and fought to slip out of her control.

For a time—she wasn't sure how long—his touch was all she thought about. Inside, the animal wasn't fighting as hard as it had been.

Minka slowly opened her eyes to find Angelo smiling down at her.

"You're doing great. Stay nice and relaxed just like that," he said. "Now, look around and take in where we are. Use your nose, your instincts. Tell me if this place feels familiar."

She looked around, not realizing until then that letting the beast out had taken longer than she'd realized. It was almost completely dark now. She scanned the slope. The plane was nowhere to be seen. She hadn't even heard it leave. The team was still there, and everyone was just sitting or lying around, apparently waiting for her to tell them which way to go.

Minka started to turn toward the ridge when something grabbed the animal's attention and snapped her focus back to the camp below. It took several moments before she—and the beast—could figure out what had distracted her, but then she picked up a strange scent coming from Diaz's direction. She tilted her head from side to side, sniffing the air.

What she smelled made no sense. At first, she thought she was simply picking up on Trevor's shifter scent. But he was on the far side of the pile of gear, and the part of the beast that was in control told her the wind shouldn't be moving the shifter's scent in Diaz's direction.

The animal part of her mind mused curiously over why Diaz smelled like Trevor, but then Minka exerted her control and forced the creature inside her to dismiss the distraction. She didn't have a lot of experience with this, but she supposed that if the two men had been sitting next to each other on the plane, there might be a scent transfer, or perhaps the two of them had gotten close with each other at some point. She knew men sometimes did that. Regardless, it meant nothing to her.

Getting back to the question Angelo had asked her, she turned and swept her gaze across the ridge. Without being told to do it, the beast began to look for details Minka had missed—a fresh tumble of rocks here, a trace of old scent there, a scrub bush broken and crushed.

As if following a line, her eyes traced the path she'd taken down from the ridge many weeks before like it was lit with small torches. They were on the right path. In fact, she'd passed no more than a few rock throws from this very place.

She turned and smiled at Angelo, only then realizing that her fangs were out. She lifted her hand to hide them from him, but he caught her fingers in his, stopping her. Then he grinned.

"This is the place, isn't it?"

Minka nodded, both amazed and relieved that Angelo never shied away from her hybrid half. She briefly wondered if her eyes were glowing green or red at that moment but then decided it didn't matter.

They glowed, and yet he didn't look away. That was the important part.

"Yes." She wasn't very good at estimating distances, so she related the distance in a term that she did understand. "This is exactly the way I came. The place I was held is only three or four hours' steady walking from here."

Angelo's grin broadened. "I knew you could do it. You ready to change back on your own now, or do you need Ivy's help?"

She smiled. "No, just yours."

# Chapter 14

Minka crouched behind the rocks at the top of the hill overlooking the hybrid research facility she'd escaped from, less than thrilled at the plan Angelo and Landon had come up with—mostly because the plan involved her staying up there by herself while everyone else was putting themselves in danger down below.

Angelo, Ivy, Derek, Powell, and Moore would enter the big building where she'd been held. That was where they thought the doctors would almost certainly be, so they wanted to put the most people on it. Landon and Diaz would take the building they thought were the guards' sleeping quarters, while Watson and Trevor would take the much smaller building that looked like an office of some kind. According to what Angelo had told her earlier, Trevor and Watson were supposed to check out any computers they found for evidence. Once they had that, they'd circle back and help Landon and Diaz keep the guards occupied. After Ivy and Angelo's team captured the doctors, everyone would meet back up on the top of the ridge; then they'd head to the location where the Osprey was supposed to pick them up.

Minka didn't know enough about military tactics to say whether the plan was a good one, but regardless, she didn't like the idea of her angel being down there without her. Angelo said she wasn't trained for this, though. She understood it, but that didn't mean she liked it.

She pulled her braid to the side and nervously ran her hand down it, watching as the teams slipped down the hillside in the darkness, moving quietly from rock to rock like ghosts. Even knowing they were there, it was hard to see all of them, especially Angelo and the other Special Forces soldiers. She was tempted to try to shift her vision so she could see Angelo better but stopped herself, worried she wouldn't be able to keep the beast under control.

Instead, she listened in on the radio earpiece Diaz had given her. She didn't have a microphone to talk into like the rest of them, but at least she'd be able to hear what was happening. Unfortunately, at the moment, nobody was saying a word.

The facility was a lot bigger than she'd remembered. Then again, she hadn't looked around much when she'd escaped. In addition to the three main buildings, there were nearly a dozen smaller ones, including one that Angelo had told her likely held ammunition and explosives and another that probably held fuel.

Below, the three groups split up and went their separate ways. Minka took deep breaths as a sense of panic she didn't understand began to build inside her. It felt like every hair on the back of her neck was tingling and standing on end. Worse, her instincts screamed that something was wrong.

But she had no idea what it was or what she could do about it. It had only been a few minutes since Angelo and the others had left her on the hilltop, but she could already see him, Ivy, and the others darting from shadow to shadow as they ran for the building where she'd been held captive. Just thinking about what the doctors had done to her in there made the beast start growling inside her, and she had to focus on thoughts of Angelo to get the rage back under control.

Even from where she was hiding, it was easy to pick out Angelo from the others. He was simply bigger. Ivy was easy to spot, too. She moved like a cat—quick, quiet, and deadly. Minka was so focused on them that she didn't realize the attack had started until there was a blinding flash from the guards' barracks and the office building as the front doors blew in.

Through the smoke and fire, she saw Landon and the others rush into the buildings. A moment later, the shooting started. Minka knew nothing about guns, but even to her inexperienced ears, it sounded like there was more than one kind of weapon being fired in there. The skin on her neck tingled even more.

Then, Minka's ears picked up a sound worse than any automatic weapon fire—deep, rage-filled, growls. And they were coming from the building Trevor and Watson had gone into. Her heart raced. *Oh God, no.* From the sounds of it, there were at least five or ten hybrids down there. How could there be so many of them on the same compound with her and she had never known?

She jumped to her feet, not sure what she was going to do, when she caught fast movement out of the corner of her eye. She whipped her head around toward the building Angelo, Ivy, and Derek had entered just in time to see a half-dozen fast-moving figures racing toward it. They were all big, but the one in the lead was head and shoulders taller than the others. He was even bigger than Angelo.

From where she was, she could clearly see the red

glow of their eyes. But even if she hadn't, she would have known what they were. They moved too fast and too aggressively to be anything other than hybrids. And they were heading straight for Angelo and his team.

Cursing at Angelo for not leaving her a way to call him with a warning, she raced down the hill. She didn't know what she was going to do when she got there, especially since she didn't have a weapon. But she sure as hell wasn't staying up on a hill while Angelo was about to be attacked by a group of monsters he didn't even know were coming.

---

Landon knew they were screwed the second they blew in the front door of the barracks and found the guards already waiting for them, weapons locked and loaded. But he and Diaz were trained for this shit and didn't stand there waiting to get popped. They spread out into the big, open room and started engaging targets.

"Watson," Landon shouted out over his radio as he dived for the floor and popped a round through a big-ass guard who was dumb enough to run right down the middle of the hallway. "We're facing a lot of hostiles over here. Any chance you two can break off what you're doing and hit them from the back side of the building?"

Instead of an answer, all Landon heard was the sound of weapons fire in his ear—and the growl of hybrids.

"I'm going to have to get back to you on that request, Captain," Watson finally shouted back. "This isn't just an admin building. It's like some kind of backup lab. There are about a half-dozen holding cells full of hybrids, and unfortunately, someone forgot to lock the cell doors on them. So we're all a little busy right now."

*Shit.*

"Copy that," Landon said.

He got up and darted behind a square column as one of the guards sent a full magazine worth of rounds buzzing down the hallway. The bullets punched holes in the walls, the furniture, and the ceiling, but fortunately, they didn't hit anything soft and squishy.

Fuck, he hoped things were better for Ivy and Angelo. He'd purposely put his wife with Angelo, knowing his best friend would do anything to take care of her. But if things were as bad over there as they were here, that might not be enough.

---

Angelo swore the moment he, Ivy, and Derek entered the research building. The urge to hurry and find the doctors had taken a momentary backseat at the scene in front of them. Even in the dim light, it was impossible to miss the holding cells along both walls, and the six people locked in them. Of their own accord, his hands slowly clenched into fists and the desire to punch someone was suddenly overwhelming.

He wasn't the only one. Beside him, Ivy growled as she looked at the abused and broken hybrids.

On the other side of her, Derek was already reaching for his medic's bag.

Angelo had expected all of the doctor's test subjects would be locals—Tajiks or Pashtuns—but four of the six hybrids seemed fair-skinned enough to be from Europe or North America. Only two of the hybrids—a woman with long hair and eyes that were completely feral, and a muscular man with deep slashes all over his chest and an American flag tattooed on his right shoulder—were even strong enough to stand and growl at them. The other four were in such bad shape that all they could do was lie there. All of them were chained to the wall or floor by their ankles. The torn, bruised, and bloody skin around the manacles showed how hard they had fought for their freedom.

Anger welled up in Angelo. This was how Minka had been treated. Suddenly, punching the doctors wasn't enough. Landon had told him in a general way how they had hurt Ivy, but now he really understood it. He decided then and there that he would kill both Klaus and Renard if he got the chance—unless Ivy got to them first, of course.

Ivy ran to the first cell and yanked on the door. Even though Angelo knew she was pulling with more force than he could ever manage, the heavy steel bars barely budged.

The sound of gunfire grew louder outside, and Angelo winced as he heard Landon shouting over the radio that they needed backup…and Watson telling him that backup wouldn't be coming from their direction.

"The guards must have figured out we were coming," Watson added. "They've unlocked all the cages over here. The place is crawling with hybrids that are acting like they haven't eaten in months and think we're dinner."

*Shit.*

It was getting heavy out there, and they were taking too long in here. Powell and Moore had peeled off to cover the rear of the building, and the vehicles near the back of the facility. The plan had been for Powell and Moore to come running if he, Ivy, and Derek needed help, but now it sounded like Watson and his team were going to need them instead.

"Powell," Angelo called into the radio, hoping to be heard over the chatter coming from the other teams. "Can you get to Trevor and Watson?"

Angelo hoped the animosity between Powell and Trevor wasn't going to get in the way here, or things could get real ugly, real fast.

Powell's voice came back over the radio immediately. "We'll try, but it might take us a bit. We're pinned down by at least four guards back here by the fuel dump. They were waiting for us the moment we came around the side of the building."

Over the open line, Angelo could hear the sounds of automatic weapons fire. *Double shit*.

"Landon," he called. "Powell and Moore are trying to get to Watson's team, but they're pinned down. You want Derek, Ivy, and me to break off and give you a hand?"

"No," Landon answered. "Get those doctors to a secure location first, then come help. We'll hold on until then."

"Roger that." Angelo jogged over to where Ivy and Derek were standing, looking at the hybrid lying on the floor of the first cell. "We need to move."

"They smell like Minka," she said. "Like me."

Angelo ground his jaw. *Dammit*.

Derek frowned. "What do you mean?"

Ivy ignored his question, instead focusing on Angelo. Her green eyes glowed so bright they practically lit up her face. "You never asked how I knew Minka had been created from my DNA the moment I saw her, but it was the scent. Like any person's scent, it's unique, but there are parts that are like mine. That's how I knew. I'm not sure if the other shifters have noticed, but I did." She glanced at the hybrids. "They have that trace of my scent, too. They were made with my DNA."

Derek's eyes went wide. "All of them?"

She nodded, and Angelo could see the horrible pain in her eyes. "All of them. We can't leave them here like this. We have to help them."

Angelo winced as he remembered yelling at Ivy about not wanting to help Minka, how he had essentially called her selfish because he thought she was more worried about keeping her marriage to Landon a secret than helping Minka. But now he finally understood it had never been about the secrets. It had been about not wanting to be responsible for other humans being tortured and experimented on—about not wanting to look at Minka and know the pain she'd gone through was Ivy's fault.

There wasn't anything Angelo could do to take that pain away, but there was one thing he could do—make sure it never happened again.

"We'll come back and get the hybrids out. I don't know how, but we'll do it, Ivy. I promise," he said. "We need to end this. We can't let Klaus and Renard get away to ever do this again. Can you find them?"

Ivy opened her mouth to argue, but Derek spoke first.

"You and Angelo go find those doctors. I'll stay here and figure out a way to get these people free. If nothing else, at least I'll keep them safe, okay?"

Ivy regarded Derek for a long moment, then she nodded. "I'm trusting you to do that."

Giving the hybrids one more long look, she turned and sniffed the air. "Klaus and Renard are here."

"In this building?" Angelo asked.

She nodded.

"Then let's go find them." He keyed the mic on his radio as he jogged after her. "Landon, I know you're in deep shit right now, but you need to get somebody over to the research building as soon as you can. Derek is trying to save some injured hybrids, and he's going to need help."

On the other end of the line, Landon didn't even hesitate. "Copy that. I'll break off here as soon as possible. Keep it together until I can."

Up ahead, Ivy had picked up her pace to a run. Angelo hurried to keep up, trying to cover every branch in the hallway and every open doorway they passed. Several of the rooms reminded him of small treatment rooms in a hospital, complete with beds and carts of equipment. Other rooms had computers and workstations that seemed more suited to a financial company than a hybrid research facility.

He was just wondering if Ivy was wrong about the doctors being there when she suddenly turned and kicked in the double doors of a random room on the left. She charged inside with a menacing growl that made the hair on his neck stand up. He sprinted the rest of the way, practically skidding into the room to cover her in case someone in there had a weapon.

But the place was empty.

Dim lights on the high ceiling barely illuminated the circular room, but Angelo had no problem figuring out what it was used for. The metal table in the center of the room was highlighted by banks of adjustable lights overhead and surrounded by trays and carts of surgical instruments that could only mean this was an operating room. This was where Klaus and Renard had tortured and experimented on Minka. And if the row of dark, reflective glass on the opposite wall was any indication, people had watched it happen.

For the first time, Angelo wished he were a shifter, so he could growl.

Ivy spun around to stare at the windows. A moment later, she let out a hiss and darted toward the glass. Lights flickered on behind the windows, revealing two men. Angelo had only seen them in the photographs put up during the mission briefing, but he easily recognized them—Johan Klaus and Jean Renard. The doctors should have looked terrified, but they didn't. If anything, they looked damn pleased.

Angelo's gut clenched.

He ran forward to pull Ivy back, but she was already ahead of him, spinning around to shove him back toward the door.

"It's a trap," she shouted.

They'd barely made it into the hallway when she jerked to a halt. Angelo stopped too, swinging his M4 around just as the doors on the other end burst open. Half a dozen hybrids charged into the building and headed their way.

Angelo squeezed the trigger as he backpedaled into the operating room. Beside him, Ivy did the same. He glanced around for something to take cover behind as the hybrids returned fire, but there was nothing in the room that a bullet wouldn't be able to punch a hole through—him and Ivy included.

"Kill the man!" one of the doctors shouted from inside the observation room. "But take the female shifter alive."

Ivy snarled. "The hell you will!"

*Damn straight*, Angelo thought as he dropped his empty magazine and slapped in a fresh one. There was no way in hell he was going to let his best friend's wife get captured by these assholes again.

---

Minka felt the beast clawing to get out as she sprinted toward the building Angelo, Ivy, and Derek had gone into. She tried to remember what Tanner had taught her about holding on to herself while letting the beast out enough to use its abilities, but that had been much easier to do when she'd been sitting on the couch in Layla's office. Now that she knew her friends were in danger, she couldn't think of anything but getting to them. The risk of losing control was worth the speed she gained when she ceded a little more of herself to the beast though, so she opened the door in her mind almost all the way.

She ran faster than she ever had in her life, faster even than any animal she'd ever seen. The feeling was exhilarating, and maybe she would have enjoyed it if she hadn't been terrified of Angelo, Ivy, and Derek getting killed by those hybrids.

Minka didn't have any idea what she was going to do when she got inside, but she would do whatever was necessary. Angelo had risked everything to save her. If that meant she had to let the beast completely free, she'd do it without hesitation.

When she reached the building, she charged through the door she'd seen the hybrids disappear through less than a minute earlier, her heart pounding in her chest. She thought she was ready, that she had enough control to do this, but the scene that met her gaze froze her muscles solid and she slid to a stumbling stop.

A dead hybrid was lying in the center of the room, blood pouring from an unbelievable number of gunshot wounds. Angelo was standing over by another set of double doors on the far side of the room, facing down two hybrids. But instead of shooting them, he'd turned his gun backward like a club and was smashing it into the hybrids over and over. His uniform was shredded across the chest and stomach, and blood dripped from his lacerated arms. She briefly wondered why Angelo didn't simply shoot the hybrids, but then she realized the weapon must be out of bullets.

On the other side of the room, two more hybrids had Ivy pinned to the floor while the really big one had her arms pulled away from her body at a vicious angle. Renard advanced on Ivy with a syringe as thick as Minka's wrist as Klaus stood off to the side, smiling.

Ivy snarled and clawed at the two creatures on top of her, tearing great, long gashes into every part of them she could reach. But the hybrids seemed impervious to the damage, or at least to the pain.

While seeing Angelo and Ivy in such danger was traumatic, it was those doctors and being in the room where they'd experimented on her that almost made her turn and run out screaming. They had strapped her down to that metal table in the center of the room, shined those bright, overhead lights into her eyes, and injected her with the serum that had destroyed her life and turned her into a monster. This was the place where her months of pain and suffering had begun.

Her legs threatened to give out on her as all the fear and terror came rushing in to crush her under its heavy weight. The beast that always raged to get out so it could claw at anything it could reach suddenly ran back into its cage and cowered.

Minka heard Angelo shouting at her, telling her to get away. She almost did it, too. But the knowledge that Angelo would gladly face pain and death himself if he knew she was safe kept her from running. While every instinct inside her said to get as far away from there as she could, her love for him made her stay and fight.

She locked her gaze on Angelo as she forced herself to take a step in his direction. He shook his head, telling her to run, but she ignored him. Instead, she used the sight of him struggling against the two hybrids to feed the panic inside her, praying it would encourage the beast to come out.

One of the hybrids raked his claws across Angelo's chest again. Blood spattered against the wall. That was all she needed.

Minka launched herself at the hybrid, her fangs and claws coming out as the beast took over. She didn't know what to do when she landed on the creature's back, but her inner beast did, so she swung the door wide to set it free. She bared her teeth, sinking them into the side of the hybrid's neck.

The hybrid howled in pain, spinning around and trying to wrestle her off. She ignored him, wrapping her legs around the creature's waist and locking her ankles together over his midsection. Digging the claws of her left hand into his back, she got her right arm over the hybrid's shoulder and sunk her claws into his chest.

She'd always hated her claws, had wanted them to go away and never come back. But now, with Angelo in danger, she gloried in having weapons she could use to protect him. She urged her beast to extend the long, curved claws as far as they would go, urged it to shred and destroy anything it could reach.

The hybrid fell backward to the hard floor, trying to smash her under his weight, yanking and clawing at her arms and legs. She dug in even deeper with her fangs, subduing the creature. The moment the hybrid went limp, she sprang to her feet, intending to lunge for the other creature still attacking Angelo.

He glanced at her. "I got this. Help Ivy."

Minka hesitated, torn, then spun around and sprinted across the room.

Renard had the needle already buried in Ivy's arm and was saying something to her, toying with her before he pumped the drug into her. Minka knew exactly what was in there. It was the same drug they'd pumped into her many times when they wanted her docile for their experiments. The drug had immobilized her while leaving her totally aware of what they were doing to her. The fear that had come with being paralyzed while they did things to her was worse than any nightmare.

Minka wasn't going to let Ivy experience that.

She leaped on the smaller of the two hybrids holding Ivy down, the claws of one hand digging into his shoulders as she reached out to claw at Renard's face at the same time. The doctor reeled back, the syringe ripping out of Ivy's arm and skittering across the floor.

Minka wanted to jump on Renard but knew she had to take care of this hybrid first. But before she could rip into him with her fangs, the big hybrid holding Ivy's arm grabbed her and yanked her off, flinging her across the room as if she were a kitten. She smashed into the wall, then fell on a cart filled with medical instruments before tumbling to the floor. Ignoring the pain, she jumped to her feet and ran back over to where Ivy was struggling against the three hybrids.

The big hybrid moved to block Minka, growling and showing fangs that were much larger than her own. She darted to the right, hoping to get around him, when a loud boom shook the building. It was immediately followed by a sharp, explosive crack, like lightning hitting. The dark windows positioned over the metal table shattered, and some of the overhead lights crashed to the floor.

Minka's beast took a step back into its cage in confusion, and she was barely able to keep her feet. She looked around to see that everyone else in the room seemed as stunned as she was. The scent of smoke filled her nose—something nearby was on fire.

She was wondering if the building they were in was on fire too, when the big hybrid suddenly lunged at her. Her beast charged out of its cage, and she ducked under the hybrid's outstretched hands, slicing her claws deep into his calf as she bounded past him to get to Ivy.

Minka let the beast have a little more control, trusting she'd be able to rein it in later.

She darted up behind the hybrid she'd clawed earlier

and swung her hand at the back of his legs. The creature screamed in pain as her claws tore into his muscles. She jumped over him as he fell to the floor, desperate to get to Ivy. But her friend was already slashing at the other hybrid who had been holding her down, her claws moving in a blur as she struck at his face, neck, and chest over and over in rapid succession.

Ivy easily avoided the hybrid's clumsy counterstrikes, tearing into the creature with calm precision. Ivy's claws found the hybrid's throat so fast even Minka's enhanced vision could barely see the blur of motion. Once that hybrid was down, Ivy dealt with the one Minka had hamstrung just as quickly.

Minka turned, looking for the doctors. As much as the big hybrid concerned her, it was the doctors the beast inside her wanted. A movement over by the double doors that led outside caught her attention. She snapped her head around just in time to see Klaus and Renard flee into the darkness. The big hybrid raced after them. The sight of the men who had tortured her escaping was too much for the beast. With a growl, the beast took over, and she ran full speed toward the doors.

Minka knew she should stay and make sure Angelo was okay. But she couldn't. No matter how much she tried to fight the beast and lock in on Angelo's scent and the image of him in her head, it did no good. The beast wanted the two men who had tortured her, and now that Minka had set it free, there didn't seem to be anything she could do to stop it.

# Chapter 15

LANDON AND DIAZ HAD JUST FINISHED CLEARING OUT the remaining guards from the barracks and were hauling ass over to the other building to help Trevor and Watson when the whole freaking world exploded.

The resounding boom was like a punch in the chest, sending him and Diaz flying. Fireballs and metal fragments flew through the air, smacking into the buildings and ground around them. All Landon could do was hug the dirt and pray nothing landed on top of them as munitions from the ammo dump kept cooking off and throwing crap everywhere.

The worst of it was just starting to slow when something else blew up on the far side of the compound. From where he was lying on the ground, Landon could feel the blast wave sweep over him. He lifted his head in time to see a big, flaming fuel drum smash into the side of the building Ivy and Angelo had gone into. *Oh God*. Whatever had blown up the ammo holding area must have gotten to the fuel area, too.

Before he could radio either of them to check in, more fuel drums started raining down, splashing liquid fire around like some kind of pissed-off medieval dragon. The whole damn compound was going to go up.

"Get to the admin building!" Landon shouted at Diaz.

He and Diaz had just scrambled to their feet when

another fuel drum hit the ground where he'd been lying just seconds before and burst into flames. *Shit*.

Landon heard a thud somewhere overhead and turned to see another fuel drum hit the admin building. *Fuck*. They needed to get those guys out of there.

He and Diaz rushed into the building to find the place was already on fire. Even through the haze, Landon could see that while this place may have started as an office, it wasn't one now. It was more like a cross between an emergency room and a prison cell block. A handful of cells closed off by steel bars lined the wall on the far side of the big room, while the entire center section was filled with carts of medical equipment, computer stations, and metal gurneys.

Right now, though, it looked more like something out of a madhouse. Flames raced and licked along the ceiling and far wall, and heavy smoke was already curling around the ceiling, making his eyes water.

Landon blinked and looked around for his guys. Trevor was crouched behind a table, ripping a big computer apart with his bare hands. A moment later, he yanked out the hard drive and dropped it into his rucksack.

A couple feet away, Watson was keeping two enraged hybrids busy by popping off shots at them every time they poked their heads out of their cells. The bodies of three dead hybrids lay on the floor halfway between the cells and where Trevor and Watson had barricaded themselves. The creatures had obviously died trying their best to get to his guys and rip out their throats. Landon and Diaz raced over to help.

Watson glanced at him. "Man, nice of you to finally show up. These things are frigging insane."

Landon opened his mouth to answer when Derek's voice came over the radio.

"Captain, if you're out there, I'm in deep shit and could really use that help about now. And if you have any explosives, I could use some of those, too."

———

Angelo had known he and Ivy were screwed the moment their M4s had run out of ammo. The one saving grace to the whole fucked-up situation was that he couldn't imagine how it could get any worse.

Then Minka had skidded into the room. That was when Angelo decided his imagination sucked because things had definitely gotten worse.

Time had stopped as Minka stood there frozen in the doorway and the red glow in her eyes dimmed. The beast had picked a shitty time to bail on Minka. He'd shouted at her to run before the hybrids—or worse, the doctors—could get to her.

But she'd stayed, and the next few minutes had been the longest of his life as he'd watched her fight the hybrids.

Angelo was still trying to finish off the hybrid trying to kill him when an explosion rocked the building, knocking him to the floor. He crawled to his feet, tossing away the broken remnants of his M4 and reaching for the knife on his belt. He would have to get a lot closer to the hybrid than he liked to use it, but he didn't have a choice.

On the far side of the room, Klaus and Renard ran for the doors, the big-ass hybrid right behind them. Angelo swore as Minka raced after them.

*Fuck.*

"Minka, stop!" he shouted.

She ignored him.

From the corner of his eye, he saw Ivy hesitate, her gaze darting from him to the doors.

"I'll deal with the hybrid," he told her. "You stay with Minka."

Ivy nodded and took off running.

Angelo moved to block the doors in case the hybrid tried to follow Minka and Ivy. He needn't have bothered. The thing charged him like a deranged bull, going from zero to sixty in the blink of an eye.

Angelo had just enough time to get his knife up before the enraged monster slammed into him like a freight train. Angelo wasn't a small guy, but the force of the impact still knocked him off his feet and slammed him to the ground. The hybrid crashed down on top of him, crushing him to the floor and knocking the air out of his lungs.

*Son of a bitch.*

With stars dancing in his vision, Angelo fought to get the knife up from in between them, but the damn thing was stuck. He knew he had to do something fast— before the hybrid started tearing into him—but the knife wouldn't move.

The hybrid didn't tear into him, though. In fact, the creature simply collapsed on him, knocking what little air had made it back into Angelo's lungs right out again. He shoved the creature off his chest and crawled out from under it. That was when he discovered his knife was shoved right through the hybrid's heart.

Angelo didn't waste time trying to figure out how he'd gotten so lucky. He jerked the knife out and scrambled to his feet, then sprinted out the doors after Minka and Ivy. He knew Ivy would try to take care of Minka, but there was still a lot that could go wrong. He had to find Minka and get her back under control before she got hurt.

Outside, he headed toward the rear of the compound where the vehicles were, sure that had to be where Klaus, Renard, and that big-ass hybrid guard had gone. And if they were going that way, so was Minka.

All around him, the compound looked like a scene from Dante's *Inferno*. Random explosions were still occurring within the wreck of the building that used to house the compound's ammo, throwing chunks of metal and wood all over the place. The smoke was so thick from the multiple fires burning, he could barely see more than ten feet in front of him. He had to trust he was heading the right way as he moved toward the motor pool.

He tried to contact Landon on the radio as he moved slowly through the thick smoke. But other than a few broken words here and there, he couldn't reach him. Shit, for all he knew, his radio had been busted during the fight...or worse.

Then from somewhere just ahead of him, he heard pistol shots ring out, quickly followed by feline growls that he was sure were Minka's.

He took off running in that direction, dodging the falling debris and raging fires, praying he reached Minka in time—and that she wouldn't be so far gone when he got there that he couldn't get her back.

<p style="text-align:center">~~~</p>

By the time Landon reached the doors leading into the research facility and darted inside, the fire on the roof was already blazing at least twenty feet high. He hadn't been able to reach anybody on the radio on the way over, so he had no idea what the hell was going on with Ivy, Angelo, or Derek. All he could say for sure was that there was no way a person could last much longer in that building—not in that fire. If it hadn't been for the short call from Derek, he would never have come in here to look for him in the first place.

Landon slipped into the big, open space, covering his face with his arm as he looked around for Ivy, Angelo, or Derek. It was hot as hell and the smoke was getting thicker by the second, but at least he could breathe. There was no sign of his people, though. All he saw were dead hybrids and a lot of blood. He ran through another set of double doors, then down a long hall. He shouted Derek's name, but there was no answer. That didn't mean anything. He doubted anyone could hear him over the roar of the flames.

Landon skidded to a stop when he reached a room full of cells and saw Derek pounding on one of the door locks with a steel bar. Though the medic was hitting the lock mechanism as hard as he could, it was obvious he wasn't going to get through the heavy-duty lock.

Landon wasn't sure if it mattered. There were six cells in the room, and all of them held hybrids, but the creatures in four of the cells, including the one Derek was working on, weren't moving at all.

The other two hybrids—a bare-chested man and a woman with a wild mane of dark blond hair—were going absolutely nuts. They were yanking at the chains around their ankles so hard Landon was worried they'd tear off their own feet. He swore when he caught sight of the American flag tattooed on the male hybrid's shoulder. Shit, that guy was almost certainly a soldier.

Derek dropped the steel bar when he saw Landon. "Thank God you're here. I found a single set of keys that I think opens the manacles around their ankles, but nothing for the cell doors. Some guard probably has it on his fucking belt." He motioned to the cells. "We need to get the others out fast. They won't last long in this smoke. Please tell me you brought some bang with you."

Landon was about to point out that they were probably wasting their time with the four hybrids who weren't moving, but then he stopped himself. Derek wouldn't care. He was a Special Forces medic. He never gave up on anyone who was injured, no matter how bad it looked.

So Landon nodded and yanked off his rucksack, dropping it to the floor. "I got explosives. Where are Ivy and Angelo?"

"They went after Klaus and Renard," Derek said.

That's what Landon figured. If he had a minute, he would have tried to get them on the radio to make sure they were okay, but with the fire spreading, he wasn't sure he and Derek were going to have enough time to blow the cell doors, much less anything else.

"We don't have time to mess around," he told Derek. "We'll rig all the doors to blow at once, then figure out how to deal with the two conscious hybrids after that."

Derek focused on cutting and molding the plastic explosives into charges while Landon strung out the detonation cord and crimped on the blasting caps. The det cord would explosively transmit the shock wave from one charge to the next, while the blasting caps would boost it enough to set off the C4.

"Keep the charges as small as possible," Landon told Derek. "We want to blow through the locks, not rip them apart and frag the hell out of the hybrids."

Around them, the flames and smoke were getting worse by the second. It was already difficult to breathe. Another few minutes, and the superheated air in the space would start searing their lungs.

Derek attached the explosive charges to the door locks, then tried his best to motion the two conscious hybrids toward the back of the cell. It didn't look like it was working. They were still yanking on the chains holding them to the floor like they were insane.

"I'm pulling the shot now," Landon shouted as he attached the firing device on the end of the last piece of det cord. "We'll just have to pray they'll be okay."

Derek looked torn as he stared at the female hybrid standing a few steps from the cell door. But finally he nodded and ran past Landon, ducking around the nearest corner.

Landon punched in the shortest delay on the countdown timer—five seconds—then pressed the green button and raced after Derek.

He'd barely made it to the corner when he heard the sharp, distinctive crack of C4 plastic explosive going off. He immediately turned around to head back and almost got run over by the male hybrid with the slashed chest hauling ass past them toward the exit, the manacle and chain dragging behind him. Landon didn't even reach for his weapon. Not that it would have done much good. The hybrid was out of sight in the blink of an eye. Landon couldn't have brought himself to shoot the man anyway. He was a soldier just trying to get away.

"What the hell happened with him?" Derek asked as they ran back to the cells.

"The explosion must have freaked him out so much he ripped his manacle right out of the wall."

"Well, we wanted to get him out—he's out," Derek said. "Let's just hope he doesn't go after any of our people."

Derek checked for a pulse on each of the four unconscious hybrids before unlocking the manacles around their ankles.

"They're alive, but just barely. Get them out of here, and I'll try to figure out how I'm going to get the woman to let me in there with her."

Landon carried each of them outside, one after another, praying that getting them into the open air might help. He was just coming back inside after he'd taken the last out when he realized they'd run out of time. The ceiling was completely engulfed by fire now, with heavy pieces starting to fall to the floor and flames running down the walls so fast it looked like a burning waterfall. Unfortunately, Derek was still having problems with the last hybrid, the totally freaked-out female.

"Why haven't you gotten her unlocked yet?" he shouted.

"I'm fucking trying," Derek said, "but I can't get close enough to unlock the chain around her ankle."

Landon hurried over to help, but that only seemed to make the hybrid more agitated. She snarled, reaching out to try to claw Derek.

*Shit.*

How the hell could they save her if she wanted to
kill them?

———~~~———

The beast was so eager to go after the doctors, it almost
got Minka killed. She'd just entered the fenced-in area
where the vehicles were parked when Renard stepped
out from behind a dirt-covered Land Rover and started
shooting at her.

She leaped to the side and rolled across the ground
toward the protection offered by another vehicle. As
fast as she moved, she still felt the hot sting as a bullet
creased a line along her back, from her right shoulder to
her left hip.

Scrambling to her feet, she ran around the vehicle,
hoping to catch Renard from behind. She came out from
behind the truck low and fast but didn't see him. She
could smell his stench, though. Then she heard footsteps farther down the line of vehicles. She immediately
changed direction, leaping on top of the Land Rover and
bounding from one vehicle to the next.

She'd just landed on a big military truck when she
felt that familiar tingle along the back of her neck. She'd
been tricked. In the beast's desire to get to Renard, it
had completely forgotten about the other hybrid…until
now. Renard had been luring her into a trap. And she
had fallen for it.

Minka twisted in midair, trying to change course, but
wasn't fast enough to avoid the bullet coming at her.
It hit her left hip, and she crashed to the ground with a
yowl of pain. She tried to spring to her feet, but her left

leg responded sluggishly, and she ended up tumbling to the ground again.

She shoved herself up with her hands, intending to crawl away if she had to, but by then it was too late. Gravel crunched on the ground in front of her, and she looked up to see Renard standing there, the big hybrid at his side. The creature held a large pistol in its hands, and it was pointed straight at her head. It seemed strange that a hybrid as big and terrifying as this one would prefer a gun over its natural weapons.

"You're one fast, vicious animal, I'll give you that, girl," Renard sneered. "But you're still just a dumb animal. I knew that all I had to do was get you separated from that feline shifter bitch and you would be easy to take down."

Trapped under the control of the beast, Minka flinched at the fact that she hadn't even thought about Ivy following her. What had they done to her?

Renard smiled and took a step closer. The beast inside Minka gave a soft growl. Renard had always liked to get as close as he could when he was going to hurt her, so he could see the pain in her eyes. He would stand within inches of her chains' limits, knowing she could not hurt him.

Well, there were no chains stopping her now. This time, there was nothing to keep the beast from making Renard pay for every single horrible thing he'd done to her and all the other people he'd tortured and killed. This time, he would be the one screaming in pain.

But then, just as she started to tense her good leg for a lunge, Renard motioned the hybrid forward. "Shoot her but don't kill her. We'll throw her in the back of the truck, and I'll deal with her later. Be quick about it. We need to help Johan before that shifter bitch gets him."

The beast inside Minka growled low and deep, preparing to go for the big hybrid instead of Renard. But the hybrid wasn't as stupid as the doctor. He moved to the side, out of Minka's attack range, and lifted the pistol, pointing it right at the base of her spine. Minka's blood went cold. The hybrid was going to paralyze her so Renard could do whatever he wanted to her when he got around to it.

# Chapter 16

"STAY BACK," DEREK ORDERED. "I THINK I ALMOST had her."

"We don't have time for this," Landon shouted. "You need to figure out how to calm her down or sedate her. We have to go—now!"

Derek moved closer to the hybrid, his hands up in a peaceful gesture. The woman tilted her head sideways in a curious way, sniffing the air a little. And holy shit, the red glow started fading from her eyes, showing some amazing slate-gray coloring. But then a beam in the ceiling in the next cell over collapsed, sending flaming pieces down all around them. The hybrid's eyes flared red again, and she leaped straight at Derek. But instead of protecting himself, Derek wrapped his arms around the hybrid, taking her down. She snarled, trying to claw him.

"There's a syringe in the top left pocket of my shirt," Derek shouted as he tried to get control of the woman's claws. "It's a sedative. Get it and inject her!"

It was damn tough with the hybrid flailing around like a Tasmanian devil, but after a few seconds, Landon found the syringe. He yanked the top off it and pushed a little on the plunger to make sure there wasn't any air in the needle.

"How much do I inject?"

"All of it, and pray it's enough!" Derek yelled,

struggling to keep the woman's claws away from his throat.

Landon got a tight grip on the syringe and jabbed the needle into her arm, fighting like hell to get it all into her. Then he tossed the needle aside and helped hold on to her. She quieted, but it took way too long. By the time Derek was able to let her go, he and Landon both had to slap their uniforms and her clothes as the burning embers raining down from the ceiling caught them on fire.

"Get the chain off her ankle and let's get the hell out of here," Landon ordered.

Derek rammed the key into the hole in the manacle. "Fuck, fuck, and triple fuck! She smashed at it so much trying to get free that it's completely mangled. The key is never going to fit in it."

Landon crawled over to check the lock as Derek scrambled to his feet and ran over to where the chain was attached to the wall. He yanked hard, but it wouldn't budge. Landon joined him, but there was no way it was coming out of the wall.

Landon glanced over his shoulder at the fire roaring down the wall toward them like some living creature, then turned back to Derek. "We're not going to be able to get her out of here. Not unless we take off her foot."

Derek shook his head violently. "No way in hell am I taking off her foot," he said, yanking on the chain again.

Landon grabbed his shoulder, stilling him. "If an enraged hybrid stronger than both of us combined couldn't get it out of the wall, we sure as hell can't."

Derek stared at him for a moment, then stubbornly went back to pulling on the chain. Landon did the same, though he knew it wasn't going to help.

"Get the fuck out of the way!" someone growled behind them.

Landon turned, expecting to see Trevor, but it was Diaz—with frigging claws, fangs, and yellow glowing eyes.

"What the hell?" he mumbled.

"Later," Diaz said. "I could hear you two bitching and moaning from halfway across the compound. Let's get her out of here before we all roast."

Landon and Derek scrambled to make room for Diaz as the smallest guy on his former A-team grabbed the chain and heaved. The chain immediately started to pull away from the wall. Diaz snarled, growled, and heaved again—then ripped the damn thing out of the concrete wall.

Landon stared, wondering if the smoke had finally gotten to him because his mind was a completely confused mess. Derek must have had the same befuddled look on his face, because Diaz bared his long frigging teeth at them and growled.

"You want me to carry the woman too, or would you rather let her die from smoke inhalation?"

"I got her," Derek said. Without another word, he scooped up the sedated hybrid in his arms and headed for the exit through the flames and falling debris.

Diaz looked at Landon, his eyes slowly changing from glowing yellow to their normal brown. "You coming, Captain?"

---

Angelo was charging toward the big hybrid before he even saw Minka lying on the ground. He was already coming in fast, but when he saw the dark blood staining the ground beside her, anger made him run even faster.

The hybrid must have sensed him because it turned his way and growled, eyes going red and fangs growing long. But it was too late for the creature to do anything to stop Angelo. He rammed his shoulder solidly into the side of the hybrid's rib cage. The pistol went flying from its hand, and Angelo felt the creature's ribs crack from the impact. A few more gave way when he slammed the hybrid to the ground.

Angelo hoped the impact would stun the creature enough to allow him to stick his knife in it and kill the thing quickly. Unfortunately, the hybrid didn't seem bothered by a few busted-up ribs. He tossed Angelo aside like he weighed nothing.

A gunshot sounded nearby, but Angelo couldn't spare a second to even look in Minka's direction—everything was moving too fast.

He and the hybrid came up swinging. Angelo ducked the first few swipes the thing took at his face with those sharp claws, and jabbed with his knife. If he could kill the damn thing, great. But disabling the creature would work, too. He simply wanted to keep it away from Minka. Unfortunately, the same couldn't be said of the raging monster with the sharp teeth and claws—it was trying to rip off Angelo's head.

Another shot rang out, and this time, Angelo instinctively looked in Minka's direction. He had a fraction of a second to realize she was okay before the hybrid smashed into him and practically caved in his chest.

Everything went fuzzy as he hit the ground. Pain exploded through his entire body, especially at the center of his back, which had come down on something particularly hard and unyielding.

Angelo tried to get air into his lungs, but they didn't seem to work. He opened his eyes to see the hybrid pulling a clawed hand back to tear out his throat. And there wasn't a whole lot Angelo could do to stop him. But he sure as hell wasn't going down without a fight, not with Minka struggling for her life a few feet away.

So he did the only thing he could think of. He lunged upward with his knife just as the hybrid's clawed hand came down. They met in the middle, Angelo's left shoulder absorbing most of the impact of its claws while his blade found its way deep into its gut.

The creature roared and plucked out the knife, flinging it aside.

Angelo rolled to the right, both to gather himself for a last-ditch punch and to get off of whatever the hell he was lying on. He reached behind his back, expecting to find a rock, but instead came up with something much more familiar and useful—a gun.

The big hybrid's eyes widened in alarm. It tried to rake Angelo with its claws, but it was too late. Angelo squeezed the trigger and put two rounds through the thing's heart at point-blank range, then another under its jaw, just in case. He would have shot the thing a couple more times, but the gun was out of bullets.

Angelo rolled over, stumbling to his feet as he searched for Minka. What he saw made his heart nearly stop.

*Fuck.*

Minka closed the distance between her and the doctor in a single lunge. Renard pulled the trigger on the gun in his hand, but she was too fast, and the round missed her completely. She hit Renard, driving him backward and slamming him to the ground. Then she swiped at the hand wrapped around the pistol, her claws digging in deep and knocking the weapon aside.

Now that she'd disarmed Renard, Minka screamed at the beast to help Angelo, but the beast was completely in charge now. As Renard tried to take a swing at her, she casually batted the hand away, playing with him. Minka darted her head closer to Renard, showing off the long fangs she was going to use to tear him apart. Renard stared up at her wide-eyed, in fear, as if he knew he was about to die at the hands of the monster he'd helped make.

And all Minka could do was watch.

Gunshots rang out nearby, distracting the beast for a moment, but not long. She leaned forward, her fangs centimeters from Renard's neck.

"Minka, stop!"

She latched on to Angelo's voice like a lifeline, using it to give her the leverage she needed to turn her head and look at him. The beast snarled at the interruption, fighting her for control, but Minka refused to give it back.

Angelo was kneeling beside her, a look of concern on his face. She tried to tell him that she needed his help to regain control, but no words came out. While Minka never wanted Renard to hurt anyone ever again, she didn't want it to be like this. She didn't want the beast in charge of her body, using her hands to kill while she was forced to watch helplessly.

Angelo moved closer, and Minka knew it would be okay once he wrapped his arms around her. He would make the beast go away.

But he didn't touch her. "Minka, I know you don't want to do this. You don't want the animal inside you running your life, taking over like this. But you have to be the one to fight this battle. I know you can do it. But you need to know it, too."

Minka began to panic. Why did her angel not simply hold her like he always had and make this all stop? Then she looked in his face and saw the love and concern there—and she knew the answer.

Angelo would be leaving soon. He wanted her to learn how to do this on her own because he wouldn't always be there for her.

Minka's heart tore a little more with that realization. But she couldn't think of that now. So she pushed her fear and pain aside, forcing herself to relax and imagine the door of the cage like Tanner had taught her. But when the image appeared, Minka was shocked to realize the door was closed…with her inside.

The beast had trapped her in the cage of her own making, and as she shoved against the door, the beast shoved back, fighting her for control. The beast was going to take over, and she'd be trapped in this cage in her own head forever.

Then she felt Angelo's hand holding hers there in the darkness. The warmth and love coming from that contact felt so very real. This was the anchor Tanner had described to her, the thing that would keep her calm and always lead her back to herself.

Minka kicked the door of the cage over and over until

she saw the bars bend. Then she shoved against the door, pushing it open.

The big, dark cat she had come to associate with the beast was waiting outside. She knew this was a fight she had to win if she wished to be truly free of the rage inside her, but this wasn't a battle she could win with rage and anger. The beast was a part of her. She needed it to survive, and it needed her.

Minka slowly approached the big cat. It snarled and reared up before her. She placed her hand against the animal's chest, feeling the rage and heat pound against her palm, but she was no longer terrified of it.

When Minka opened her eyes, the darkness of the surrounding night let her know her eyes had returned to normal. She looked over and saw Angelo still kneeling beside her, his face etched with worry. She let her eyes shift, so she could see him better.

Angelo smiled and reached out to gently pull her off Renard and move her to the side, a few meters away from the doctor.

"Don't fucking move," Angelo ordered the man.

Tears trickling down her cheeks, Minka wrapped her arms around Angelo, squeezing him tightly and wishing she never had to let him go. "You saved me."

Angelo pulled back enough to look at her. "No, you saved yourself. That was a fight you had to have with the beast, and you won."

Minka would have argued with him, but right then Ivy jogged into the clearing. She eyed Renard, then put an arm around Minka.

"Are you okay?" she asked.

Minka nodded. She couldn't describe the feeling of

closeness that now existed between her and Ivy, but a part of her thought it must have been what it was like to have a sister.

A noise in the gravel caught Minka's attention, and she turned to see Renard trying to reach for the gun Minka had knocked out of his hand earlier. Ivy was on the man before he even got close to it, flipping him over and growling at him.

"Don't make me chase you," Ivy snarled. "Your buddy Klaus did that, and it didn't work out too well for him. He died of a heart attack just as the chase was getting interesting."

Renard's eyes widened, and he held up his hands in surrender. "Okay, okay. I give up!" He swallowed hard, his gaze darting from Ivy to Minka and Angelo, then back to Ivy again. "Please don't kill me. I'll do whatever you want. I'll tell you anything you want to know about Klaus and his hybrid research—anything you want, just don't kill me."

Ivy's eyes narrowed. "Tell me about Thomas Thorn and his connection to Keegan Stutmeir."

"Shouldn't we wait until we get everyone else together before we start questioning him?" Angelo interrupted.

Ivy shook her head. "No. I want to hear what he has to say now—before Powell and Moore show up."

Renard looked confused for a moment but then started talking, speaking so fast that Minka could barely keep up as Renard told them how Thorn had funded Stutmeir and his efforts to create man-made shifters for more than four years, and how he'd continued funding the hybrid work after Stutmeir's death.

"Klaus communicated with him constantly," Renard

said. "Thorn sent him detailed orders on where he wanted us to focus our efforts. He made Klaus and me very rich men in return for us creating a serum that would give him an army of hybrids."

Ivy's eyes narrowed. "Someone would have figured out they were different from other soldiers the first time he used them."

"That's what we tried to tell him," Renard said. "But he didn't care. He wanted us to hurry up and perfect the serum, and when we were too slow, he threatened us. That's why Klaus found us another backer for our work."

"Who was it?" Ivy asked.

Renard shook his head. "I don't know the person's name. Klaus told me that it was someone else on the DCO Committee. All I cared about were the new hybrid protocols that were provided to us."

"When did you start working for this new person?" Ivy asked.

"In December."

Ivy glanced at Angelo, her green eyes glinting. "That's right after we destroyed the hybrid lab down in Costa Rica. Whoever this other person on the Committee is, they must have decided they didn't want to start from scratch."

"So they tracked down Klaus and Renard and bought them off, then turned over all the research from Costa Rica to them," Angelo added.

"And it worked," Renard said. "We blended their work with our process and came up with the perfect hybrid/shifter blend." He gestured to the dead hybrid on the ground a few feet away. "They possess all of the strengths of a shifter with none of the control issues of our previous hybrid strains."

Minka felt sick at the gloating tone in Renard's voice. How many people had died in horrible pain so he and Klaus and whomever they'd worked for could create their perfect hybrid/shifter blend? Renard had probably never even bothered to count.

"Where are all these detailed reports and communications you had with Thorn and this new person?" Ivy asked Renard.

He pointed at a big research building several hundred meters away engulfed in flames. "In a mainframe computer in the lab—or what's left of it."

Ivy turned to see where he was pointing. Then her eyes went wide. "Oh God. Derek and the hybrids are in there." She threw Angelo a quick look. "Bring Renard."

Then she was gone, racing across the smoke- and fire-filled compound so fast she was almost a blur.

"What the hell did she mean?" Renard asked. "Bring me where?"

Angelo snorted as he pulled Renard to his feet. "Back to Washington, DC, so you can finger Thorn and send him to prison—or wherever they send psychos like him."

"You can't!" Renard protested, trying to pull free. "I won't last five minutes once Thorn knows where to find me. I'm not going."

"I wasn't asking," Angelo said.

Renard swore, yanking his arm away and giving Angelo a panicked shove. Before Minka knew it, the doctor was running. He had to have known he could never get away from them. Then she saw the pistol lying on the ground. Renard wasn't combat trained like Angelo, but he had a head start. He would reach the gun before Angelo could stop him.

Minka was moving before she realized what she was doing, her body instinctively responding. She had to get to Renard before he made it to that pistol.

~~~

"How long have you…?"

Landon let his voice trail off as he and Diaz watched Derek slowly come to the realization that he wasn't going to be able to save any of the unconscious hybrids Landon had carried out of the burning building. Three of them had been dead by the time Landon and the others had gotten out there with the sedated female, but Derek had really thought they had a shot at pulling the last one back from the brink.

Landon had finally reached Ivy on the radio a few moments ago, telling her where they were and asking for an update. Before that, he and Diaz had helped Derek, taking turns giving CPR to the frail, broken creature and doing everything the medic told them. But there was nothing any of them could do that could repair the damage the young man had endured. He and Diaz knew that already, but Derek was still leaning over the body with fingers pressed to the creature's throat, trying to find a pulse that wasn't there.

Diaz stared down at the ground. "How long have I been turning into a monster you mean? It started right after getting bitten by that hybrid in Washington State. That damn thing infected me."

Landon frowned. He remembered Diaz getting bitten in the fight. "You can't turn into a hybrid by getting bitten, Diaz. Trust me on that one."

Diaz shrugged. "Apparently you can, because I sure

as hell wasn't like this until that hybrid took a chunk out of me."

"If that's the case, why do your eyes glow yellow like a shifter, instead of red like a hybrid?" Landon asked.

A muscle in Diaz's jaw flexed, but he didn't respond. "It's not exactly something I've taken the time to study."

Landon put a hand on his shoulder. "There are some people at the DCO who can probably tell you what's going on."

Diaz pulled away and shook his head violently. "No fucking way. I'm a Special Forces soldier to the core. I don't want to get mixed up with that freaky shit of yours. And if they find out I'm a hybrid, that's where I'll end up. I don't want to work in an organization where I have to worry about my partner shooting me in the back or scientists cutting me open to see what makes me tick. You can't ever tell a soul about this."

"I won't, and neither will Derek," Landon promised. "But it's going to be hard to hide it for long. Ivy will figure it out at some point when she picks up your scent—if she hasn't already. Sooner or later, someone else will figure it out, too."

"I'll take later then." Diaz gave him a pointed look. "And in the meantime, I'm going to stay as far away from Ivy as I can."

Derek pulled his hand away from the hybrid's throat and came over to sit down on the ground beside them. He looked really tired.

"They never had a chance," he said softly. "Too much internal damage from all the crap the doctors pumped into them, I guess." Derek glanced at the female hybrid lying on the jacket he'd spread out on

the ground a few feet away. "What's going to happen
to her?" he asked.

Landon followed his gaze. He didn't know why, but
the woman looked familiar. It was almost like he'd seen
her before. "Ivy and I will take care of her, and so will
Zarina, Layla, and Tanner. We'll make sure she's safe."

Derek nodded and looked like he would have said
more when Diaz's head jerked up.

"Ivy's coming."

---

Angelo swore as he stumbled back, stunned the gutless,
piece of shit doctor had actually caught him off guard. If
the guy thought he could outrun Angelo, he was stupid
as well as a coward. But then Angelo saw the pistol on
the ground.

*Shit.*

He was already praying Renard was a bad shot when
a blur of movement flew past him.

Minka hit Renard just as the man rolled over and
lifted the weapon. She didn't make a sound as she raked
him with her claws and tore open his throat, letting
momentum carry her over him. She hit the ground and
did a perfect tuck and roll before coming to a stop and
spinning back around in a balanced crouch.

She'd moved so damn fast, Angelo feared the beast
had resumed control again, but the moment Minka spun
around, he saw that her eyes were bright green, not red.
As he watched, the vivid glow faded, replaced by her
natural dark eye color, and her claws retracted.

Even though he knew Renard had to be dead, Angelo
hurried over to Minka, just in case. One look at the

doctor was enough to assure Angelo the guy wasn't going to be experimenting on anyone ever again.

He pulled Minka into his arms. "I'm sorry you had to do that."

"So am I," she said, the words muffled against his chest. "But at least it was me doing it for the right reasons, and not the beast doing it for the wrong ones. I can live with that."

They held each other for a few more minutes until Angelo remembered the bullet Minka had taken in the hip. He pulled away to see how bad it was, but it had already closed up and stopped bleeding. He couldn't believe she could heal so fast.

Angelo gently smoothed back the hair that had come loose from her braid. "Why didn't you stay up on the hill, where it was safe?"

"Because I saw the hybrids," she said. "I was worried about you."

He closed his eyes for a moment, then bent to rest his forehead against hers. "We should probably go tell Ivy and Landon about Renard."

Minka nodded. "I doubt they'll be very happy."

At that moment, Angelo wasn't too worried about that. Minka was safe and in control of herself. The sick fucks who had tormented her were dead, and it appeared that all their research had gone up in flames. He was just a soldier and couldn't give a shit about all the covert crap; in his opinion, the night had ended exactly the way it should have.

---

Angelo and Minka found Ivy huddled over the body of the female hybrid. He worried at first that the hybrid was dead like the others, but then he saw her chest slowly rising and falling. Derek was kneeling beside the hybrid, tending a wound around the woman's ankle. Diaz and Landon were standing to one side, watching.

Ivy lifted her head as Angelo and Minka moved closer. Her eyes darted behind them, then back again, clearly looking for Renard.

"He tried to get away," Angelo said before she could ask. "He left Minka no choice."

Angelo expected Ivy to be pissed, but instead, her expression softened as she stood and walked over to them. "You okay?" she asked Minka.

Minka nodded. "Yes. The bullet went right through, and my hip doesn't hurt at all now."

Ivy gave her a small smile. "That's not what I meant."

Minka looked down at the ground. "I would have preferred if I hadn't had to kill Renard. I know you were hoping he'd help you put Thomas Thorn in prison, but I didn't have a choice. He was going to shoot Angelo."

Ivy sighed and pulled Minka in for a hug. Minka wrapped her arms around Ivy and squeezed her tight. Angelo heard a few sniffles but chose to ignore them. The other guys were smart enough to do the same.

"I'm just glad you're still you," Ivy said when she stepped back. "That's more important to me than anything else."

Minka smiled and reached up to wipe the tears from her cheeks.

"I'm sorry I let you face Renard and that hybrid alone," Ivy said. "I thought Klaus was trying to get around you to attack you from behind, and by the time

I figured out he was leading me away from you, it was too late to get back to help."

"It's okay." Minka glanced at Angelo, then reached out to take his hand. "Angelo got there in time."

He started to give her a smile when the sound of footsteps made him stiffen. He looked up to see Trevor, Watson, Powell, and Moore coming toward them across the smoky, fire-ravaged compound.

"We almost got overrun by the last of the hybrids," Trevor said as he and the other guys came over. "We would have been screwed if Powell and Moore hadn't shown up."

Angelo eyed the two men. It was obvious from the claw marks on their uniforms and tactical vests that they'd been in the thick of things. "What happened to the two of you out there?"

Powell shrugged. "We got pinned down by some guards, then a handful of those damn hybrids showed up. Next thing we know, the frigging ammo storage blew up. Luckily, the flames took down most of the hybrids. Otherwise, we'd be dead."

Moore glanced at the bodies on the ground, paying special attention to the sedated female hybrid. "Did you find the doctors?"

"Yes," Ivy said. "But Klaus had a heart attack while I was trying to run him down, and Minka was forced to kill Renard when he pulled a weapon."

Powell and Moore exchanged looks.

"Heart attack, huh?" Powell said, glancing at Ivy. "That's too bad. I'm sure Thorn would rather we'd brought them back alive."

Ivy shrugged. "We tried. I'm sure he'll understand."

"I'm sure he will."

Giving Ivy a nod, Powell and Moore walked over to check on Derek and the hybrid.

"You believe their story?" Landon asked softly after the two men had moved out of earshot.

Trevor snorted. "Oh, I'm sure they got into it with some guards and a few hybrids. There were so many running around here, it would have been impossible not to. But I have no fucking doubt they blew the ammo point and fuel dump themselves. Those places were demoed in such a way to scatter flaming debris everywhere and burn this whole place down, which is probably what Thorn and Dick sent them here to do."

"Do you think there's anything on those hard drives you grabbed?" Landon asked.

Trevor shrugged. "Don't know. I guess we'll find out soon enough."

"I hope so," Ivy said. "Because with both Renard and Klaus dead—and yes, Klaus really did die from a heart attack—we've got nothing else on Thorn except what Renard told us about his involvement. And his statements won't mean much in a court of law."

Landon nodded, then turned and looked around at all the chaos filling the area. "Diaz, Trevor, let's get a makeshift litter put together for the injured hybrid, then let's get the hell out of here."

Beside Angelo, Minka took a step closer to him. "I guess the mission is over now, right?"

He nodded and slipped an arm around her shoulders, pulling her to his side. If Watson noticed, he didn't let on.

Minka wrapped her arm around Angelo's waist,

resting her head against his chest. She didn't say any-thing, but he knew what she was thinking. In a few hours, she would be getting back on a bird for the States, and he'd go with his team to their base camp in northern Afghanistan. Hell, for all he knew, they might come right back here to Tajikistan. Either way, he and Minka were going to have to say good-bye.

The thought scared the hell out of him.

# Chapter 17

MINKA TRIED HARD TO HOLD BACK TEARS AS SHE boarded the Osprey with Angelo. They found two seats in the back. It was as close to privacy as they could get on the small aircraft. Everyone must have known they needed some time together because they all sat up front. The thump of the rotors made talking almost impossible, but there wasn't really anything to say anyway. Mostly because she and Angelo had said what they needed to while the crew had prepared the aircraft for takeoff.

"When we get to Bagram, I'm going to have to go with my team," Angelo had said. "But I'll be coming off this deployment in a month or two. I have a lot of leave time saved up, and I'm going to spend every minute of it with you. If you want me to, I mean."

"Of course I want you to," she'd said, but on the inside, she didn't know how it was going to work. She couldn't imagine living without Angelo by her side, but that simply was not a possibility. Angelo wasn't only a soldier; he was Special Forces, which meant he deployed—a lot.

So she'd nodded as he talked about his current enlistment and possible options after that, like getting out of the army. But those things would be years from now, and with the way her heart was breaking at the thought of being separated from him for just a few weeks, it all seemed so far away.

But she put up a good front because that was what she knew Angelo needed.

Minka leaned her head against his shoulder as the aircraft took off. She was tired and her eyes felt heavy. The physical fighting, as well as the internal fight she'd had with the beast, had taken a lot out of her. But she didn't want to waste this time with Angelo sleeping. So she held his hand and stayed awake the whole trip back. And if she let out a few tears, she made sure he didn't see them.

—⁂—

By the time they got back to the air base in Bagram, Angelo knew that Minka was barely holding it together. But what could he do? He had to go back with his team. Watson and the rest of the A-team had been completely out of contact with the battalion for almost two days, and he'd been gone for over a week. If he knew Major Bennett, the man would be waiting for them the moment they stepped off the aircraft.

At best, he and the others would be heading back out to Tajikistan. At worst, they'd be going back to a Commander's Inquiry on why their team had been involved in an unauthorized combat operation in a friendly nation. Either way, he probably wouldn't have much of a chance to say good-bye to Minka after they stepped onto the tarmac.

He and Minka waited until everyone else but the crew chief had left. The man pointedly ignored them, going about his business of conducting ground checks as if they weren't there.

Turning in his seat, Angelo carefully cupped Minka's

cheek and kissed her. "I love you, Minka," he said softly.
"I'm coming back to you, I promise. You just need to
hold on for a little while. Can you do that?"

Tears filled her eyes, but she nodded, and he liked to
think she was happy. "Yes, I can hold on and wait for
you. Because I love you, too."

He couldn't believe how amazing those simple words
made him feel. God, he wished they could stay there,
just like that, but if he was right about Bennett—or
anyone else from the battalion waiting for him—it
would be better to go out and meet them on the flight
line. Forcing them to come inside and get him would
only make things worse.

Giving Minka another kiss, he stood up and offered
his hand to her. She wiped away her tears, then took his
hand and rose gracefully to her feet. Even after getting
shot in the hip, she moved like a dancer—or a cat. That
would be a better way to put it.

Outside, they joined Landon and Ivy, then walked
around the aircraft toward the row of buildings that lined
the runway. Sure enough, Major Bennett was there,
standing beside a somber-looking Lieutenant Watson
and the rest of the team. Bennett gave Angelo a disap-
proving look, but that expression paled in comparison to
the one he directed at Landon.

"Homeland Security invading foreign countries these
days, Captain?" Bennett asked, then held up his hand.
"Don't answer that. I don't want to know." He eyed
Minka and Ivy next, no doubt wondering what they
were doing with members of his A-team. He opened his
mouth as if he was going to ask, then shook his head. "I
don't want to know about them, either."

Bennett held out a thick envelope to Angelo. "I don't have a clue why the hell this keeps happening, Sergeant Rios, but you've been transferred to Homeland Security. Can't say I'm shocked, but I am disappointed." He scowled at Watson. "By the way, Lieutenant, your promotion orders to Captain are waiting for you back at the S1 shop. Maybe as your first official act as the new captain and commander of this fucked-up A-team, you can try to hold on to the rest of your troops before the fucking DHS takes them all."

Giving Watson a nod, the major turned and strode off.

Angelo stared at the envelope in his hand. He didn't have to open it to know what was in it. Ten copies of his transfer orders, an out-processing form already completed by someone in the admin section, and a copy of his close-out performance evaluation report—the last eval he'd be getting with the 5th Special Forces Group, at least for now.

He was still wrapping his mind around that when the guys gathered around him, clapping him on the back and congratulating him. He didn't know what they were congratulating him for. His head was spinning so fast, he couldn't keep up.

Less than a minute later, Watson herded the guys away, saying he had to get them back to the battalion for another ops brief. The next thing Angelo knew, he was standing with Ivy, Landon, and Minka.

"What the hell just happened?" he finally asked.

Landon grinned. "Obviously, John must think you'd be a good addition to the DCO, as Minka's partner I'm guessing. And when John wants something, he usually gets it. You're moving to DC, man, to be part of the covert crap you hate so much."

"What do you mean, 'partner'?" Minka asked, looking excited and a little scared at the same time. "I love the idea of being Angelo's partner, but I can't go out and kill people all the time."

Ivy smiled. "John isn't like that, Minka. He would never ask you to do something that isn't in your nature. He's very good at finding what people and teams are good at and having them do that for the DCO. There are lots of jobs that don't require killing people. Conducting surveillance, reconnaissance operations, tracking down kidnap victims—the list is almost endless."

Minka turned to look at Angelo, the excitement in her eyes quickly outpacing the fear. "Is this really happening?"

He nodded, his heart pounding as the revelation grew that his life, and Minka's, had suddenly taken a complete 180-degree turn. "I think it is."

Minka bit her lip. "And you are okay with this? I know how close you are with your teammates. Will you be okay leaving them?"

Angelo considered that. In some ways, he felt like he was turning his back on his team, on the army, on everything he'd been for the entirety of his adult life. But one look at Minka's face told him it was what he needed to do. A thought suddenly hit him then, putting everything into perspective. If his father had been given an opportunity like this fifteen years ago, would he have taken it? And if he had, would his mom still be alive?

He smiled down at Minka, knowing in his heart he was never going to regret doing this for her. "I'm very okay with it."

Minka laughed and threw her arms around his neck. Angelo hugged her back. If anyone was looking at them, they were probably wondering what the heck was going on out there, but right then all Angelo cared about was the fact that Minka was happy. And so was he.

She suddenly stepped back to give him a confused look. "Does this mean we'll be staying at Landon's apartment?"

Ivy laughed and put her arm around Minka's shoulders, turning to lead her toward the military passenger terminal where they'd be getting a flight to the States.

"You're going to find this out soon enough, but people like us get paid better than trigger pullers like Landon and Angelo." Ivy threw a grin their way. "So no, you won't be staying at Landon's small apartment because you'll be able to afford a much nicer one."

Angelo couldn't help but chuckle as Minka's eyes widened. "I'm going to get paid? Will I be able to buy one of those iPod music boxes, too?"

"Yes, you can buy an iPod if you want," Ivy said. "You can even buy two, so Angelo can have his own."

"That would be silly," Minka said. "Angelo can just listen to mine anytime he wants since we'll be living together."

Angelo only half listened as Landon reminded them about the DCO's no-fraternization policy and how he and Minka would need to keep their relationship a secret. Ultimately, he didn't care what games he had to play to keep Minka at his side. That was where she was supposed to be, and that was all that mattered.

—⁂—

Minka slowly rode up and down on Angelo's cock in their big, new bed. She was still getting used to that word—*cock*—and hadn't been able to say it out loud yet, but she thought she might soon. She was getting very comfortable making love with Angelo and was very eager to learn everything there was to know about sex. Right then, he was showing her how much fun they could have making slow, gentle love. He was buried deep inside her, and she was rotating her hips in small, tight circles, which created an absolutely magical sensation between the folds of her pussy—another new word for her.

Angelo had a firm grip on her bottom and refused to let her move any faster. It was torturous, especially since she could have orgasmed in ten seconds if he'd just let her. But he liked to tease her, and she liked to let him.

The past several weeks since learning they would be a team had been amazing. First, before coming back to the States, they'd taken a few days to stop by and visit her parents. It had been a complete surprise to her, but Angelo had insisted.

"They need to know you're okay," he'd told her.

Her parents had been in tears when she and Angelo showed up at the door. She'd given them a very abbreviated version of what had happened, only saying she'd been kidnapped by evil men and that Angelo had rescued her. The most important part was that Angelo had saved her life and that they were in love. When she'd explained she'd be working with him in the United States at a very good job and have her own apartment, her mother had been tearful but happy. Her father, on the other hand, had bluntly asked Angelo if he loved Minka. When Angelo said he did, her father had just as pointedly asked if Angelo intended to marry her. Both Minka and her mother had been mortified, but Angelo only smiled.

"Yes, I do," he said. "As soon as she'll have me. But she's a strong woman. She'll only marry me when she wants to."

Her father had laughed at that and brought out the vodka.

After coming back to Washington, DC, they'd found this beautiful apartment. Minka still could not believe she had enough money to live in a place like this. Even better, John had arranged it so Angelo could officially live here too, even though they had to maintain a silly story about him sleeping in the spare bedroom and that he was only living there so he could help her maintain control over her hybrid nature.

They were still working with John regarding exactly what kind of work they would be doing at the DCO. At that moment, everything was leaning toward training them to be a search-and-recon team. They would go all over the world, finding people in trouble and figuring out what kind of extra DCO resources would be needed to help them out. This was work Minka honestly felt she and Angelo could do.

She leaned forward and kissed Angelo, boldly finding his tongue with hers. She had to focus to keep her fangs from slipping out and nicking him. He never complained, but it was something she wanted to work on. She enjoyed kissing him and didn't want anything getting in the way of that.

Angelo slid one hand into her hair, weaving his fingers in and tugging a little as his other hand gripped her bottom. *Mmm*. That felt so good—especially when he thrust into her at the same time. Angelo had already proven to her many times over that her climax was always more intense when she let it build for a while.

Angelo was getting close, too. She could tell from the thundering beat of his heart and his quick, deep thrusts. She loved making him come hard, thrilled she could make him feel as good as he did her.

Angelo's gaze locked with hers, and she knew her eyes were glowing green. Minka couldn't begin to tell him how much she appreciated the fact that it didn't bother him.

She purred as she felt the first tingles of orgasm deep inside her, in that place where her beast resided. Now that she'd come to accept that part of herself and could control it, she didn't mind when the beast shared in her pleasure. They were two parts, living as one. Neither could live without the other, and now, she would never dream of denying the beast this happiness.

Minka circled her hips faster, like she did when she was dancing. Angelo groaned, his dark eyes turning molten. He liked when she did that. He called her his little feline belly dancer.

As the sensations grew stronger and Angelo's grip on her bottom tightened, Minka pressed her lips to his ear. "I love you. Forever."

Those words always sent her angel over the edge. With a hoarse groan, he plunged deep into her, bringing her to climax. She yowled and threw her head back as she came. He yanked her more tightly against him, and she splayed her hands on his chest, panting for breath. Her claws were out now, but she was careful not to sink them into his muscles. Even during climax, she was able to maintain enough control for that.

When the last whispers of her orgasm had faded away, she collapsed against him and lay there gasping, enjoying the pleasant tremors that rippled through her.

Angelo licked her neck, nipping and kissing there. "I love you, too. You know that, don't you?"

Minka pushed herself up on her hands and smiled at him. "I know. And I'll never forget."

# Epilogue

JOHN CHECKED HIS REARVIEW MIRROR AS HE DROVE along Highway 123 toward his home near Tyson's Corner. He didn't expect anyone to be following him, but lately, he'd gotten the feeling that something was off. Then again, spying on the Committee and uncovering secrets would make anyone paranoid.

Unfortunately, Landon and Ivy hadn't been able to hand him a smoking gun to put Thomas Thorn away for the rest of his life, but they'd definitely confirmed a lot of John's suspicions. Thanks to the information Renard gave them, he now knew for a fact that Thorn had funded Keegan Stutmeir and the hybrid program, albeit without proof, of course. But it was just a matter of time before they found the evidence they needed.

The mission to Tajikistan had also confirmed there was a second player in the hybrid game. The hard drives Trevor had taken showed that someone on the Committee had provided Klaus with technical information on the Costa Rican hybrid strain. If John had to guess, he'd say it was Rebecca Brannon or Xavier Danes.

John turned down the main road toward the high-rise complex where he lived. The third thing the Tajikistan mission had clarified was the hybrid family tree. They'd thought the different hybrids were part of the same group, but now they knew differently. The hybrids Stutmeir had created—the ones John liked to think of as the first generation—were all dead, except for Tanner. The Costa Rican variants—the second-generation hybrids—were almost all gone too, except for a few that might have escaped into the jungle. Of course, there was a distinct possibility that whoever was behind the operation in Central America still had the formula for that variant. Only time would tell on that.

Then, there was the third-generation hybrid/shifter blend made from Ivy's DNA. There was Minka, the unidentified woman Landon had brought back with them, and the unidentified male who'd gotten away. John had people out looking for the man, but Tajikistan was a rough country, and it might take a while to find him—if he was even still alive.

Finally, there were the fourth-generation variants Landon and the rest of the team had fought in Tajikistan. Zarina thought they were probably a blend of the second- and third-generation hybrids. He'd sent in another team to scout out the area to look for survivors, but they hadn't found any. That still worried the hell out of John. With the control they'd demonstrated, the creatures would be seriously dangerous if someone could find the formula and create more of them. But Klaus and Renard were dead, so hopefully their research had died with them.

John pulled into the private parking garage of his apartment complex, nodded at the security guard, then got on the elevator. He had to swipe a card through a reader, enter in a six-digit pin number, then stand in the middle of the car for a visual ID scan. That was the only way to get the elevator to take him to the top floor.

As he stepped out of the elevator, the big, muscular

man sitting behind the desk outside John's front door
looked up. John hated the idea of having a guard at his
apartment, but if he had to have one, he was glad it was
Morgan Gerard. John had no idea what kind of animal
DNA Morgan had, but whatever it was, it made him
strong as hell and patient as the day is long. Morgan
was what Adam called a "hidden shifter," a person who
had some kind of animal DNA mixed with his own but
not necessarily the type that would make him useful as
a weapon to the DCO. Shifters like Morgan existed in
the shadows, never showing up on the DCO's radar,
which was exactly the way Adam and these low-level
shifters liked it.

Morgan nodded in his direction, then went back to his
book. From his appearance, people tended to think the
big man was some kind of dumb jock, but one look at
the cover of the quantum physics book he was reading
would tell anyone that wasn't the case.

John opened his door and walked into the large, beau-
tifully decorated penthouse apartment. He was about to
call out that he was home when a little girl came running into the living room, her long, shiny hair streaming
behind her. John bent down and scooped her up, spinning around in a circle.

"Daddy's home!" She giggled.

"How's my Boo?" he asked, kissing her on the cheek
and making her laugh even more. Boo wasn't really her
name, but after seeing *Monsters, Inc.* a few years ago,
she'd decided she liked the name more than she did her
own. And his eight-year-old daughter could be very
forceful when it came to getting what she wanted. Just
like her mother.

John turned to see Cree coming out of the kitchen, her dark, wavy hair down around her mocha-skinned shoulders, her sometimes blue—sometimes gray eyes twinkling. God, he didn't know how she did it, but somehow, his shifter wife looked more beautiful every day.

"Good day at the office?" she asked with a smile as she kissed him.

He nodded. "I'll tell you all about it later."

She opened her mouth to say something, but Boo interrupted.

"Daddy, Uncle Adam came to visit. He's been making me laugh at all the funny faces he can do."

John glanced at Cree. "Adam makes funny faces?"

He honestly couldn't see the former assassin playing peekaboo with his daughter. But then again, he rarely ever saw the man smile, so what the hell did he know?

Cree smiled. "I guess. He's waiting in the office." She gave Boo a kiss. "Want to hang out with Milan for a while before dinner?"

John looked over to see the slender, incredibly graceful woman coming to stand near the island that separated the kitchen from the living room. She'd moved so quietly, he hadn't even heard her. A hidden shifter like Morgan, Adam's pretty, dark-haired wife smiled as she came over.

She took Boo's hand as he set his daughter on her feet. "Come on, Boo. Let's go to your room and play with your dolls while your mommy and daddy talk to Uncle Adam."

"I stopped by and visited Jayson Harmon on the way home," John said as he and Cree crossed the living room to the home office. "You remember I told you about

him? The lieutenant from Landon's former Special
Forces A-team who's been recovering from injuries
he got in Afghanistan. I offered him a job at the DCO
weapons range."

Cree stopped to look at him in surprise. "So you're
going to put Layla in the field, then?"

John shook his head. "I didn't say that. I told Layla
I'd allow her to train to be a field agent. She has a long
way to go before I'd even consider it. I offered him a
job because he's a good man who needs someone to
give him a chance. And he can more than handle the job.
He's qualified on nearly any weapon you can name, he
knows how to repair and maintain them, he's good with
explosives and tactics, and as a bonus, he already has a
top secret security clearance."

"Did he take the job?"

John nodded. It had been hard as hell convincing the
former soldier that it wasn't some kind of pity offering
because of his connection to Landon and Layla. "It took
some persuading, but in the end, he took it. The man's
got a lot of pride, but he's not stupid. He knows a good
deal when he hears it."

"And how do you think he'll handle it when he discovers the DCO employs genetically enhanced humans
and that his girlfriend is one of them?" Cree asked.

John smiled. "Something tells me he's not going to
be that shocked."

Then, if and when Layla was ready to become a field
agent, hopefully he'd be able to team her up with Jayson.
He'd seen them together, and there was definitely a
spark. But Layla wasn't the only one who had a long
way to go before she'd be ready for field work; Jayson

did too, and John wasn't sure either of them was ever going to get there—or if they could even stay together long enough to make it that far.

Adam was seated in the leather wingback chair, gazing out at the setting sun, which reflected off his dark-blond hair and emphasized the angular planes of his face. He hadn't changed at all in the ten years John had known him, reminding him once again that he didn't have a clue how old Adam was.

John sat down in the chair opposite Adam. Cree perched on the arm and crossed her legs.

Adam turned to look at him with those unsettling eyes of his that had taken John a long time to get used to. A combination of orange and yellow, his pupils were partially slitted. He blinked, his eyes shifting back to their normal hazel green. "Did you find anything on the hard drives they brought back from Tajikistan?"

John casually pulled Cree onto his lap, where she fit perfectly. "Nothing we can use to drag Thorn into court. On the good side, at least now we know what the facts are. We just have to keep digging in the right places to get solid evidence."

"We already have evidence." Adam regarded him with eyes that seemed even colder than usual. "Thorn is behind the hybrid program, and because of him, a lot of people have died—scientists and doctors he ordered kidnapped, homeless veterans in Atlanta, hikers and campers in Washington State his doctors experimented on, all those research subjects that Landon and Ivy found all over the world. They're all dead at his hands. What other evidence do you need? I can slip into that big, gaudy mansion of his and kill him in two minutes."

John clenched his jaw. He and Adam had already had this conversation. "We're not going to do that, and you know it."

"Why not?" Adam asked. "You act like the DCO doesn't kill people every day. Your operatives killed Klaus, Renard, and a slew of human guards and hybrids. What the hell makes Thorn any better than them? Why does he get to live while they all died?"

"He's not any better than them. He's ten times worse," John said. "There's a difference between killing a man who's pointing a gun at you and walking into his house in the dead of night and executing him."

Adam regarded him coldly. "And you're saying the DCO hasn't done exactly that before as well?"

"Dammit, you know we have. And you also know how extreme the circumstances have to be before I ever authorize something like that," John continued before Adam could interrupt. "There must be a clear indication that significant lives will be lost and that there's no other alternative."

Adam swore, his eyes flashing color. He had good reason to hate Thorn. "You don't think more people are going to die because of Thorn?"

"They very well might," John agreed. "But saying they might isn't enough to justify an execution."

Adam's eyes returned to their usual icy coolness, but he didn't say anything.

John sighed. "You knew this was the way it was going to be ten years ago when you and I agreed to work together to figure out which member of the Committee was abusing their position and using the DCO for their own purposes. All along, the plan was to put that person

in prison, not kill them. Just because we've finally figured out that Thorn is that person doesn't mean anything
has changed. You said you were comfortable following
my lead on this. Have you changed your mind?"

Adam stared out the window for a long time before
answering, his jaw clenching. "No."

John had to stop from letting out another sigh,
this time in relief. Adam was a good man, but he was
also dangerous as hell, and it would be stupid to ever
forget that.

"So we go back to digging through email servers or
hoping one of Thorn's people makes a mistake and leaks
something incriminating," Adam said, turning his head
to look at John again. "We've been waiting for that to
happen for years. What makes you think anything will
be different now?"

John smiled. "Because now we know exactly what
we're looking for."

Adam lifted a brow. "We do?"

"We do," John said. "Renard told Ivy that Klaus
had every single communication with Thorn saved on
a computer in a research building that burned down—
orders from Thorn, money transfers, research data, status
updates on every success and every failure. I'm betting
Thorn has that same information saved somewhere, too.
All we need to do is find it."

He expected Adam to take a shot at his logic, but the
shifter simply regarded him for a long time in silence
before finally nodding. "A man like Thorn would
want to keep information like that somewhere close
by," Adam said. "That means his home or his office
at Chadwick-Thorn. Are you seriously considering

trying to slip one of your people into Thorn's office or private residence?"

"I won't have to," John said. "Not if Thorn invites them in."

"Ivy and Landon?" Cree frowned. "You think he trusts them that much."

John nodded. "It's one of the unexpected benefits of Klaus and Renard ending up dead. Thorn assumes Ivy and Landon manipulated events to make it happen on his orders. He's already invited them over for another meeting at his corporate office. If we get lucky, they'll have the freedom to move around Chadwick-Thorn on their own. From there, who knows?"

Adam considered that. "Are you sure you want to put them in that kind of situation? If Thorn or Frasier get even a whiff that Ivy and Landon are up to something, they're dead. And if he realizes they're following your orders, you'll be next—or someone you love will be."

John looked at Cree. She looked right back at him.

"I know," he said. "Ivy and Landon will be careful. Besides, it's not like I have anyone better to send in after Thorn and his secrets."

Even Adam couldn't argue with that. He glanced at his watch, then got to his feet. "I need to be going."

"I thought you and Milan were going to stay for dinner," Cree said.

Adam grabbed his overcoat from the back of the chair and shrugged into it. "I'll be back by then, but I have some other business I need to take care of first."

Adam didn't volunteer what that business might be, and John didn't ask. Their friendship was based on a strong foundation of letting the other person keep his own secrets. John knew that whatever Adam was up to, it almost certainly had to do with taking down Thorn or keeping an eye on something else related to the DCO.

Milan came out of Boo's room as they walked into the living room. Adam whispered something to Milan that John couldn't hear, then smiled and leaned close, his forehead almost touching hers. There was something about the quiet, graceful woman that brought out a different side in the former assassin.

Adam gave Milan a quick kiss, then a nod in John's direction before letting himself out. Milan motioned that she'd be back in Boo's bedroom, then disappeared down the hallway.

Cree turned and looked at John. The heat in her eyes was unmistakable, and he felt an answering warmth gathering somewhere just below his belt. It made him realize how long it had been since they'd had a chance to spend some alone time together. Days off were in short supply for a person in his position.

"Dinner won't be done for another hour," she said. "And Milan is watching Boo."

John grinned.

Taking his hand, Cree turned and led him toward their bedroom. Once inside, John closed and locked the door behind them. Then he scooped his wife up in his arms and carried her over to the bed. Cree had taught him a long time ago to grab their moments when they could because in their line of work, they never knew when they might get the chance again.

Here's a sneak peek at book four in Paige Tyler's sizzling SWAT series

# *TO LOVE A WOLF*

It must be payday. Either that, or God hated him. As Landry Cooper strode across the bank's lobby and got in line behind the twenty other people already there, he wasn't sure which.

He'd been so exhausted after work he hadn't even bothered to shower and change into civvies at the SWAT compound like he usually did. Instead, he'd come straight to the bank in his combat boots, military cargo pants, and a dark blue T-shirt with the Dallas PD emblem and the word "SWAT" on the left side of his chest. He couldn't wait to get home and throw everything in the wash, so he could grab something to eat and fall into bed.

He bit back a growl as the man at the front of the line plunked down a cardboard box full of rolled coins on the counter and started lining up the different denominations in front of the teller.

"You've got to be kidding me," he muttered.

A tall, slender woman with long, golden-brown hair a few people ahead gave him a quick, understanding smile over her shoulder. He smiled back, but she'd already turned around. He waited, hoping she'd glance his way again, but she didn't.

He hated going to the bank, but his SWAT teammate

had finally paid off the bet they'd made months ago about whether his squad leader and the newest member of the team would end up being a couple. Instead of giving Cooper the hundred bucks in cash like a normal person, Brooks had given him a frigging check.

When Officer Khaki Blake had walked into the training room for the first time, every pair of eyes in the room immediately locked on her—except for Cooper's. Oh, he'd noticed she was attractive. But he'd been more interested in watching how the rest of the SWAT team reacted. While most of the guys had checked her out with open curiosity, none of their hearts had pounded as hard as his squad leader's, Corporal Xander Riggs. Cooper had immediately pegged Khaki as *The One* for Xander, and vice versa.

But just because Cooper accepted the concept of *The One* didn't mean he bought into the idea there were women in the world for him and the other remaining thirteen single members of the Pack. Cooper wasn't jaded when it came to love, but he wasn't naive, either.

The two people ahead of Cooper finally got fed up and walked away. He quickly stepped forward and found himself behind the attractive woman who'd smiled earlier. He couldn't help noticing she looked exceptionally good in a pair of jeans. Or that her long, silky hair had the most intriguing gold highlights when the light caught them just right. She smelled so delicious he had to fight the urge to bury his nose in her neck. Damn, he must be more tired than he thought. If he wasn't careful he'd be humping her leg next.

He opened his mouth to say something charming, but all that came out was a yawn big enough to make his jaw crack. The woman in front of him must have heard it too, because she turned around.

"And I thought I've been waiting in line a long time," she said, giving him a smile so breathtaking it damn near made his heart stop. "You look like you're ready to fall asleep on your feet."

Cooper knew he should reply, but he was so mesmerized by her perfect skin, clear green eyes, and soft lips that he couldn't do anything but stare. He felt like a teenager back in high school again.

"Um, yeah. Long day," he finally managed.

What the hell was wrong with him? He'd never had a problem talking to a beautiful woman before. But in his defense, he'd never been in the presence of a woman this gorgeous.

He gave himself a mental shake. *Get your head in the game before she thinks you're a loser and turns around again.*

"Catching bad guys, huh?" she asked.

"Something like that." He gave her his best charming smile. "Luckily, I'm off duty for the night."

She laughed, and the sound of it was so beautiful it almost brought him to his knees. Crap, he actually felt a little light-headed. He chalked it up to being out in the hot Texas sun all day. That could be hard on anyone, even a werewolf.

She regarded him with an amused look. "Is that your way of saying you're free for dinner?"

Could she read his mind? "Depends. Would you say yes if I asked you out?"

Her lips curved. "I might. Although most guys tell me their names before asking me out on a date."

Cooper chuckled. He'd been attracted to her from the moment he saw her, but after talking to her, he was even more mesmerized. He'd always appreciated a woman who was confident enough to hold up her end of a verbal sparring match, but she seemed more than capable.

He held out his hand. "Landry Cooper, at your service. Now that you know my name, how about dinner?"

He might have imagined it, but when she slipped her smaller hand into his much larger one, he could have sworn he felt a tingle pass between them—and it had wasn't because of static electricity.

"I'm Everly Danu," she said. "And dinner sounds great."

*Everly.* Even her name was beautiful.

Cooper opened his mouth to ask Everly if she wanted to grab something that night—the hell with going home and falling into bed—when voices nearby caught his attention.

"*Are we still robbing the place with the cop here?*" a male voice whispered.

"*We're in too deep to back out now*," another deeper voice said softly. "*We were already going to kill the guard anyway. Just make sure to take out the cop fast.*"

Cooper snapped his head around. He scanned the crowded bank, looking for anyone who stood out, and immediately zeroed in on a man standing by the entrance. Average height with light brown hair, the guy was wearing mirrored sunglasses and a black windbreaker. On his own, the man wasn't that remarkable, but the small radio receiver in his ear sure as hell was. It wasn't hard to miss the telltale bulge under the man's left arm or the way he kept glancing at Cooper in between keeping an eye on the door, either.

Cooper swept the bank lobby with his gaze, looking for the man's accomplice. He found him sitting by the manager's desk. Thanks to the same identical sunglasses and black windbreaker the guy was wearing, he was easy to spot.

Cooper quickly ID'd two other men—one positioned a few feet away from the bank's security guard, the other near the row of windows that looked out onto the main road. Both of them were wearing sunglasses and windbreakers.

The guy by the door checked his watch, then nodded at his friend over by the security guard. Cooper tensed. Shit, these assholes were really going to hit the bank with an armed cop standing right in the middle of them. Were they suicidal or just plain stupid?

Cooper's hand dropped to the Sig .40 on his belt.

"Landry?" Everly asked, her voice trembling a little. "Is something wrong?"

He didn't want to take his eyes off the four guys about to hit the bank, but Everly's growing fear was so strong he could practically taste it on the air. Finding it impossible to ignore, he tore his gaze from the four men and turned back to Everly.

"I don't want to alarm you, but the bank is about to be robbed," he said softly. "I need you to stay calm, okay?"

COMING JUNE 2016

# Acknowledgments

I hope you enjoyed *Her Fierce Warrior*! After meeting Minka and Angelo in *Her Perfect Mate* (Book 1 in the X-Ops series), so many readers have been waiting for their story, even if they didn't know the two of them would end up together. If you read the acknowledgments in *Her Perfect Mate*, then you already know that Angelo's character was inspired by a friend of ours named Angelo Riguero who was tragically and senselessly murdered in 2012. He was thrilled when I told him that he inspired the SF soldier in the X-Ops series, and giving him his own happily ever is our way of remembering and honoring him. I like to think Angelo knows all about *Her Fierce Warrior* and is smiling down from heaven right now.

This whole series would not be possible without some very incredible people. In addition to another big thank-you to my hubby for all his help with the action scenes and military and tactical jargon, I'd like to thank my agent, Bob Mecoy, for believing in us and encouraging us and being there when we need to talk; my editor and go-to-person at Sourcebooks, Cat Clyne (who loves this series as much as I do and is always a phone call, text, or email away whenever I need something); and all the other amazing people at Sourcebooks, including my fantastic publicist Amelia Narigon, and their crazy-talented art department. The covers they make for me are seriously drool-worthy!

Because I could never leave out my readers, a huge thank-you to everyone who has read my books and Snoopy danced right along with me with every new release. That includes the fantastic people on my amazing Street Team, as well as my assistant, Janet. You rock!

I also want to give a big thank-you to the men, women, and working dogs serving in our military, as well as their families.

And a very special shout-out to our favorite restaurant, P.F. Chang's, where hubby and I bat story lines back and forth and come up with all of our best ideas, as well as a thank-you to our fantastic waiter, Andrew, who sends our order to the kitchen the moment we walk in the door!

Hope you enjoy the fifth book in the X-Ops series coming soon from Sourcebooks, and look forward to reading the rest of the series as much as I look forward to sharing it with you.

If you love a man in uniform as much as I do, make sure you check out my other action-packed paranormal/romantic-suspense series from Sourcebooks called SWAT (Special Wolf Alpha Team)!

Happy Reading!

# About the Author

Paige Tyler is the *New York Times* and *USA Today* best-selling author of sexy, romantic fiction. She and her very own military hero (also known as her husband) live on the beautiful Florida coast with their adorable fur baby (also known as their dog). Paige graduated with a degree in education but decided to pursue her passion and write books about hunky alpha males and the kick-butt heroines who fall in love with them. Visit www.paigetylertheauthor.com.

She's also on Facebook, Twitter, Tumblr, tsu, Wattpad, Google+, Instagram, and Pinterest.

# Hungry Like the Wolf

SWAT: Special Wolf Alpha Team

## by Paige Tyler

*New York Times* and *USA Today* bestselling author

—•—

### She's convinced they're hiding something

The team of sharpshooters is elite and ultra-secretive—they are also the darlings of Dallas. This doesn't sit well with investigative journalist Mackenzie Stone. They must be hiding something…and she's determined to find out what.

### He's as alpha as a man can get

Gage Dixon, the SWAT team commander, is six-plus feet of pure muscle and keeps his team tight and on target. When he is tasked to let the persistent—and gorgeous—journalist shadow the team for a story, he has one mission: protect the pack's secrets.

### He'll do everything he can to protect his secret

But keeping Mac at a distance proves difficult. She's smart, sexy, and just smells so damn good. As she digs, she's getting closer to the truth—and closer to his heart. Will Gage guard their secret at the expense of his own happiness? Or will he choose love and make her his own…

—•—

**For more Paige Tyler, visit:**

www.sourcebooks.com

# Wolf Trouble

SWAT: Special Wolf Alpha Team

## by Paige Tyler

*New York Times* and *USA Today* bestselling author

---

### He's in trouble with a capital T

There's never been a female on the Dallas SWAT team and Senior Corporal Xander Riggs prefers it that way. The elite pack of alpha-male wolf shifters is no place for a woman. But Khaki Blake is no ordinary woman.

When Khaki walks through the door, attractive as hell and smelling like heaven, Xander doesn't know what the heck to do. Worse, she's put under his command and Xander's protective instincts go on high alert. When things start heating up both on and off the clock, it's almost impossible to keep their heads in the game and their hands off each other...

---

### For more Paige Tyler, visit:

www.sourcebooks.com

# In the Company of Wolves

SWAT: Special Wolf Alpha Team

## by Paige Tyler

*New York Times* and *USA Today* bestselling author

---

The new gang of thugs in town is ruthless to the extreme—and a pack of wolf shifters. Special Wolf Alpha Team discovers this in the middle of a shoot-out. When Eric Becker comes face to face with a female werewolf, shooting her isn't an option, but neither is arresting her. She's the most beautiful woman he's ever seen—or smelled. Becker hides her and leaves the crime scene with the rest of his team.

Jayna Winston has no idea why that SWAT guy hid her, but she's sure glad he did. Now what's a street-savvy thief going to do with a hot alpha-wolf SWAT officer?

---

**Praise for Paige Tyler's SWAT series:**

"Bring on the growling, possessive alpha male… A fast-paced and super-exciting read that grabbed my attention. I loved it." —*Night Owl Reviews*, Top Pick, 5 Stars

**For more Paige Tyler, visit:**

www.sourcebooks.com